THE PROSE EDDA

SNORRI STURLUSON (1179–1241) was born in western Iceland, the son of an upstart Icelandic chieftain. In the early thirteenth century, Snorri rose to become Iceland's richest and, for a time, its most powerful leader. Twice he was elected law-speaker at the Althing, Iceland's national assembly, and twice he went abroad to visit Norwegian royalty. An ambitious and sometimes ruthless leader, Snorri was also a man of learning, with deep interests in the myth, poetry and history of the Viking Age. He has long been assumed to be the author of some of medieval Iceland's greatest works, including the *Prose Edda* and *Heimskringla*, the latter a saga history of the kings of Norway.

JESSE BYOCK is Professor of Old Norse and Medieval Scandinavian Studies at the University of California, Los Angeles, and Professor at UCLA's Cotsen Institute of Archaeology. A specialist in North Atlantic and Viking Studies, he directs the Mosfell Archaeological Project in Iceland. Prof. Byock received his Ph.D. from Harvard University after studying in Iceland, Sweden and France. His books and translations include *Viking Age Iceland*, *Medieval Iceland: Society, Sagas, and Power*, *Feud in the Icelandic Saga*, *The Saga of King Hrolf Kraki* and *The Saga of the Volsungs: The Norse Epic of Sigurd the Dragon Slayer*.

SNORRI STURLUSON

The Prose Edda

Norse Mythology

Translated with an Introduction and Notes by
JESSE L. BYOCK

PENGUIN BOOKS

PENGUIN CLASSICS

Published by the Penguin Group
Penguin Books Ltd, 80 Strand, London WC2R 0RL, England
Penguin Group (USA) Inc., 375 Hudson Street, New York, New York 10014, USA
Penguin Group (Canada), 10 Alcorn Avenue, Toronto, Ontario, Canada M4V 3B2
(a division of Pearson Penguin Canada Inc.)
Penguin Ireland, 25 St Stephen's Green, Dublin 2, Ireland
(a division of Penguin Books Ltd)
Penguin Group (Australia), 250 Camberwell Road,
Camberwell, Victoria 3124, Australia (a division of Pearson Australia Group Pty Ltd)
Penguin Books India Pvt Ltd, 11 Community Centre,
Panchsheel Park, New Delhi – 110 017, India
Penguin Group (NZ), cnr Airborne and Rosedale Roads, Albany,
Auckland 1310, New Zealand (a division of Pearson New Zealand Ltd)
Penguin Books (South Africa) (Pty) Ltd, 24 Sturdee Avenue,
Rosebank 2196, South Africa

Penguin Books Ltd, Registered Offices: 80 Strand, London WC2R 0RL, England

www.penguin.com

First published in Penguin Classics 2005

027

Set in 10.25/12.25 pt PostScript Adobe Sabon
Typeset by Rowland Phototypesetting Ltd, Bury St Edmunds, Suffolk
Printed in Great Britain by Clays Ltd, St Ives plc

ISBN-13: 978-0-140-44755-2

www.greenpenguin.co.uk

Contents

Acknowledgements

First, I want to thank Russell Poole, who translated the section *Poetic References from Skaldskaparmal.* His knowledge of kennings and poetic language was an important contribution to this volume. Much of this translation was done in Iceland where Kristján Jóhann Jónsson, Eysteinn Björnsson, Aðalsteinn Davíðsson, Ingunn Ásdísardóttir, Gísli Sigurðsson, Peter Foote and Paul Taylor generously read parts of the manuscript and made many comments. Vésteinn Ólason also graciously offered his time and the resources of the Árni Magnússon Manuscript Institute. Robert Guillemette turned his artistry to the World Tree. Efrain Kristal, the authority on Jorges Luis Borges who translated the *Edda* into Spanish, offered many valuable insights. My editor at Penguin Classics, Laura Barber, deserves credit for making this book more succinct. I am fortunate for the assistance of my talented students at the University of California, Brian O'Camb, David Lassen and Natalie Operstein. I greatly appreciated the support of the UCLA Center for Medieval and Renaissance Studies and especially thank Deborah Kennel and Karen Burgess. The Fulbright Commission, The John Simon Guggenheim Memorial Foundation, the National Endowment for the Humanities and the UCLA Academic Senate all helped bring this project to fruition.

I wish to dedicate this volume to Franz Bäuml, Albert Lord, Richard Tomasson and Eugen Weber, teachers from whom I learned.

Introduction

The *Prose Edda* is Scandinavia's best-known work of literature and the most extensive source for Norse mythology. In straightforward prose interspersed with ancient verse, the *Edda* recounts the Norse creation epic and the subsequent struggles of the gods, giants, dwarves and elves in that universe. Woven throughout is the gods' tragic realization that the future holds one final cataclysmic battle, Ragnarok, when the world will be destroyed. The *Edda* also tells heroic stories about legendary warriors and their kin, stories which incorporate shards of ancient memory. The powerful supernatural tales and heroic lore captured in the *Edda* have influenced modern culture, inspiring most notably Richard Wagner's *Ring* cycle and J. R. R. Tolkien's *The Lord of the Rings*. The *Edda* also influenced poets W. H. Auden and Henry Wadsworth Longfellow, the fabulist Jorge Luis Borges, and a host of writers and artists in other genres, including fantasy, comic books and film.

Over the centuries the *Prose Edda* has been known as the *Younger Edda*, *Snorri's Edda*, and simply the *Edda*. Many of the stories contained in the *Prose Edda* have counterparts in ancient verse known as eddic poetry – anonymous poems collected and written down in a separate work called the *Poetic Edda* around the same time that the *Prose Edda* was compiled in the thirteenth century. In many instances the *Prose Edda* incorporates stanzas of eddic poems directly into its prose, citing these verses as sources.

The *Prose Edda* also adopts stanzas and references from another group of poems, called skaldic poetry. The two forms of poetry, eddic and skaldic, are closely related, and most skalds, as

Old Norse poets were called, could work in either form. The major differences between the two are that skaldic poetry employs more intricate word choices and metres than does eddic poetry, and that skaldic poems, unlike eddic poems, are frequently attributed to individual skalds who composed them.

Both the *Eddas* – poetry and prose – were written in Iceland during the thirteenth century, and they are based in large part on the oral tradition that stemmed from the earlier Viking Age. This era, from roughly 800 to 1100, was a time when Scandinavian seafarers explored, raided and settled distant lands, including the previously uninhabited Iceland. Old Norse was the language spoken throughout Scandinavia during the Viking period, and the two *Eddas* were written in Old Icelandic, a branch of Old Norse that had changed little from the time Iceland was settled in the late 800s. The *Eddas*, like Iceland's sagas, were written in the native language and they were meant to be read aloud, enabling a single manuscript to speak to many, literate and non-literate alike. The content of the *Eddas* did not go through an intermediate stage of being written and transmitted in Latin, the language of the Church, as did most other non-Icelandic writings from the Middle Ages that give information about Norse myth and legend. For example, the *Prose Edda* differs from the *Gesta Danorum* (*History of the Danes*), which was written in Latin around the year 1200 by the Danish cleric Saxo Grammaticus for Denmark's archbishop and was strongly influenced by his classical learning.

Geographical and political circumstances help to explain why the *Prose Edda* and the *Poetic Edda* were written in the form they were in medieval Iceland. This was an immigrant society formed by colonists from many parts of the Viking world, but especially from Norway and from Norse colonies in the British Isles. In a frontier setting on the far northern edge of the habitable world, the Icelanders held fast to the cultural memories brought by the early settlers, which provided them with a sense of common origin and helped bind them into a cohesive cultural group. Additionally, the Icelanders made the transition from their traditional religious beliefs to Christianity in a manner distinctly different from the contemporaneous conversion in the Norwegian mother culture. There, Christian missionary kings forcefully uprooted the belief in the old gods. The Icelanders, rather than shedding blood among themselves as did the Norwegians, peacefully accepted the new religion through a political compromise in the year 1000 at their annual national assembly, the Althing. This collective decision sanctioned a gradual transition to the new belief system. The old forms of worship faded within a few decades of the conversion, but the Icelanders continued long afterwards to value stories from the pagan times as a cultural heritage rather than a creed.

Despite the Icelanders' attachment to the Old Scandinavian past, thirteenth-century Icelanders often followed mainland Scandinavia in adopting elements of continental European culture. Many new tastes reached Iceland, especially via Norway, and among the imports came new forms of poetic expression including rhymed verse, sung dances (precursors of the ballad), French romances and Christian religious narratives, which competed with traditional eddic and skaldic poetry. In response to the new trends, the *Edda* was written as a handbook for those aspiring Icelandic skalds who wanted to master the traditional forms of verse and the older stories essential to the imagery of Old Norse poetry. Rather than reconstructing cultic practices of the old religion, which had ceased two centuries earlier, the *Edda* concentrates on what was still known at the time of its composition: myths, legends and the use of traditional poetic diction. It is evident that the one or more authors who compiled the *Edda* wanted to continue knowledge of Old Scandinavian poetry and the culture that surrounded it.

Even though the *Edda* relies heavily on native traditions, a good argument can be made that it also shows awareness of two Latin literary genres of the Middle Ages: writings about mythology and about language and poetics. Some scholars propose that Latin treatises may have influenced those parts of the text that treat technical poetic terminology and systems of poetic classification. Further, almost everyone agrees that the writer of the *Edda* knew at least something of the ideas current in the general Latin learning of the Middle Ages, whether or not he himself knew Latin.

The Title *Edda* and the Question of Authorship

The origin of the use of the word *edda* as a title is elusive. In thirteenth-century Icelandic, the term *edda* meant 'great-grandmother', which would have been a fitting title for a compilation of traditional stories, but we will never know for sure how the name came to be applied. The original thirteenth-century manuscript is long lost, and it is not known whether the word *edda* was even its title. The name *edda* first appears in the surviving fourteenth-century manuscripts as a subtitle, referring to only a part of the compilation. Two related terms, *edduregla* and *eddulist*, referring to the rules and the art of poetry, also appear in fourteenth-century manuscripts. From these terms and their usage, we infer that the word *edda* had become associated with traditional verse, and by late medieval times the *Edda* was regarded in Iceland as the authoritative handbook for training poets in traditional verse forms.

It has long been assumed that the learned and quarrelsome Icelandic chieftain Snorri Sturluson is the author of the *Edda*. The main evidence for Snorri's authorship is the following short passage from the *Codex Upsaliensis*, an early fourteenth-century Icelandic manuscript containing the *Edda*:

> This book is called *Edda*. Snorri Sturluson compiled [literally, assembled] it in the way that it is arranged here. First it tells about the Æsir [the gods] and Ymir [the primordial giant], then comes the poetic diction section with the poetic names of many things and lastly a poem called the *List of Meters* which Snorri composed about King Hakon and Duke Skuli.[1]

This passage outlines the main contents of the *Edda*, and although Snorri is named as the compiler of the work, it is not clear from the passage whether Snorri is the author of more than the *List of Metres*. The other main manuscripts of the *Edda* are also ambiguous about Snorri's connection to the work; nevertheless, the mentions of Snorri in the manuscripts have greatly influenced Snorri's acceptance as the author of the entire work.

But who was Snorri? He was the son of Sturla, an upstart chieftain from western Iceland, whose sons and grandchildren lent the family name of Sturlung (the descendants of Sturla) to the Sturlung Age, a turbulent time in the history of Iceland in the first half of the thirteenth century. Born in 1178 or 1179, Snorri was two years old when his life took an unexpected turn. Jon Loptsson, Iceland's most powerful and cultured leader, offered to raise Snorri in order to settle a feud. It was unusual for a child to be fostered in this way by a man of a higher social status than his father, so Snorri's father saw this offer as a sign of respect. Snorri spent the next sixteen years at Oddi, Jon Loptsson's estate and an important centre of learning in medieval Iceland. When he left Oddi, Snorri married one of the wealthiest women in Iceland and soon became a prominent chieftain. In 1215, and again in 1222, Snorri was elected the Althing's law-speaker, the highest official position in the Old Icelandic Free State. As a sign of his status, Snorri built at the site of the Althing an unusually large turf building, where he and his men lived during the two-week period of the assembly, and it is instructive that this thirteenth-century Christian chieftain named this residence Valhalla, after the hall of the chief Norse god Odin.

Snorri was extremely ambitious and his life was full of disputes and enemies. To increase his prestige and power at home, he sailed to Norway two times, where he made ill-advised alliances with conflicting factions within the Norwegian royal family. In the 1230s the number and reach of Snorri's enemies in Iceland and Norway grew dangerously. He had married his daughters to rising Icelandic chieftains, but the marriages ended and the alliances failed. In the year 1241, two of Snorri's former sons-in-law, recruited by the Norwegian king, who was extending his power to Iceland, attacked and surprised Snorri at his estate at Reykjaholt in western Iceland. They found him hiding in his cellar and killed him.

Snorri is mentioned in many thirteenth-century Icelandic writings, and they allow us to know more about him than about most other individuals in medieval Europe. Still, we can only guess at some aspects of Snorri's life, including the extent of his writings. The books that tradition attributes to him, the *History of the Kings of Norway* (*Heimskringla*) and the *Prose Edda*, indicate that he spent time gathering information for his future writings during his travels in Scandinavia. The opening section of *Heimskringla*, which covers the earliest mythic and legendary period, is called the *Saga of the Ynglings*. Like the *Edda*, this work tells ancient stories, and intersperses its prose with eddic and skaldic verses. However, the stories of the two works are often distinguished by differences of fact and detail.

The Parts of the *Edda*

The *Edda* is divided into four parts. It begins with a short *Prologue*, a self-standing unit that differs significantly from the rest of the *Edda* in sentence structure, subject matter and the kind of genealogical information it gives. In a Norse culture that was in the process of absorbing elements of classical learning, the *Prologue* attempts to elevate the status of the *Edda* by equating Norse stories with those from the Graeco-Roman tradition. It also tries to make the *Edda*'s stories more palatable to medieval Christians by harmonizing Norse beliefs with Christian concepts. The *Prologue* may have been part of the original text, or some or all of it may have been added later.

The second and main section is known as *Gylfaginning* and is the core of the *Edda*. No one can learn about Scandinavian mythology without it, since it is our best source for the story of the creation, the struggles of the gods, and the events leading to the destruction of the universe. The text of *Gylfaginning* is remarkably similar in all the important manuscripts of the *Edda*. *Gylfaginning* means the 'deluding [*ginning*] of Gylfi', a reference not to the stories that King Gylfi of Sweden learns from the Æsir, but to Gylfi's realization that he was the victim of an elaborate optical illusion.

Gylfaginning is written entirely as a dialogue between Gylfi and three formidable god-like figures who are at the centre of the deception. Gylfi disguises himself as a traveller named Gangleri, a name meaning 'strider', 'walker', or 'wanderer', and journeys to visit the Æsir. This mysterious people is said to be newly arrived in the North, and Gangleri seeks to discover the source of their power. In the Æsir's majestic but illusory hall, Gangleri/Gylfi meets three manifestations of Odin: High, Just-as-High and Third. These strange, lordly individuals sit on thrones one above the other. Gangleri questions them and, story by story, they reveal what they know.

Gangleri's dialogue with Odin's three manifestations resembles contests of wisdom found in eddic poems such as *The Lay of Vafthrudnir* (*Vafþrúðnismál*), where Odin pits his mastery of mythic knowledge against the giant Vafthrudnir. Norse wisdom contests were adversarial, and Gangleri is told at the start that he will not escape unharmed unless he grows wiser. Gangleri's method is to probe the Æsir with questions such as 'Who is the highest or the oldest of all the gods?' 'How were the earth and the sky made?' The richly detailed answers often touch on troubling topics, many anticipating the destruction of the world.

The third section is called *Skaldskaparmal* (*Skáldskaparmál*) , and, unlike *Gylfaginning*, it varies considerably from manuscript to manuscript. The name *Skaldskaparmal* is telling. *Skáld*, as mentioned earlier, is the Old Norse word for 'poet'. *Skapr* means 'creation' or 'craft', while *mál* is 'language' or 'diction', hence *Skáldskaparmál* means the 'language of poetry' or 'poetic diction'. The stories in *Skaldskaparmal* give background for references and allusions found in Old Norse verse, and these explanations are a priceless repository of Scandinavian lore. (See Appendix 2 for a discussion of the poetic devices, kennings and *heiti*.)

There is little doubt that *Gylfaginning* and *Skaldskaparmal* were written at different times and in somewhat different styles. Whereas *Gylfaginning* is entirely in dialogue, *Skaldskaparmal* is written in a combination of dialogue and third-person storytelling. It would seem that these two sections of the *Edda* were gathered into one book only after they were written separately. Still, the two fit remarkably well together, containing almost no repetition. Both *Skaldskaparmal* and *Gylfaginning* tell myths, but *Skaldskaparmal* also recounts tales of legendary heroes. Some of these heroic legends can be dated to a time before the Viking Age known as the Migration Period, from the fifth to the seventh centuries, when warrior bands and tribes invaded the collapsing Roman Empire. Stories that originated during this era became the basis for epic cycles that were popular during the Viking Age, and continued to be told in the thirteenth century when the *Edda* was written. Among the stories gathered into *Skaldskaparmal* are those of kings and warriors whose fame springs from a mixture of history and myth. One of these is the legendary King Jormunrek, also known as Ermanaric in late Roman and Old English sources. This tragic figure ruled over a vast East Gothic kingdom of horsemen on the Ukrainian steppes until suddenly attacked by the Huns in the year 376. *Skaldskaparmal* also tells the story of the ancient Danish warrior King Hrolf Kraki, who, much like King Arthur in the Celtic lore or Charlemagne in the Frankish legends, surrounded himself with twelve champions. Hrolf's warriors and berserkers are treated more fully in *The Saga of King Hrolf Kraki*, an episodic collection of Old Scandinavian tales that has similarities to the Old English epic *Beowulf*.

Sigurd the dragon slayer, whose lineage is traced to Odin, is the best-known hero in *Skaldskaparmal*. He and his Volsung family serve as the basis of a series of epic stories, including those about Attila the Hun and the Burgundian tribesmen who covet Sigurd's treasure, the Rhine Gold. Sigurd becomes entangled in a tragic love triangle with a Burgundian princess, who later marries Attila, and a Valkyrie, who disobeys Odin. Extensive versions of the Sigurd story also survive in *The Saga of the Volsungs*, the *Poetic Edda*, *Thidrek's Saga* and the South German epic poem *The Nibelungenlied*, where Sigurd is known as Siegfried. Richard Wagner made Siegfried the hero of his *Ring* cycle, but most closely followed the storyline of what happened to Sigurd and his Volsung ancestors found in the *Eddas* and *The Saga of the Volsungs*.

The fourth and final section of the *Edda* is the poem *List of Metres*, called *Hattatal* (*Háttatal*) in Old Icelandic. There is no doubt about *Hattatal*'s authorship: it was composed by Snorri Sturluson, probably early in his career, as an attempt to curry favour with the Norwegian King Hakon Hakonarson and his father-in-law Skuli, a jarl (earl), who was given the title of duke. *Hattatal* is an ambitious, somewhat pedantic work, whose 102 stanzas demonstrate often small differences in poetic metres and obscure usages of poetic devices. Prose commentary offering technical explanations is interspersed among the verses of this long poem. The poem is a treasure for those with a knowledge of Old Icelandic and interested in the intricacies of Norse poetry. Because of the technical and obscure nature of *Hattatal*, it is not included in this nor in most translations. (Appendix 2 contains a sample stanza from *Hattatal*, followed by an example of the prose commentary.)

The Mythology of the *Edda*

In the period before the conversion to Christianity, Viking Age Scandinavians had no single, organized religion; instead they shared a common view of the universe and a belief in the same pantheon of Norse gods and other supernatural creatures. Two groups of gods, the Æsir and the Vanir, war with each other, eventually making a lasting truce. Thereafter they live together in harmony, fusing so effectively into a single group that all gods become known as Æsir, even though the Vanir retain their identity as a small, separate family. The home of the gods is at Asgard, a compound name whose first part *As-* refers to the Æsir and whose second part *gard* (related to the English word 'yard') means an 'enclosure'. Hence Asgard is the 'enclosed region where the Æsir live'.

The gods have special attributes, but many pay for their powers with a related loss. Odin, the god who sees all, loses an eye; Tyr, a god of war and council, breaks his pledge and loses his right hand (crucial for making oaths and wielding weapons); Freyja, the goddess of household prosperity, leaves her hearth to search for a husband who has wandered off. Unlike the gods of Greek and Roman mythology, the Æsir rarely quarrel among themselves over control of human or semi-divine heroes, nor do they enjoy the complacency of immortality. Their universe is constantly in danger, and their actions frequently have unanticipated consequences, as in the creation story, when Odin and his brothers slay the giant Ymir and use his body to fill Ginnungagap, the primeval void. While this act gives rise to the world of the *Edda*, the slaying also unleashes the power of the giants, the gods' enemies.

Throughout the mythology of the *Edda*, three figures serve as catalysts for much of the action. Two are gods, Odin and Thor, while the third, Loki, is a trickster-like figure. Odin is an old god who figures in the mythologies of other northern peoples, where he was known as Woden, Wodan, Wotan and Wuotan, but we know him best in the context of Scandinavian mythology, where he serves as patron of aristocrats, warriors and poets. The *Edda* is an especially important source about Odin and refers to him by many names, including All-Father, the High One and Val-Father, which means 'Father of the Slain'. Odin has both priestly and martial roles: as the god of death, who decides the fates of warriors, Odin travels between the worlds of the living and the dead on his eight-legged horse, Sleipnir; and as the god of sovereignty, he leads the Æsir with his skills in magic, prophecy and governance. Odin knows that all will be lost at Ragnarok and constantly seeks the knowledge to forestall the coming doom. Two ravens, whose names Hugin and Munin refer to the mind's divided ability for thought and memory, sit on his shoulders. Every morning they fly over the world, gathering information that they pass on to Odin, who remembers everything. In a sense, Odin is the repository of the world's knowledge. He is also a dangerous and fickle god, who is known to withdraw his favour from formerly victorious warriors.

Norse mythology hints at Odinic cults, with Odin being worshipped through a combination of ecstatic and seemingly shamanistic rituals. From the eddic poem *The Sayings of the High One* (*Hávamál*), he is said to have hanged himself in a sacrificial ritual on a tree. Barely surviving this ordeal, Odin gains arcane knowledge, including the use of runes, the ancient Scandinavian alphabet sometimes used for magical purposes. In the poem, Odin chants:

I know that I hung
on the wind-swept tree
all nine nights
with spear was I wounded
and given to Odin,
myself to me,
on that tree which no one knows
from which roots it grows.

Bread I was not given,
no drink from the horn,
downwards I glared;
up I pulled the runes,
screaming I took them,
from there I fell back again.

The second major god is Thor, Odin's eldest son by Earth, whom the *Edda* says is Odin's daughter and wife. Thor is a god of the sky, and in the Germanic regions south of Scandinavia he was called Donar, meaning 'Thunder'. From the sky, this good-natured god controls the storms and brings life-giving rain, the source of the earth's abundance. Thor was widely worshipped by farmers and seamen, and his name was a prominent element in names for men, women and places, such as Thorsteinn, Thorgerd and Thorsness, names that continued to be popular even after the introduction of Christianity.

Thor is especially known for killing giants and driving a chariot pulled by two goats across the heavens. A great fighter, he undertakes most of the actual combat against the gods' enemies, and his children are also powerful warriors. Thor's most cherished possessions are his hammer, iron gloves and belt or girdle of power. The contrast between him and his father is great. Whereas Odin is cunning and thoughtful, Thor is generally forthright and quick to act, relying on brute strength, but at times he is depicted as foolish and gullible. In one story, a giant tricks Thor into thinking that he is in a house, when he is actually in the thumb of the giant's glove. Even though Thor is sometimes naive, he is a shrewd fighter, and his enemies, such as the Midgard Serpent and the giant Utgarda-Loki, fear him when he raises his hammer.

Optical illusions, such as the one that fooled Thor when he thought he was in a house, occur frequently in the *Edda*, and are called *sjónhverfing* (sight altering), a visual deception that usually is the result of spells or chants. The *Edda* uses different terminology when describing incidents in which the actual physical appearance of things or people changes. In such instances the text often employs the word *hamr*, meaning 'shape' in the supernatural sense, and variants of the phrase *at skipta hömum*, 'to shift in shape' (*hömum* from *hamr*). The concepts involved reveal the belief that certain people and objects have special powers to bring about a metamorphosis. Loki, the third major figure in the *Edda*, is one of these shape-changers, as when he puts on Freyja's falcon shape (*valshamr*). Loki's ability to don a *hamr* and change his appearance fits well with his other trickster-like characteristics. Tricksters, found in stories from cultures as disparate as ancient Mesopotamia and the Americas, are at times cultural heroes while at other times they are antisocial individuals. Often tricksters live at the margins of society and are neither completely good nor thoroughly bad. Always on the move, they delight audiences with their adventures, mishaps and humour. As shape-changers, tricksters sometimes switch genders according to the needs of the moment.

Loki acts as an inexhaustible mischief-maker, and he often provides both the cause of the gods' dilemmas as well as the solutions. The *Edda*'s description of him reveals his many sides.

> Loki is pleasing, even beautiful to look at, but his nature is evil and he is undependable. More than others, he has the kind of wisdom known as cunning, and is treacherous in all matters. He constantly places the gods in difficulties and often solves their problems with guile. (p. 39)

The stories about Loki and his offspring are often conflicting. When first mentioned in the *Edda*, Loki is referred to as one of the Æsir, but other stories in the *Edda* make it clear that he is not a god. Rather, he is the son of the giant Farbauti and a woman named Laufey, characters about whom we know almost nothing. Also there is no convincing evidence of a Loki cult, and few if any place names can be connected with him, suggesting that if he was a god he was not publicly worshipped.

Loki's position is ambiguous. He is frequently an antagonist of the gods, but he is also one of the gods' main helpers and strangely connected to Odin. The eddic poem *Loki's Flyting* (*Lokasenna*) says that Loki is Odin's blood brother. At times Loki appears almost as the All-Father's darker side, and both Odin and Loki are complex and dangerous characters. Both engage in trickery, womanizing, shape-changing and betrayal, but Loki also changes his sex, as when he becomes a mare, giving birth to Odin's horse Sleipnir. Repeatedly, Loki wins wagers by deceiving creatures such as the dark elves, who wield creative forces and forge treasures. In this way he obtains for the gods their greatest prizes, including the ship Skidbladnir, Thor's hammer Mjollnir, Odin's spear Gungnir and the All-Father's magical ring Draupnir. This last treasure drips eight gold rings of equal weight every ninth night. Loki also changes his shape to evade the gods' anger, as when he changes into a salmon.

Like many tricksters, Loki's appetites are prodigious. On one journey, he consumes vast quantities of food in an eating contest. In *Loki's Flyting,* he boasts about bedding many of the goddesses, and his unions are especially varied, indicating the multifaceted aspects of his character. His wife Sigyn is counted among the Æsir, and he has two sons with her, but he also sires three monstrous children with the ogress Angrboda: Hel, the Midgard Serpent and the wolf Fenrir.

Loki is also creative, and in some ways he fulfils the role of a cultural hero, bringing useful tools to the world. Along with acquiring the special weapons that the gods use to defend the world, Loki is responsible for the creation of the fishing net. Humour is central to his character. At times his actions are plainly funny, and he frequently displays a wit marked by a legalistic mastery of language. In one instance, after losing a life-and-death wager with a dwarf, Loki saves himself by arguing that his opponent has a right to his head but not to his neck.

The three gods of the Vanir family, Njord, Frey and Frey's twin sister Freyja, also figure prominently in the *Edda* as fertility gods. Njord is an ancient god of abundance and well being. He appears to be related to an older deity named Nerthus, a fertility or earth goddess, who, according to the first-century Roman historian Tacitus, was worshipped on an island in the Baltic. By the Viking Age, Njord is a male god whose realm is the sea. In the *Edda*, Njord marries Skadi, the daughter of a giant. Rather than live with her husband, Skadi chooses to return to her father's home in the mountains, and this story of marital incompatibility has overtones of an ancient tale illuminating the difference between life on land and in the sea.

Njord's son Frey is said to control the bounty of the earth and is devoted to pleasure. It is instructive that this god of fertility at times cannot control his desires. In one central story, he endangers the gods by trading his sword for the hand in marriage of the lovely giantess Gerd, and at Ragnarok the gods will greatly miss this weapon. From many sources we know Frey was worshipped throughout much of the northern world. In the Baltic region, he was called Yngvi Frey. Although we have no sure explanation for the meaning of Yngvi, it was a name that was widely known, and Yngvi Frey appears to be the mythical ancestor of the tribe of Ingvaeones mentioned by Tacitus in his *Germania*, while in Old English writings Frey is called Ing (Yngvi). Yngvi Frey was especially important in Sweden at Old Uppsala, where he was revered as the divine ancestor of the royal dynasty called the Ynglings, after him. A branch of this Swedish royal family moved to Norway and was also called the Ynglings. In Norway, they founded a Viking Age dynasty in the Vik region near modern-day Oslo. Through the conquests of the long-lived King Harald Fairhair (*c.* 860–930), the Ynglings became Norway's medieval royal house, with Ynglings remaining on the throne until the fourteenth century.

The *Edda* tells us that, compared to the gods, 'The goddesses are no less sacred, nor are they less powerful' (p. 30). They are called *gydjur*, a general term meaning female gods, and *asynjur*, meaning, more specifically, female Æsir. In Asgard, the goddesses own a beautiful sanctuary named Vingolf, and the most prominent among them have their own halls. Frigg, Odin's wife and the chief goddess, owns the magnificent dwelling Fensalir. Little is known about Frigg's parentage, but she is more clearly defined as the mother of Baldr, the most beautiful of the gods, whose tragic death she tries to prevent. Like her husband Odin, Frigg has considerable powers and can see into the future, but, unlike Odin, she rarely uses her talents.

Although Frigg holds the highest rank, it is Freyja who plays a larger role in the *Edda*. Freyja has her own hall, named Folkvangar, where she alone decides the seating. Throughout Scandinavia, women worshipped Freyja as the female deity of love and fertility and as the goddess of pleasure and household prosperity. The *Edda* tells that Frejya delights in love and songs and that her great sorrow is the disappearance of her husband Od. Like many gods of fertility, Freyja and her Vanir family show a tendency towards incest, and the eddic poem *Loki's Flyting* hints that Freyja and Frey were the children of Njord and his sister. In the same poem Loki accuses Freyja of having incestuous relations with her brother. Contention swirls around Freyja: giants lust after her, and at times the gods and Loki covet her possessions. One of her treasures is the famous Brisingamen, the 'Necklace of the Brisings', made by four dwarves, and, according to the Icelandic *Short Saga of Sorli*, Odin has Loki steal it. The Old English poem *Beowulf* speaks of a similar mysterious piece of jewellery called the *Brosinga mene* (the necklace of the Brosings).

The *Edda* also mentions many lesser goddesses and other types of supernatural women. These include Idunn, who guards the apples of immortality, and Eir, who brings healing. Gefjun, whose name means 'She Who Gives', appears in one story as the founding mother of the main Danish island of Sjaelland. The virgin Fulla is a mysterious goddess. She serves as Frigg's attendant and carries a box made of ash wood, but we know nothing about its contents. Supernatural women include Norns, who shape men's lives at birth, and Valkyries, whom Odin sends into battle. On the battlefield, Valkyries choose warriors to be slain and taken to Odin's Valhalla, where his swelling army of warriors enjoys a vibrant afterlife, feasting and fighting daily in preparation for Ragnarok. Another female figure wielding supernatural power is Hel. Gloomy and cruel, she does not appear to be a goddess but presides in the underworld over those who die of disease and old age. A fearsome creature, Hel is described as half black and half white, and even some gods, such as Baldr, the son of Odin and Frigg, cannot escape her grasp. At Ragnarok, Loki leads into battle all of the dead from the realm of his daughter Hel.

Giants, Dwarves, Elves and Monsters

The gods are integrally connected to other supernatural creatures, some of whom are specifically linked to the earth, and others of whom are threatening monsters. Modern mythographers use the Greek term 'chthonic' to describe creatures who are connected to the earth, and in the *Edda*, such beings fall into several categories. One type is the *jötnar* or *thursar*, Old Norse terms which roughly translate to the English word 'giants'. Their home is in Jotunheim (Giant Land) or Utgard (Outer Enclosure), from where they threaten gods and men. The killing of the primal giant Ymir at the beginning of time is an essential feature of the Norse creation story. As part of this creation the giants face a survival test. When Ymir falls, so much blood gushes from his wounds that all the original giants except Bergelmir and his wife are killed in the resulting flood. The frost giants, the perpetual antagonists of the gods, are descended from this lone couple.

Although the *jötnar* and *thursar* often resemble our notion of giants, the equivalence is not exact. In the *Edda*, for example, Norse giants are not always exceptionally large, and we learn from descriptions of giantesses that some were of similar size to the gods with whom they intermarry. Giants are portrayed in the *Edda* as complex social beings with characteristics similar to those of the gods. Giantesses and ogresses are also memorable characters in the *Edda*, and their range of types is so broad that it is scarcely possible to classify such women as belonging to a single group. Sometimes they are oafish, troll-like beings, but at other times giant women are of such beauty in the eyes of the gods that they wish to marry them. Odin's connection with the giants, male and female, is especially close. His mother, Bestla, is the daughter of a giant, and Odin frequently seeks knowledge from these creatures.

Dwarves (*dvergar*) appear many times in the *Edda* and are rarely described in a sympathetic light. The *Edda* recounts that the dwarves emerge first of all the creatures who live in the flesh of the primordial giant Ymir. 'They were maggots at that time, but by a decision of the gods they acquired human understanding and assumed the likeness of men, living in the earth and the rocks' (p. 22). We can only guess why the gods changed the nature of the dwarves, but the answer may be connected to the history of forging or smithying. The Old Icelandic sources tell us that, in the earliest times, the Æsir were master smiths who worked metal, wood, stone and especially gold. The eddic poem *The Sibyl's Prophecy* (*Völuspá*) tells us that the period following the creation of the universe was a special age, before the era was spoiled by the arrival of mysterious women from Giant Land. For reasons that are unclear to us, the gods thereafter abandoned forging, leaving this essential art to the dwarves. Sometimes willingly but often under duress, the dwarves become the major smiths or artisans of the gods. From their underground world, these craftsmen produce precious objects and forge the implements used by the gods to prevail over the natural and social worlds. The *Edda* lists the names of many dwarves, including Durin, Dvalin, Dain, Gandalf, Thorin, Bifur, Bafur, Bombur, Nori, Oin, Fili, Kili, Throin, Gloin, Dori, Ori and Oakenshield, who are familiar to modern readers through J. R. R. Tolkien's writings.

The *Edda* frequently mentions elves, but mostly in passing. A line in *The Sibyl's Prophecy*, 'What of the Æsir? What of the elves?', implies that elves (*alfar*) were also important in Old Scandinavian mythology. The elves, it seems, lived apart from other beings and at different places, such as Alfheim and Vidblain. There were various types of elves, including light and dark ones, and the latter, who lived at Svartalfaheim, seem to

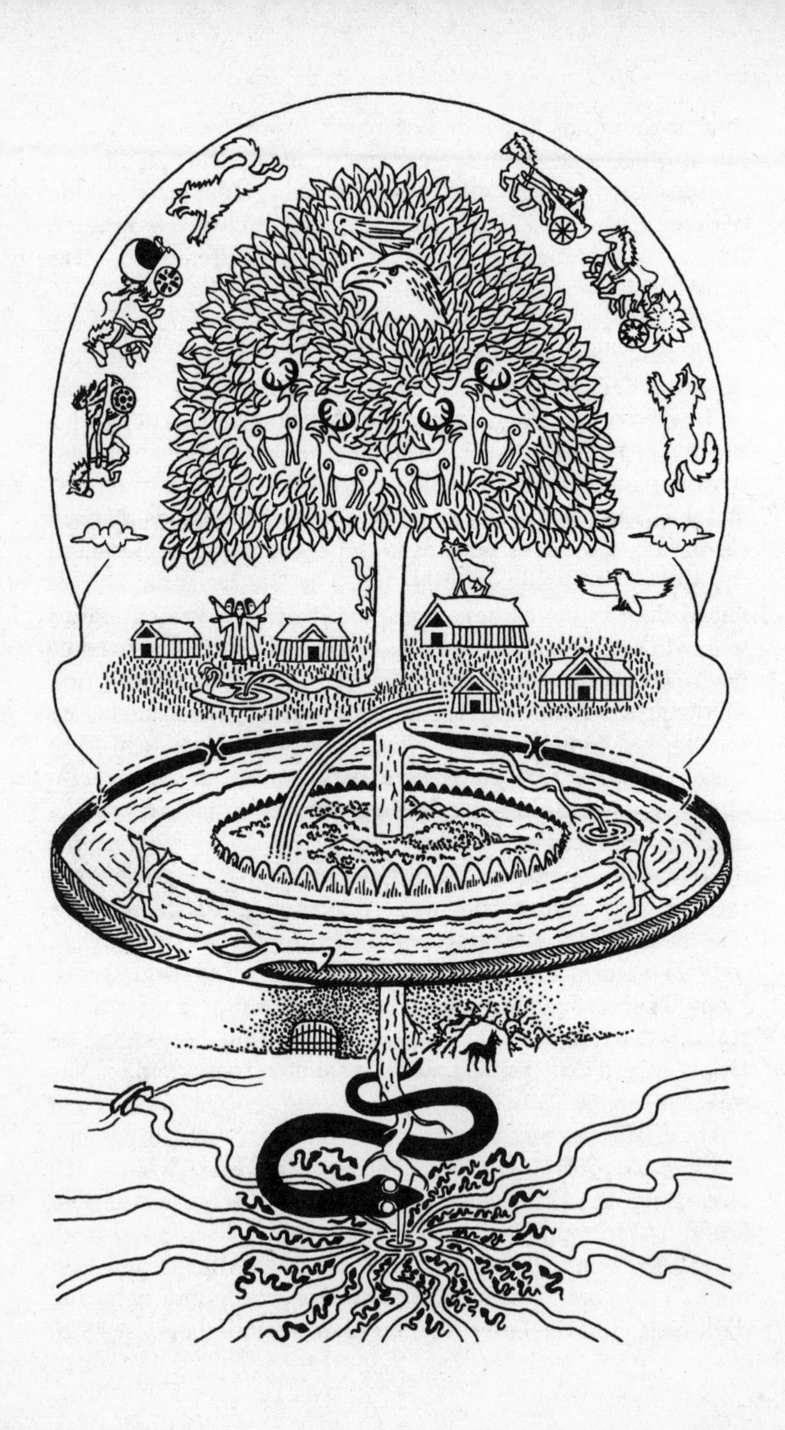

The World Tree, Yggdrasil

Rising into the heavens, the World Tree Yggdrasil was a living entity, whose branches spread over the lands. This *axis mundi* or cosmic pillar at the centre of the world is described as a giant ash, binding together the disparate parts of the universe and serving as a symbol for a dynamic cosmos. Above the branches and foliage of the tree are the heavens, formed from the skull of the primordial giant Ymir, and held in place by four dwarves. In the heavens, Sun and Moon are pulled by chariots and chased by wolves. The giant Hraesvelg, in the shape of an eagle, beats his wings, blowing the winds. In response to the question, 'How should one refer to the sky?', a passage in the *Edda* tells us: 'By calling it Ymir's head and hence the giant's skull, the burden or heavy load on the dwarves, the helmet of the dwarves West, East, South and North, the land of the sun, moon, heavenly bodies, constellations and winds, or the helmet or house of the air, of the earth and of the sun' (p. 112). Below the tree's branches lies Asgard, the home of the gods and the prophetic women called norns. From Asgard, the Rainbow Bridge, Bifrost, leads down to Midgard (Middle Earth), the home of men. A wall encloses Midgard, separating it from the outer region, Utgard, the land of the giants. Beyond Utgard is the outer sea, in which the encircling Midgard Serpent lies, biting its tail. Below is the underworld, containing monsters, serpents and a great hound, as well as the realm of the dead and seething rivers. For a fuller discussion of the World Tree and the Norse cosmos, see Appendix 1.

be dwarves. Other indications of the importance of elves in the supernatural world of Old Scandinavia include place names connected with their veneration. Many folk tales and medieval sagas also speak of elves. For example, *Kormak's Saga*, a rich source of folk religion and sorcery in medieval Iceland, provides insight into the role of elves. After a duel, the wounds of Kormak's opponent are slow in healing, and he seeks the advice of a sorceress, who says: 'Not far from here is a small hill in which elves live. Get the bull that was slaughtered by Kormak. Redden the surface of knoll with its blood and make a feast for the elves from the meat. Then you will get better.'[2]

Among the monsters who most threaten the gods are the children of Loki. One is the wolf Fenrir, who in the final battle swallows the sun, another is the gigantic Midgard Serpent, who lies in the outer sea, encircling all lands, and the third is Hel, who oversees the realm of the dead. The gods are so fearful of Fenrir that they decide to bind the wolf while still a cub. Only mighty Tyr, a god of war and battle, calms the young wolf long enough to allow the other gods to bind it with a magic fetter, although Tyr loses his hand in the process.

The *Edda* in Iceland and Beyond

Written on the far northern edge of the medieval world, the *Edda* is an extraordinary document for its invaluable insights into the language and techniques of Viking Age skalds, and this was one of the principal reasons that Icelanders took care to preserve the *Edda* by repeatedly copying it. Iceland was an unusually literate society in the Middle Ages, and copying manuscripts of all kinds was a pastime that remained popular among the Icelanders down to the beginning of the twentieth century. In the medieval period, Icelandic manuscripts were made of calf skin (vellum) and were expensive to produce. In early modern times, Icelanders began to import inexpensively manufactured blank paper books, and one piece of evidence of the *Edda*'s continuing popularity is that over 150 paper copies of the *Edda* survive, many from the nineteenth century.

The *Edda*'s wealth of information about Old Norse mythology was another reason for the Icelanders' continued interest in the work. It was also the major reason why, starting in early modern times, the *Edda* gained fame outside Iceland. The *Edda*'s entrance into the wider world of western culture is itself a story. In the sixteenth century, Denmark was an aggressive power in Northern Europe, seeking primacy in Scandinavia and, in common with the rulers of states elsewhere in Europe, the Danish kings strove to enhance their ambitious political agenda by documenting the antiquity and legitimacy of their history. For this purpose, the Danish state adopted as its own the mythic and heroic past of all Scandinavia.

Iceland became a possession of the Danish king in the late fourteenth century, and by the sixteenth century the Danes had discovered that Iceland's medieval manuscripts were a treasure trove, containing information about Scandinavia's past found nowhere else. Icelanders sent manuscripts to the king as gifts, and these and many others found their way into the archives and royal libraries in Copenhagen. The Danish king went so far as to command the Icelanders not to sell their manuscripts outside the kingdom. With the royal government as patron, Icelandic students and scholars were invited to Copenhagen to study and work on the manuscripts. Among the most important of these scholars was the humanist Arngrimur Jonsson (1568–1648), whose influential book *Brevis Commentarius de Islandia* (*Short Commentary About Iceland*), published in Copenhagen in 1593, brought Iceland's medieval writings, including the *Edda*, to the attention of scholars outside Denmark. Jonsson's popular work fuelled a growing awareness of the *Edda* beyond Scandinavia that eventually led to a series of translations of the *Edda* into modern languages. The first translation of *Gylfaginning* into English appeared in London in 1770, as part of a book by Bishop Percy entitled *Northern Antiquities*. This book soon gained a readership, and in 1809 Sir Walter Scott reprinted it in Edinburgh with his own additions. By the nineteenth century, readers of most major European languages were able to learn about the gods, giants, dwarves, elves and other creatures who populated the cosmos of Old Scandinavian belief and imagination. For allowing us to glimpse this complex universe, we owe a debt of gratitude to Snorri Sturluson and the other Icelanders who contributed to writing and preserving the *Edda*.

NOTES

1. *Snorre Sturlusons Edda: Uppsala-Handskriften DG 11*, vol. II, transcribed by Anders Grape, Gotfried Kallstenius and Olof Thorell (Uppsala, 1977), p. 1.
2. *Kormáks Saga* in *Vatnsdæ la Saga*, ed. Einar Ól. Sveinsson. *Íslenzk fornrit* VIII (Reykjavik, 1939), chapter 22. For an English translation of *Kormak's Saga*, see *Sagas of Warrior-Poets*, ed. Diana Whaley (London and New York, 2002).

Further Reading

STUDIES

Ciklamini, Marlene, *Snorri Sturluson* (Boston, 1978).

Clunies Ross, Margaret, *Skáldskaparmál* (Odense, 1987).

Davidson, H. R. Ellis, *Gods and Myths of Northern Europe* (London and New York, 1981).

De Vries, Jan, *The Problem of Loki* (Helsinki, 1933).

Dubois, Thomas A., *Nordic Religions in the Viking Ages* (Philadelphia, 1999).

Dumézil, Georges, *Gods of the Ancient Northmen* (Berkeley, 1973).

Edda: A Collection of Essays, ed. R. Glendinning and H. Bessason (Manitoba, 1983).

Faulkes, Anthony, 'Descent from the Gods', *Mediaeval Scandinavia* 11 (1978–9), pp. 92–125.

—, 'The Sources of Skáldskaparmál', in *Snorri Sturluson*, ed. A. Wolf, *Script Oralia* 51 (Tübingen, 1993), pp. 59–76.

Gade, Kari E., *The Structure of Old Norse dróttkvætt Poetry* (Ithaca, NY, 1995).

Harris, Joseph, 'The Masterbuilder Tale in Snorri's Edda and Two Sagas', *Arkiv för Nordisk Filologi* 91 (1976), pp. 66–101.

Lindow, John, *Norse Mythology* (Oxford, 2002).

McTurk, Rory, 'Fooling Gylfi', *Alvíssmál* 3 (1994), pp. 3–18.

Nordal, Gudrun, *Tools of Literacy* (Toronto, 2001).

Poole, Russell, *Viking Poems on War and Peace* (Toronto, 1991).

Quinn, Judy, 'Eddu list', *Alvíssmál* 4 (1995), pp. 69–92.

See, Klaus von, 'Snorri Sturluson and the Creation of a Norse Cultural Ideology', *Saga-Book* 25, 4 (2001), pp. 367–93.
Snorrastefna, ed. Úlfar Bragason (Reykjavik, 1992).
Specvlvm Norroenvm, ed. U. Dronke *et al.* (Odense, 1981).
Turville-Petre, E. O. G., *Myth and Religion of the North* (London, 1964).
Uspenskij, Fjodor, 'Towards Further Interpretation of the Primordial Cow *Auðhumla*', *Scripta Islandica* 51 (2000), pp. 119–32.

PRIMARY TEXTS FOR NORSE MYTH AND LEGEND

The Poetic Edda, tr. C. Larrington (Oxford, 1996).
The Saga of King Hrolf Kraki, tr. J. L. Byock (London and New York, 1998).
The Saga of the Volsungs, tr. J. L. Byock (London and New York, 1999).
The Saga of the Ynglings, in *Heimskringla*, tr. L. M. Hollander (Austin, Tex., 1999), pp. 6–50.
Saxo Grammaticus, *The History of the Danes, I–IX*, ed. H. E. Davidson, tr. P. Fisher (Cambridge, 1996).
Seven Viking Romances, tr. H. Pálsson and P. Edwards (London and New York, 1985).
Tacitus, Publius Cornelius, *The Agricola and The Germania*, tr. H. Mattingly, revised S. A. Handford (London and New York, 1970).

THE ICELANDIC AND OLD NORSE BACKGROUND

Byock, Jesse L., *Viking Age Iceland* (London and New York, 2001).
Foote, Peter G., and David M. Wilson, *The Viking Achievement* (London, 1970).

Haywood, John, *The Penguin Historical Atlas of the Vikings* (London and New York, 1995).
Kristjánsson, Jónas, *Eddas and Sagas* (Reykjavik, 1997).

REFERENCE WORKS

Medieval Scandinavia: An Encyclopedia, ed. P. Pulsiano *et al.* (New York, 1993).
Orchard, Andy, *Dictionary of Norse Myth and Legend* (London, 2002).
Simek, Rudolf, *Dictionary of Northern Mythology* (Cambridge, 1993).

EDITIONS OF THE PROSE AND POETIC EDDAS

Faulkes, Anthony, *Edda by Snorri Sturluson: Prologue and Gylfaginning* (Oxford, 1982) and *Edda by Snorri Sturluson: Skáldskaparmál*, 2 vols. (London, 1998).
Helgason, Jon and Anne Holtsmark, *Edda: Prosafortellingene av Gylfaginning og Skáldskaparmál* (Copenhagen, 1968).
Jónsson, Finnur, *Edda Snorra Sturlusonar* (Copenhagen, 1931).
Neckel, Gustav, *Edda: Die Lieder des Codex Regius, Vol. I, Text* (Heidelberg, 1927).

Note on the Translation

All modern editions of the *Prose Edda* rely on the largely intact vellum *Codex Regius* manuscript (Gks 2367 quarto) from the first half of the fourteenth century. This manuscript, however, has gaps, and three other key manuscripts provide the majority of the missing passages and variant readings. They are the vellum *Codex Upsaliensis* from the early fourteenth century, the mid-fourteenth-century vellum *Codex Wormianus* and a paper book, *Codex Trajectinus*, a copy from around 1600 of an earlier vellum manuscript now lost. This translation from the Old Icelandic draws its text from the modern editions of the *Edda* cited in the Further Reading.

The *Prose Edda*, all or parts of it, was translated into English three times during the last century, by Arthur Brodeur (New York, 1916), Jean Young (Cambridge, 1954) and Anthony Faulkes (London, 1987). Only the Faulkes' translation includes *Hattatal*. The chapter and section headings in this translation are my own, and I believe that they will facilitate the reading of the *Edda* and its use as a source. Also, where *Gylfaginning* incorporates stanzas from eddic poems into its prose, the names of the poems and the corresponding stanzas are given.

This book contains three appendices designed for those readers who want more information on the World Tree and cosmos, the devices of Old Norse verse, and which eddic poems were used as sources for *Gylfaginning*. At the end of the book there is also an extensive Glossary of Names. I compiled this index to provide the reader with a tool for locating the characters (both supernatural and human), groups, places, animals and objects that appear in the text. Also at the end of the volume the reader will find genealogies and notes. In the Glossary, Notes and Further Reading I include Old Icelandic spellings; elsewhere accents are dropped and the spelling of proper names and special terms are anglicized, usually by omitting the Old Norse endings and replacing non-English letters with their closest equivalents. I do not strive for complete consistency, especially when a name is familiar to English speakers in another form; thus, I use *Valhalla* rather than *Valhöll*. My goal throughout is to produce an accurate translation in a clear modern idiom that best reproduces the nature of the original prose.

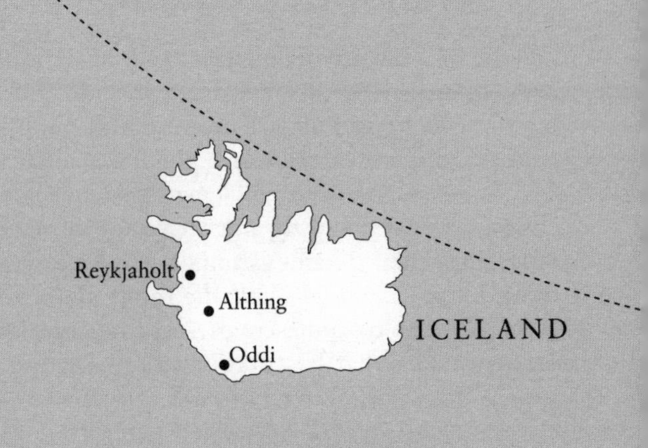

N

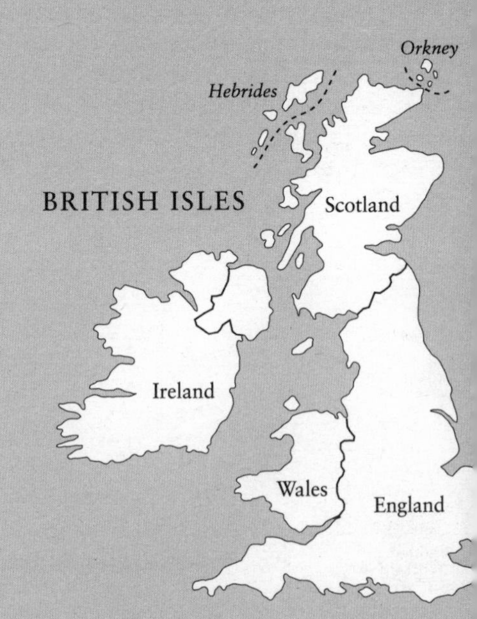

Atlantic
Ocean

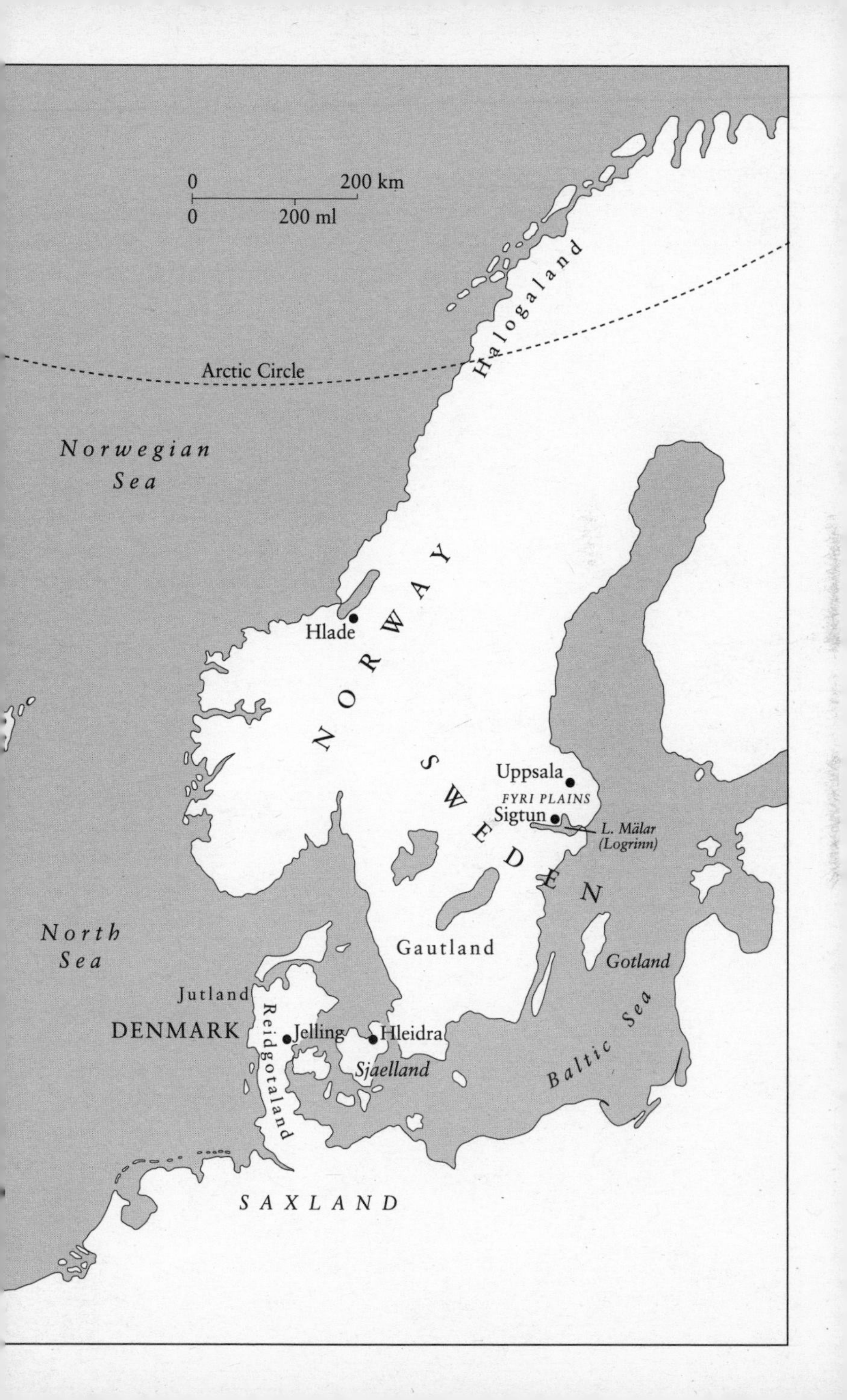
0
200 km
0
200 ml
Halogaland
Arctic Circle
Norwegian Sea
NORWAY
Hlade
SWEDEN
Uppsala
FYRI PLAINS
Sigtun
L. Mälar (Logrinn)
North Sea
Gautland
Gotland
Jutland
DENMARK
Reidgotaland
Jelling
Hleidra
Sjaelland
Baltic Sea
SAXLAND

THE PROSE EDDA

PROLOGUE

1. IN THE BEGINNING

In the beginning, almighty God created heaven and earth and all that pertains to them. Lastly he created two people, Adam and Eve, and from them came clans, whose descendants multiplied and spread across the whole world. But as time passed, people became dissimilar from one another. Some were good and held to the right beliefs, but the large majority turned to the desires of this world and neglected God's commandments. For this reason God drowned the world and all its living things in a flood, except for those who were on the ark with Noah. After Noah's flood, eight people remained alive, and they inhabited the world and from them are descended the families of man.

Again, as before, when their numbers had grown and they had settled throughout the world, the majority of mankind loved worldly desires and ambition. They abandoned their obedience to God, going so far that they no longer desired to name God. Who then was able to tell their sons about God's wondrous deeds? Thus they lost God's name, and nobody could be found anywhere in the world who knew his maker. Nevertheless, God granted men the earthly gifts of wealth and happiness to enable them to enjoy the world. He also gave them the wisdom to understand all earthly things and all the separate parts that could be seen of the sky and the earth.

People thought about these things, wondering what it could mean that the earth and animals and birds were in some ways similar, even though their natures were not alike. One of the earth's features is that, when the high mountains are dug into, water springs up, and even in deep valleys it is not necessary to dig down any further for water. The same is true in animals and birds, whose blood is equally close to the surface on the head and feet. A second characteristic of the earth is that grass and flowers bloom every year, but in the same year everything withers and drops off. So it is with the animals and the birds: hair and feathers grow on them, but each year these fall away. The third characteristic of the earth is that when it is opened or dug into, grass grows over the soil that is closest to the surface. People think of rocks and stones as comparable to the teeth and bones of living creatures. Thus they understand that the earth is alive and has a life of its own. They also know that, in terms of years, the earth is wondrously old and powerful in its own nature. It gives birth to all living things and claims ownership over all that dies. For this reason, they gave it a name and traced their origins to it.

From their ancestors, people also learned that the earth, the sun and the heavenly bodies remain constant after many hundreds of years have been reckoned. But the paths of the heavenly bodies change unequally, some have longer courses whereas others shorter. From such observations, people supposed that perhaps a controlling being was guiding the heavenly bodies, deciding their paths according to his wishes, and that this being would be very powerful and mighty. They surmised that, if he ruled over the main elements of nature, he existed before the heavenly bodies. They also perceived that, if he ruled the movement of the heavenly bodies, he governed the sun's shining, the moisture from the air, and also the resulting fruits of the earth and the winds in the sky that raised storms at sea.

People did not know where his kingdom was. Because of this, they believed that he ruled over all things on earth and in the sky, in the heavens and the heavenly bodies, and in the sea and the weather. In order to recount these beliefs and to fix them in memory, they gave their own names to all things, and the nature of their beliefs changed in many ways as different nations were established and languages branched out. People understood all matters in an earthly way because they had been granted no spiritual wisdom. Therefore they reckoned that all things were fashioned from material substances.

2. THE THREE PARTS OF THE WORLD

The world was divided into three parts. From the south towards the west up to the Mediterranean Sea is the part called Africa. Its southern region is hot and scorched by the sun. The second part begins in the west and continues northward towards the sea; it is called Europe or Enea. Its northern regions are so cold that no grass grows and no one can subsist there. Starting in the north and continuing across the eastern continent all the way to the south is the region called Asia.[1] Everything in that part of the world is beautiful and stately, and the earth produces gold and gemstones. The middle of the world is also there. Just as the earth in that region is more beautiful and better in all ways than other places, so too the people there are most endowed with all blessings: wisdom and strength, beauty, and every kind of skill.

3. THE PEOPLE OF TROY AND THOR

Near the middle of the world, a building and a living hall were constructed, which became the most renowned that have ever been. The place was named Troy and is found in the region we call Turkey. It was built much larger than others and in many ways with greater skill; neither cost nor the resources of the country were spared. There were twelve kingdoms with one high king, and to each kingdom belonged many groups who paid tribute. In the city there were twelve main chieftains. These rulers were superior in all human attributes to the other people who had preceded them in the world.

One of the kings was named Munon or Mennon. He was married to Troan, the daughter of Priam, the chief king. They had a son who was named Tror, the one we call Thor. He was brought up in Thracia by a duke named Loricus, and when he was ten years old he received his father's weapons. So great was his beauty that, when he was among other people, he stood out as elephant ivory does when inlaid in oak. His hair was more beautiful than gold. By the time he was twelve years old, he had acquired his full strength. Then he was able to lift from the ground ten bearskins, all in a pile. Next he killed his foster-father Loricus and his wife Lora, or Glora, and took possession of the realm of Thracia. We call that place Thrudheim. Afterwards he travelled widely through many lands, exploring all parts of the world, and on his own he overcame all manner of berserkers[1] and giants, as well as one of the greatest dragons and many beasts.

In the northern part of the world he came across the prophetess called Sibyl, whom we call Sif, and he married her. No one knows Sif's ancestors. She was the loveliest of women, with hair like gold. Their son, named Loridi, was much like his father. Loridi's son was Einridi, his son Vingethor, his son Vingenir, his son Moda, his son Magi, his son Seskef, his son Bedvig, his son Athra, whom we call Annar, his son Itrmann, his son Heremod, his son Skjaldun, whom we call Skjold, his son Biaf, whom we call Bjar, his son Jat, his son Gudolf, his son Finn, and his son Friallaf, whom we call Fridleif. He had a son named Voden, the one we call Odin, an excellent man because of his wisdom and because he had every kind of accomplishment. His wife, named Frigida, we call Frigg.[2]

4. ODIN'S JOURNEY NORTHWARD

Odin had the gift of prophecy, as his wife also did, and through this learning he became aware that his name would become renowned in the northern part of the world and honoured more than other kings. For this reason he was eager to set off from Turkey, and he took with him on his journey a large following of people, young and old, men and women. So, too, they took with them many precious things. Wherever they went on their travels, tales of their splendour were told, making them seem more like gods than men. They journeyed without stopping until they had reached the north, where they entered the region now called Saxland. There Odin settled down for a long time, taking possession of much of the land.

Odin had three of his sons guard the country. One of them, Veggdegg, was a powerful king who ruled over East Saxland. His son was Vitrgils, whose sons were Vitta, the father of Heingest, and Sigar, the father of Svebdegg, whom we call Svipdag. Odin's second son, named Beldegg, we call Baldr; he held the land that is now called Westphalia. His son was Brand, and his son was Frjodigar, whom we call Frodi; his son was Freovin, his son was Wigg, whose son Gevis we call Gavir. Odin's third son was named Siggi, whose son was Rerir. The men of this family ruled in what is now called France, and from them come the family called the Volsungs.

From all of them, numerous and great families descend.

5. ODIN'S JOURNEY CONTINUES AND THE ÆSIR SETTLE IN THE NORTH

Then Odin set out, travelling north, and arrived in the country called Reidgotaland. He took possession of all that he wanted in that land and made his son Skjold ruler. Skjold's son was named Fridleif and from him are descended the kindred known as the Skjoldungs, the family of the kings of Denmark. What is now called Jutland was then called Reidgotaland.

He then went northward to what is now called Sweden, where a king named Gylfi lived. When the king learned of the journey of these Asians, who were called Æsir, he went to meet them, offering to grant Odin as much authority in his kingdom as he wanted. Wherever they stayed in these lands a time of peace and prosperity accompanied their journey, so that all believed the newcomers were the cause. This was because the local inhabitants saw that they were unlike any others they had known in beauty and intelligence. Recognizing the land's rich possibilities, Odin chose a place for a town, the one that is now called Sigtun.[1] He appointed leaders and, in accordance with the customs of Troy, he selected twelve men to administer the law of the land. In this way he organized the laws as they had been in Troy, in the manner to which the Turks were accustomed.

Then he went north, continuing until he reached the ocean, which people believed surrounded all lands. There, in what is now called Norway, he placed his son in power. This son was named Saeming, and Norway's kings, as well as its jarls and other important men of the kingdom, trace their descent to him, as it is told in *Haleygjatal.*[2] Odin also had with him his son named Yngvi, who after him became a king in Sweden, and from whom those kinsmen called the Ynglings are descended.

The Æsir and some of their sons married women from the lands where they settled, and their families increased. They spread throughout Saxland and from there throughout all the northern regions so that their language – that of the men of Asia – became the native tongue in all these lands. People think, because the names of their ancestors are recorded in genealogies, they can show that these names were part of the language that the Æsir brought here to the northern world – to Norway, Sweden, Denmark and Saxland. In England, however, some names of ancient regions and places lead one to believe that the names originally came from another language.

GYLFAGINNING
(THE DELUDING OF GYLFI)

I. KING GYLFI AND THE WOMAN GEFJUN

King Gylfi ruled over the lands now called Sweden. It is said that he offered a travelling woman, in return for the pleasure of her company, a piece of ploughland in his kingdom as large as four oxen could plough in a day and a night. But this woman, named Gefjun, was of the Æsir. She took four oxen from Jotunheim [Giant Land] in the north. They were her own sons by a giant, and she yoked them to the plough, which dug so hard and so deep that it cut the land loose. The oxen dragged this land westward out to sea, stopping finally at a certain channel. There Gefjun fastened the land and gave it the name Sjaelland.[1] The place where the land was removed has since become a body of water in Sweden now called Logrinn [the Lake],[2] and in this lake there are as many inlets as there are headlands in Sjaelland. So says the poet Bragi the Old:

> Gefjun dragged from Gylfi
> gladly the land beyond value,
> Denmark's increase,
> steam rising from the swift-footed bulls.
> The oxen bore eight
> moons of the forehead and four heads,
> hauling as they went in front of
> the grassy isle's wide fissure.

2. GYLFI ENCOUNTERS THE THREE CHIEFTAINS OF THE ÆSIR[1]

King Gylfi was a wise man skilled in magic. He was amazed that the Æsir knew so much that everything went according to their wishes. He wondered whether this was because of their own nature or whether it came from the divine power of the gods they worshipped. He set out on a secret trip to Asgard and changed into the likeness of an old man to disguise himself. But the Æsir, because they had the gift of prophecy, were the wiser in such matters. Before his arrival they foresaw his coming and, in preparation for him, they conjured up visual illusions.[2] When he entered the fortress, he saw a hall. It was so high that he could scarcely see over it, and golden shields covered its roof like shingles. As Thjodolf of Hvin[3] says, Valhalla [Hall of the Slain] was roofed with shields:

> On their backs they let shine
> hall shingles of Svafnir [Odin],
> when bombarded with stones,
> those resourceful men.

Gylfi saw a man in the doorway of the hall. He was juggling short swords and had seven in the air at once. The man spoke first, asking the visitor's name. Gylfi named himself Gangleri, saying that he had travelled over trackless paths. He asked for a night's lodging and inquired who owned the hall. The man answered that it belonged to their king.

'I can take you to see him; then you can ask him his name yourself.' The man then turned and went ahead into the hall. Gylfi followed him and immediately the door closed after him. He saw many living areas there and groups of people. Some were playing games, some were drinking, and some had weapons and were fighting. He looked around, and it seemed to him that much of what he was seeing was incredible. Then he said:

'All doorways
before entering
gaze into carefully;
one never knows
where on the benches
enemies are sitting.'

(*Sayings of the High One.* 1)

He saw three thrones, each one higher than the other. Three men sat there, one in each seat. He asked the name of their ruler. The man guiding him replied that the king was in the lowest of the high seats; he was called High. Next came the one called Just-as-High, while the one highest up was called Third.[4]

Then High asked the new arrival if there was some more pressing cause of his visit, although he was welcome to food and drink as were all in the hall of the High One. Gylfi replied that he wanted to know first whether there was a wise man in the hall. High said that Gylfi would not escape unharmed unless he grew wiser, adding:

'Stand forward while you inquire;
The one who recounts shall sit.'

3. THE ALL-FATHER

Gangleri began to question: 'Who is the highest or the oldest of all the gods?'

High replied, 'He is called All-Father in our language, but in Asgard the Old, he has twelve names: one is All-Father, a second is Herran or Herjan [Lord], a third is Nikar or Hnikar [Thruster], a fourth is Nikuz or Hnikud [Thruster], a fifth is Fjolnir [Wise One], a sixth Oski [Fulfiller of Desire], a seventh Omi [Resounding One], an eighth Biflidi or Biflindi [Spear Shaker], a ninth Svidar, a tenth Svidrir, an eleventh Vidrir [Ruler of Weather] and a twelfth Jalg or Jalk [Gelding].'

Then Gangleri asked, 'Where is this god? What is he capable of doing and what outstanding deeds has he done?'

High replied, 'He lives through all ages and governs all things in his realm. He decides all matters, great or small.'

Then Just-as-High said, 'He made heaven, earth and the skies and everything in them.'

Then Third said, 'Most important, he created man and gave him a living spirit that will never die, even if the body rots to dust or burns to ashes. All men who are righteous shall live and be with him in that place called Gimle or Vingolf. But evil men go to Hel[1] and from there into Niflhel[2] [Dark Hel], which is below in the ninth world.

Gangleri then asked: 'What did he do before heaven and earth were created?'

High answered, 'Back then, he was with the frost giants.'

4. NIFLHEIM AND MUSPELLSHEIM

Gangleri asked, 'What was the beginning, or how did things start? What was there before?'

High answered, 'As it says in *The Sibyl's Prophecy*:

> Early of ages
> when nothing was.
> There was neither sand nor sea
> nor cold waves.
> The earth was not found
> nor the sky above.
> Ginnungagap[1] was there,
> but grass, nowhere.' (*The Sibyl's Prophecy. 3*)

Next Just-as-High said, 'Niflheim [Dark World] was made many ages before the earth was created, and at its centre is the spring called Hvergelmir [Roaring Kettle]. From there flow those rivers called Svol, Gunnthra, Fjorm, Fimbulthul, Slid and Hrid, Sylg and Ylg, Vid and Leiptr. Also there is Gjoll, which lies next to Helgrind [Gates of Hel].'

Then Third said, 'First, however, there was that world in the southern region which is called Muspell.[2] It is bright and hot.

That region flames and burns and is impassable for foreigners and those who cannot claim it as their native land. Surt [Black One] is the name of he who waits there at the land's edge to defend it. He has a flaming sword, and when the end of the world comes, he will set off to battle and defeat all the gods, burning the whole world with fire. So it is said in *The Sibyl's Prophecy*:

> Surt comes from the south
> with the fiery destruction of branches.
> The sun shines from the sword
> of the gods of the slain.
> Stone cliffs tumble
> and troll witches stumble.[3]
> Men tread the Road to Hel
> as the sky splits apart.' (*The Sibyl's Prophecy*. 52)

5. GINNUNGAGAP AND THE EMERGENCE OF YMIR

Gangleri asked: 'How were things set up before the different families came into being and mankind increased?'

High replied, 'When those rivers, which are called Elivagar [Storm Waves], came so far from their source, the poisonous flow hardened like a slag of cinders running from a furnace, and became ice. When this ice began to solidify and no longer ran, poisonous drops spewed out and froze into icy rime [hoarfrost]. Then layer by layer, the ice grew within Ginnungagap.'

Then Just-as-High said, 'That part of Ginnungagap, which reached into the northern regions, became filled with thick ice and rime. Inside the gap there was mist and wind-whipped rain. But the southern part of Ginnungagap grew light because of sparks and glowing embers flowing from Muspellsheim.'

Then Third spoke: 'Just as coldness and all things grim came from Niflheim, the regions bordering on Muspell were warm and bright, and Ginnungagap was as mild as a windless sky. It thawed and dripped at the point where the icy rime and the warm winds met. There was a quickening in these flowing drops and life sprang up, taking its force from the power that sent the heat. The likeness of a man appeared and he was named Ymir. The frost giants call him Aurgelmir, and from him come the clans of the frost giants, as it says in *The Shorter Sibyl's Prophecy*:

All the seeresses[1] are
from Vidolf,
all the wizards
from Vilmeid,
but the sorcerers are
from Svarthofdi
and all the giants
come from Ymir. (*The Lay of Hyndla*. 33)

'Here as the giant Vafthrudnir says:

From where Aurgelmir first came,
the wise giant,
among sons of giants.

When poison from Elivagar
splashed out in drops
it grew until forming a giant,
from there all our clans
have come;
therefore they are all so cruel.'
(*The Lay of Vafthrudnir*. 30–31)

Then Gangleri asked, 'How did the families grow from that point or how did it come about that others came into being? And do you believe that the one whom you were just talking about is a god?'

High answered: 'In no way do we accept him as a god. He was evil, as are all his descendants; we call them frost giants. It is said that as he slept he took to sweating. Then, from under his left arm[2] grew a male and a female, while one of his legs got a son with the other. From here came the clans that are called the frost giants. The old frost giant, him we call Ymir.'

6. THE PRIMEVAL COW AUDHUMLA, YMIR AND THE BIRTH OF ODIN

Gangleri asked, 'Where did Ymir live, and what did he live on?'

'Next it happened that as the icy rime dripped, the cow called Audhumla was formed. Four rivers of milk ran from her udders, and she nourished Ymir.'

Then Gangleri asked, 'On what did the cow feed?'

High replied, 'She licked the blocks of ice, which were salty. As she licked these stones of icy rime the first day, the hair of a man appeared in the blocks towards the evening. On the second day came the man's head, and on the third day, the whole man. He was called Buri, and he was beautiful, big and strong. He had a son called Bor, who took as his wife the woman called Bestla. She was the daughter of Bolthorn the giant, and they had three sons. One was called Odin, another Vili and the third Ve. It is my belief that this Odin and his brothers are the rulers of heaven and earth. We know that is his name, and it is what we call the one whom we know to be the greatest and the most renowned, and you too can easily call him that.'

7. BERGELMIR AND THE APPEARANCE OF THE SECOND RACE OF FROST GIANTS

Then Gangleri asked, 'How did they get on together? Who among them was the most powerful?'

'The sons of Bor killed the giant Ymir,' answered High. 'When he fell, so much blood gushed from his wounds that with it they drowned all the race of the frost giants except for one who escaped with his household. The giants call that one

Bergelmir. He, together with his wife, climbed up on to his wooden box,[1] and there they kept themselves safe. From them come the races of the frost giants, as is said here:

> Countless winters[2]
> before the earth was created
> back then Bergelmir was born;
> that is the first I remember
> when the wise giant
> was placed on the box.'
>
> (*The Lay of Vafthrudnir*. 35)

8. THE WORLD IS CREATED FROM YMIR'S BODY

Gangleri answered, 'What did Bor's sons do next, if you believe they are gods?'

High said, 'It is no small matter to be told. They took Ymir and they moved him into the middle of Ginnungagap and made from him the world. From his blood they made the sea and the lakes. The earth was fashioned from the flesh, and mountain cliffs from the bones. They made stones and gravel from the teeth, the molars and those bones that were broken.'

Then Just-as-High said, 'With the blood that gushed freely from the wounds, they made the sea, and by fashioning that sea around, they belted and fastened the earth. Most men would think it impossible to cross over this water.'

Then Third added: 'They also took his skull and from it made the sky. They raised it over the earth and under each of the four corners they placed a dwarf. These are called East, West, North and South. Then they took the embers and sparks shooting out from Muspellsheim and flying randomly. These they placed in the middle of the Ginnung Sky, both above and below, to light up heaven and earth. They fixed places for all these burning elements. Some were placed up in the heavens, whereas for others, which had moved about under the heavens, they found places and established their courses. It is said in the old sources that, from then on, times of day were differentiated and the course of years was set. So it is said in *The Sibyl's Prophecy*:

> Sun did not know
> where she had her home.
> Moon did not know
> what strength he had.
> The stars did not know
> where their places were. (*The Sibyl's Prophecy*. 5)

'This was before the earth was created,' Third added.

Then Gangleri said, 'I hear of great happenings. It was wondrous work and skilfully done, but how was the earth set in order?'

Then High answered: 'It is circular around the edge and surrounding it lies the deep sea. On these ocean coasts, the sons of Bor gave land to the clans of the giants to live on. But further inland they built a fortress wall around the world to protect against the hostility of the giants. As material for the wall, they used the eyelashes[1] of the giant Ymir and called this stronghold Midgard[2] [Middle Earth]. They took his brain, threw it up into the air, and from it they made the clouds. As is said here:

> From Ymir's flesh
> was the earth created,
> from the bloody sweat, the sea,
> cliffs from bones,
> trees from hair,
> and from the head, the heavens;
>
> And from his eyelashes
> the gentle gods made
> Midgard for the sons of men;
> and from his brains
> all the oppressive
> clouds were formed.'
>
> (*The Lay of Grimnir*. 40–41)

9. MEN ARE CREATED AND ASGARD IS BUILT. THE ALL-FATHER SEES EVERYTHING

Then Gangleri said, 'It seems to me that they accomplished great things when the earth and the sky were made, the sun and the moon set in their places and the days divided. But the people who inhabit the world, where did they come from?'

Then High answered, 'The sons of Bor were once walking along the seashore and found two trees. They lifted the logs and from them created people. The first son gave them breath and life; the second, intelligence and movement; the third, form, speech, hearing and sight.[1] They [Bor's sons] gave them clothing and names. The man was called Ask [Ash Tree] and the woman, Embla [Elm or Vine]. From them came mankind and they were given a home behind Midgard's wall.'

High said: 'Next they made a stronghold for themselves in the middle of the world, and it was called Asgard. We call it Troy. There the gods lived together with their kinsmen, and as a result many events and happenings took place both on the earth and in the sky. One place there is called Hlidskjalf [Watch-tower]. When Odin sat in its high seat, he could see through all worlds and into all men's doings. Moreover, he understood everything he saw. His wife was called Frigg, Fjorgyn's daughter, and from this family has come the kindred we call the family of the Æsir. They lived in Old Asgard and the realms that belong to it; each member of this family is divine. For these reasons he can be referred to as All-Father, since he is the father of all the gods and men and of everything that has been accomplished by his power. Earth was his daughter[2] and his wife. With her he had his first son, and this is Asa-Thor [Thor of the Æsir]. He has strength and might, and because of this, he defeats all living creatures.'

10. NIGHT AND DAY

'A giant called Norfi or Narfi lived in Giant Land. He had a daughter named Night, who was black and swarthy like her kinsmen. She was married first to the man called Naglfari; their son was named Aud [Wealth]. Next she was married to Annar [Second]. Their daughter was named Earth. Finally she married Delling, who was from the family of the gods. Their son was Day, and he was as bright and beautiful as his father's people. Then All-Father took Night and her son Day. He gave them two horses and two chariots and placed them in the sky to ride around the earth every twenty-four hours. Night rides first with the horse called Hrimfaxi [Frost Mane], and every morning foam from the horse's bit sprinkles the earth. Day's horse is called Skinfaxi [Shining Mane], and with its mane it lights up all the sky and the earth.'

11. SUN AND MOON

Then Gangleri said, 'How does he steer the course of the sun and the moon?'

High said: 'There was a man named Mundilfari who had two children. They were so fair and beautiful that he called one Moon [Mani] and the other, a daughter, he called Sun [Sol], marrying her to the man named Glen. But the gods were angered by this arrogance, and they took the brother and sister and placed them up in the heavens. There they made Sun drive the horses that drew the chariot of the sun, which the gods, in order to illuminate the worlds, had created from burning embers flying from Muspellsheim. The horses are called Arvak and Alsvinn. In order to cool them, the gods placed two bellows under their shoulders; according to some lore, the bellows are called Isarnkol. Mani guides the path of the moon and controls its waxing and waning. He took from the earth two children named Bil and Hjuki. They had been walking from the well called Byrgir, carrying between them on their shoulders the pole called Simul with the pail called Soeg. Vidfinn was the name of their father. These children follow Mani, as can be seen from the earth.'

12. THE WOLVES

Then Gangleri asked, 'The sun moves quickly and it is almost as though she fears something. She cannot go faster on her journey even if she were afraid of her own death.'

Then High answered, 'It is not surprising that she moves with such speed. The one chasing her comes close, and there is no escape for her except to run.'

'Who is chasing her?' asked Gangleri.

High said, 'There are two wolves, and the one who is chasing her is called Skoll. He frightens her, and he eventually will catch her. The other is called Hati Hrodvitnisson. He runs in front of her trying to catch the moon. And, this will happen.'

Then Gangleri asked, 'Of what family are the wolves?'

High replied, 'An ogress lives to the east of Midgard in the forest called Jarnvid [Iron Wood]. The troll women who are called the Jarnvidjur [the Iron Wood Dwellers] live in that forest. The old ogress bore many giant sons, all in the likeness of wolves, and it is from here that these wolves come. It is said that the most powerful of this kin will be the one called Managarm [Moon Dog]. He will gorge himself with the life of all who die, and he will swallow the moon,[1] spattering blood throughout the sky and all the heavens. Because of this, the sun will lose its brightness while the winds will turn violent, roaring in from all directions. So it is said in *The Sibyl's Prophecy*:

> In the East the old one lives[2]
> in Iron Wood
> and there she bears
> Fenrir's brood [the wolves].

From all of them comes
one in particular,
the ruin of the moon
in the shape of a troll.

He gorges himself on the life
of doomed men,
reddens the gods' dwelling
with crimson gore.
Dark goes the sunshine,
for summers after,
the weather all vicious.
Do you know now or what?'

(*The Sibyl's Prophecy.* 40–41)

13. BIFROST [THE RAINBOW BRIDGE]

Then Gangleri said, 'What is the path from the earth to the sky?'

Then, snickering, High answered: 'Your question shows little knowledge. Haven't you heard that the gods built a bridge from the earth to the sky and it is called Bifrost? You will have seen it, and possibly you call it the rainbow. It has three colours and great strength, and it is made with more skill and knowledge than other constructions. Sturdy though it is, it will break when the sons of Muspell ride over it [at Ragnarok]. Then their horses will swim across great rivers and so they will advance.'

Then Gangleri said, 'Since they can do whatever they wish, it seems to me that the gods did not build the bridge reliably if it will break.'

High replied, 'The gods deserve no blame for the construction. Bifrost is a sound bridge, but nothing in this world can be trusted when the sons of Muspell attack.'

14. ASGARD AND THE ORIGIN OF THE DWARVES

Then Gangleri said: 'What did All-Father do, once Asgard was built?'

High replied, 'In the beginning he assigned rulers, asking them to judge with him people's fate and to oversee the arrangements of the stronghold. This was done at the place called Idavoll [Eternally Renewing Field] in the middle of the stronghold.[1] Their first task was to build the temple where they placed their seats – twelve in addition to All-Father's throne. That building is the best and the largest on earth. Outside and inside everything seems to be made of gold, and the place is called Gladsheim [Home of Joy]. They built a second hall, a sanctuary, which belonged to the goddesses,[2] and it was exceptionally beautiful. People call this building Vingolf [Friendly Quarters].

'Next they set up forges and made hammer, tongs and anvil, and with these they fashioned all other tools. Following this, they worked metal, stone, wood and great quantities of gold, such that all their furniture and household utensils were of gold. That age is called the Golden Age before it was spoiled by the arrival of the women who came from Giant Land.[3]

'Next the gods took their places on their thrones. They issued their judgments and remembered where the dwarves had come to life in the soil under the earth, like maggots in flesh. The dwarves emerged first, finding life in Ymir's flesh. They were maggots at that time, but by a decision of the gods they acquired human understanding and assumed the likeness of men, living in the earth and the rocks. Modsognir was a dwarf and Durin another. So it says in *The Sibyl's Prophecy*:

> Then all the powerful gods went
> to their thrones of fate,
> the most sacred gods, and
> decided among themselves
> that a troop of dwarves

should be created
from the waves of blood[4]
and from Blain's limbs.
There in men's likeness
were made many
dwarves in the earth,
as Durin said. (*The Sibyl's Prophecy.* 9–10)

'And these, says the prophetess, are the names of these dwarves:

Nyi, Nidi,
Nordri, Sudri,
Austri, Vestri,
Althjolf, Dvalin,
Nar, Nain,
Niping, Dain,
Bifur, Bafur,
Bombor, Nori,
Ori, Onar,
Oin, Modvitnir,
Vig and Gandalf,
Vindalf, Thorin,
Fili, Kili,
Fundin, Vali,
Thror, Throin,
Thekk, Lit, Vitr,
Nyr, Nyrad,
Rekk, Radsvinn. (*The Sibyl's Prophecy.* 11–13)

'But these, too, are dwarves and they live in the rocks, whereas those mentioned before live in the ground:[5]

Draupnir, Dolgthvari,
Haur, Hugstari,
Hledjolf, Gloin,
Dori, Ori,

Duf, Andvari,
Heptifili,
Har, Siar. (*The Sibyl's Prophecy*. *13* and *15*[6])

'These came from Svarin's mound to Joruvellir [Pebble Plains] at Aurvangar [Mud Fields], and Lofar is descended from them. These are their names:

Skirpir, Virpir,
Skafinn, Ai,
Alf, Ingi,
Eikinskjaldi,
Fal, Frosti,
Finn, Ginnar.' (*The Sibyl's Prophecy*. *15–16*)

15. THE ASH YGGDRASIL, THE NORNS AND THE THREE WELLS

Then Gangleri said, 'Where is the central or holy place of the gods?'

High answered, 'It is at the ash Yggdrasil. There each day the gods hold their courts.'

Then Gangleri asked, 'What is there to tell about that place?'

Then Just-as-High said, 'The ash is the largest and the best of all trees. Its branches spread themselves over all the world, and it stands over the sky. Three roots support the tree and they are spread very far apart. One is among the Æsir. A second is among the frost giants where Ginnungagap once was. The third reaches down to Niflheim, and under this root is the well Hvergelmir; but Nidhogg [Hateful Striker] gnaws at this root from below.

'Under the root that goes to the frost giants is the Well of Mimir. Wisdom and intelligence are hidden there, and Mimir is the name of the well's owner. He is full of wisdom because he drinks of the well from the Gjallarhorn.[1] All-Father went there and asked for one drink from the well, but he did not get this until he gave one of his eyes as a pledge. As it says in *The Sibyl's Prophecy*:

Odin, I know all,
where you hid the eye
in that famous
Well of Mimir.
Each morning
Mimir drinks mead
from Val-Father's pledge.
Do you know now or what?
(*The Sibyl's Prophecy*. 28)

'The third root of the ash is in heaven, and under that root is the very holy well called the Well of Urd. There the gods have their place of judgment. Every day the Æsir ride up over Bifrost, which is also called Asbru [Bridge of the Æsir]. The horses of the Æsir are named as follows: Sleipnir [Fast Traveller] is the best; Odin owns him, and he has eight legs. The second is Glad, the third Gyllir, the fourth Glaer, the fifth Skeidbrimir, the sixth Silfrtopp, the seventh Sinir, the eighth Gils, the ninth Falhofnir, the tenth Gulltopp and the eleventh is Lettfeti. Baldr's horse was burned with him. Thor, however, walks to the court; wading those rivers named as follows:

Kormt and Ormt
and the two Kerlaugs,
through these Thor will
wade each day
when he goes to judge
at the ash Yggdrasil,
because the bridge of the Æsir
burns with fire –
holy waters seethe.' (*The Lay of Grimnir*. 29)

Then Gangleri said, 'Does fire burn over Bifrost?'

High replied: 'The red you see in the rainbow is the burning fire. The frost giants and the mountain giants would scale heaven if Bifrost could be travelled by all who wanted to do so. There are many beautiful places in heaven and everything is divinely protected. A handsome hall stands under the ash beside the well. Out of this hall come three maidens, who are called Urd [Fate], Verdandi [Becoming] and Skuld[2] [Obligation]. These maidens shape men's lives. We call them the norns. There are yet more norns, those who come to each person at birth to decide the length of one's life, and these are related to the gods. Others are descended from the elves, and a third group comes from the dwarves, as is said here:

Born of very different parents
I believe the norns are,
they do not share kinship.
Some are of the Æsir,
Some are of the elves,
Some are the daughters of Dvalin.'

(*The Lay of Fafnir.* 13)

Then Gangleri said, 'If the norns decide the fates of men, then they do so in a terribly uneven manner. Some people enjoy a good and prosperous life, whereas others have little wealth or renown. Some have a long life, but others, a short one.'

High said: 'The good norns, the ones who are well born, shape a good life. When people experience misfortune, it is the bad norns who are responsible.'

16. THE CREATURES OF THE ASH TREE YGGDRASIL

Then Gangleri said, 'What more of importance can be said about the ash?'

High replied, 'There is much to be told. An eagle sits in the branches of the ash, and it has knowledge of many things. Between its eyes sits the hawk called Vedrfolnir [Wind Bleached]. The squirrel called Ratatosk [Drill Tooth] runs up and down the ash. He tells slanderous gossip, provoking the eagle and Nidhogg. Four stags called Dain, Dvalin, Duneyr and Durathror move about in the branches of the ash, devouring the tree's foliage.[1] In Hvergelmir there are so many serpents with Nidhogg that no tongue can count them. As it says here:

> The ash Yggdrasil
> endures hardship,
> more than men know.
> A stag bites from above
> and its sides rot;
> From below Nidhogg gnaws.
>
> (*The Lay of Grimnir*. 35)

'So it is said:

> More snakes
> lie under the ash Yggdrasil
> than any old fool imagines.
> Goin and Moin,
> they are Grafvitnir's sons,
> Grabak and Grafvollud, and
> Ofnir and Svafnir
> will always, I believe,
> eat away the tree's shoots.
>
> (*The Lay of Grimnir*. 34)

'It is also said that those norns who live beside Urd's Well draw water every day from the spring and that they splash this, mixed with the mud that lies beside the well, over the ash so that its branches will not wither or decay. That water is so sacred that all things which come into the spring become as white as the membrane called *skjall* [skin] which lies on the inside of the eggshell. As it says here:

> I know an ash,
> it is called Yggdrasil,
> a high, holy tree,

splashed and coated with white clay.
From it come the dews
that fall in the valleys.
It will always stand
green over Urd's Well. (*The Sibyl's Prophecy.* 19)

'People call the dew, which falls to the earth, honey dew, and bees feed on it. Two birds nourish themselves in the Well of Urd. These are called swans, and from them comes the species of bird with that name.'

17. THE HIGH ONE TELLS OF OTHER PLACES IN HEAVEN

Then Gangleri said, 'You know much to tell about the heavens. Are there other significant places besides the one at Urd's Well?'

High said, 'There are many magnificent places there. One is called Alfheim [Elf World]. The people called the light elves live there, but the dark elves live down below in the earth. They are different from the light elves in appearance, and far more so in nature. The light elves are more beautiful than the sun, while the dark elves are blacker than pitch. One place is named Breidablik [Gleaming Far and Wide], and no place there is more beautiful. There also is the place called Glitnir [Radiant Place]; its walls, columns and pillars are of red gold, and its roof is of silver. Then there is that place called Himinbjorg. It stands at heaven's end, right at the far edge of the bridge where Bifrost enters heaven. There is also the great place called Valaskjalf; it belongs to Odin. The gods built it and roofed it with pure silver. Inside this hall is Hlidskjalf, as this throne is called. When All-Father sits in this seat, he sees over all the world.

'At the southern reaches of heaven's end is a hall, the most beautiful of them all and brighter than the sun. It is called Gimle. It will remain standing when both heaven and earth are gone, and good and righteous men will inhabit that place through all ages. As *The Sibyl's Prophecy* says:

I know a hall, standing
fairer than the sun
better than gold
at Gimle.
Worthy men
will live there
through the days of all time
enjoying happiness.'

(*The Sibyl's Prophecy*. 64)

Then Gangleri said, 'What will protect this place when Surt's fire burns heaven and earth?'

High answered: 'It is said that a second heaven lies to the south and above this heaven. It is called Andlang [Long and Wide]. Still further up, there is a third heaven called Vidblain [Wide Blue]. We believe that this region is in heaven, but now only the light elves live there.'

18. THE ORIGIN OF THE WIND

Then Gangleri said: 'From where comes the wind? It is so strong that it whips the great oceans and stirs up fire. But as strong as it is, no one can see it, so wondrously is it made.'

High said, 'I can easily tell you that. At the far northern end of heaven sits a giant named Hraesvelg [Corpse Gulper]. He has the shape of an eagle, and when he beats his wings to take flight, the winds blow out from under them. As is said here:

Hraesvelg, he is called,
who sits at heaven's end,
a giant in eagle's shape.
From his wings,
it is said, the winds
blow over all men.'

(*The Sibyl's Prophecy*. 37)

19. SUMMER AND WINTER

Then Gangleri asked, 'Why is there such a difference between the heat of summer and the cold of winter?'

High answered, 'A wise man would not have asked, because everyone can answer this. But if you are a man of such little learning that you have not heard this before, then I would rather that you, in your ignorance, ask than continue to be unaware of what one ought to know. Svasud is the name of the father of Summer. He is a man so content that from his name comes the expression "it is *svasligt*", referring to what is pleasant. The father of Winter is alternately called Vindloni or Vindsval [Wind Chill]. He is the son of Vasad [Damp Cold]. These are cruel and cold-hearted kinsmen, and Winter takes its nature from them.'

20. ODIN THE ALL-FATHER

Then Gangleri said, 'Which Æsir ought men to believe in?'

High answered, 'There are twelve Æsir whose nature is divine.'

Then Just-as-High added: 'The goddesses are no less sacred, nor are they less powerful.'

Then Third said, 'Odin is the highest and oldest of the gods. He rules in all matters, and, although the other gods are powerful, all serve him as children do their father. Frigg is his wife. She knows the fates of men, even though she pronounces no prophecies. So it is said here, when Odin himself spoke with one of the Æsir called Loki:[1]

"You are raving, Loki,
and out of your mind,
why, Loki, do you not stop?
Frigg knows,
I believe, the fate of all,
though she herself says nothing."

(*Loki's Flyting*. 21, 29, 47)

'Odin is called All-Father, because he is the father of all the gods. He is also called Father of the Slain [Val-Father], because all who fall in battle are his adopted sons. With them he mans Valhalla and Vingolf, and they are known as the Einherjar. He is also called Hanga-God [God of the Hanged], Hapta-God[2] [God of Prisoners] and Farma-God [God of Cargoes], and he named himself in many other ways on his visit to King Geirrod:

"I call myself Grim
and Gangleri,
Herjan, Hjalmberi,
Thekk, Thrid,
Thunn, Unn,
Helblindi, Har,
Sann, Svipal,[3]
Sanngetal,
Herteit, Hnikar,
Bileyg, Baleyg,
Bolverk, Fjolnir,
Grimnir, Glapsvid, Fjolsvid,
Sidhott, Sidskegg,
Sig-Father, Hnikud,
All-Father, Atrid, Farmatyr,
Oski, Omi,
Jafnhar, Blindi,
Gondlir, Harbard,
Svidur, Svidrir,
Jalk, Kjalar, Vidur,
Thror, Ygg, Thund,
Vak, Skilfing,
Vafud, Hroptatyr,
Gaut, Veratyr."' (*The Lay of Grimnir. 46–50*)

Then Gangleri said, 'You have given him a large number of names. Truly,[4] it would be a mark of great learning to be able to relate all the events that lie behind each of these names.'

Then High said, 'To go carefully through all of that requires much wisdom. Nevertheless, it can quickly be said that most names were given, because, with all the different branches of languages in the world, each of the peoples needed to change his name to their own tongue to worship and to pray. But some names derive from events that took place on his travels. They have formed into tales, and you will never be called a wise man if you are unable to recount these great events.'

21. THOR

Then Gangleri said, 'What are the names of the other Æsir? How do they occupy themselves? What have they done of importance?'

High replied: 'Thor is the foremost among them. Called Thor of the Æsir [Asa-Thor] and Thor the Charioteer [Oku-Thor], he is the strongest of all gods and men. He rules at the place called Thrudvangar [Plains of Strength], and his hall is called Bilskirnir. There are five hundred and forty living spaces[1] in the hall, and it is the largest building that men have erected. So it says in *The Lay of Grimnir*:

Five hundred rooms
and forty more are found,
I believe when counted in Bilskirnir.
Of those residences
whose roofs I recognize,
my son's I know is largest.

(*The Lay of Grimnir*. 24)

'Thor has two male goats called Tanngniost [Tooth Gnasher] and Tanngrisnir [Snarl Tooth]. He also owns the chariot that they draw, and for this reason he is called Thor the Charioteer. He, too, has three choice possessions. One is the hammer Mjollnir. Frost giants and mountain giants recognize it when it is raised in the air, which is not surprising as it has cracked many a skull among their fathers and kinsmen. His second great treasure is his Megingjard [Belt of Strength]. When he buckles it on, his divine strength doubles. His third possession, the gloves of iron, are also a great treasure. He cannot be without these when he grips the hammer's shaft. No one is so wise that he can recount all of Thor's important deeds. I myself can tell you so many significant tales about him that hours would pass before I have said all I know.'

22. BALDR

Then Gangleri said, 'I would like to hear about the other Æsir.'

High said, 'Odin's second son is Baldr, and there is much good to tell about him. He is the best, and all praise him. He is so beautiful and so bright that light shines from him. One plant is so white that it is likened to Baldr's brow.[1] It is the whitest of all plants, and from this you can judge the beauty of both his hair and his body. He is the wisest of the gods. He is also the most beautifully spoken and the most merciful, but one of his characteristics is that none of his decisions is effective. He lives at the place called Breidablik. It is in heaven, and no impurity may be there. As is said:

Breidablik it is called
where Baldr has
made for himself a hall,
in that land
where I know there are
the fewest perils. (*The Lay of Grimnir. 12*)

23. NJORD AND SKADI

'The third god is named Njord. He lives in heaven at the place called Noatun [Enclosure for Ships]. He rules over the movement of the winds, and he can calm sea and fire. One invokes him in seafaring and fishing. He is so rich and prosperous that he can grant wealth in lands or valuables to those who ask for his aid. Njord is not of the Æsir family. He was brought up in Vanaheim, but the Vanir sent him as a hostage to the gods. In return they took as a hostage from the Æsir the one called Hoenir, and his exchange contributed to the peace between the gods and the Vanir.

'Njord has a wife called Skadi, the daughter of Thjazi the giant. Skadi wanted to live in the home that her father had owned up in the mountains at Thrymheim [Thunder Home]. But Njord wanted to be near the sea. They came to an agreement that they would stay nine nights in Thrymheim, and the next three nights at Noatun.[1] But when Njord returned to Noatun from the mountain, he said:

"Hateful for me are the mountains,
I was not long there,
only nine nights.
The howling of wolves
sounded ugly to me
after the song of swans."

'Then Skadi said this:

"Sleep I could not
on the sea beds
for the screeching of the bird.
That gull wakes me
when from the wide sea
he comes each morning."

'Then Skadi went up to the mountains and lived in Thrymheim. She travels much on skis, carries a bow and shoots wild animals. She is called the ski god or the ski lady, as is said:

Thrymheim it is called
where Thjazi lived,
the mighty giant.
But now Skadi,
pure bride of gods,
lives in her father's old house.

(*The Lay of Grimnir*. 11)

24. FREY AND FREYJA

'After this, Njord of Noatun had two children. The son was called Frey and the daughter Freyja. They were beautiful and powerful. Frey is the most splendid of the gods. He controls the rain and the shining of the sun, and through them the bounty of the earth. It is good to invoke him for peace and abundance. He also determines men's success in prosperity. Freyja is the most splendid of the goddesses. She has a home in heaven called Folkvangar [Warriors' Fields]. Wherever she rides into battle, half of the slain belong to her. Odin takes the other half, as it says here:

> Folkvang it is called,
> and there Freyja decides
> the choice of seats in the hall.
> Half the slain
> she chooses each day,
> and half belong to Odin.
>
> (*The Lay of Grimnir*. 14)

'Her hall, Sessrumnir [With Many Seats], is large and beautiful. When she travels, she drives a chariot drawn by two cats. She is easily approachable for people who want to pray to her,[1] and from her name comes the title of honour whereby women of rank are called *frovur* or ladies.[2] She delights in love songs, and it is good to call on her in matters of love.'

25. TYR

Then Gangleri said, 'The Æsir seem to me to be very powerful, and it is not surprising that there is so much strength in you, since you know so much about the gods and are aware of to whom each kind of prayer should be directed. Are there still more gods?'

High answered: 'Tyr[1] is the name of another of the Æsir. He is the boldest and most courageous, and it is very much up to him who wins in battle. For men of action, he is good to invoke. The expression goes that a man is Tyr courageous if he is the type who advances out in front, never losing his courage. Tyr is so wise that a clever person is said to be Tyr wise. It is a mark of his daring that when the Æsir tried to lure the wolf Fenrir in order to place the fetter Gleipnir on him, the wolf would not trust the gods to free him until finally they placed Tyr's hand as a pledge in the wolf's mouth. Then, when the Æsir refused to free him, the wolf bit off the hand at what is now called the wolf joint. Because of this, Tyr is one-handed, and men do not think of him as a peace maker.

26. BRAGI

'One of the gods is called Bragi. Though renowned for his wisdom, he is mostly known for his eloquence and his way with words. He is the most knowledgeable about poetry, and because of him poetry is named *brag*. From his name comes the usage whereby a person, more skilled with words than others, is called *bragr* or the foremost of men or women.

'His wife is Idunn. In her private wooden box[1] she keeps the apples which the gods bite into when they begin to grow old. They all become young again, and so it will be right up to Ragnarok.'

Then Gangleri said, 'It seems to me that the gods are greatly dependent upon Idunn's care and good faith.'

High said, as he laughed, 'Misfortune once came close. I could tell you about those events, but first you shall hear the names of still more Æsir.

27. HEIMDALL

'Heimdall is one. He is called the white god and is powerful and sacred. Nine maidens, all sisters, gave birth to him as their son. He is also known as Hallinskidi and Gullintanni [Gold

Toothed], as his teeth are gold. His horse is called Gulltopp [Golden Forelock]. He lives near Bifrost at a place called Himinbjorg. He is the watchman of the gods and sits at heaven's end, where he keeps watch over the bridge against the mountain giants. He needs less sleep than a bird, and he can see equally well by night or by day a distance of a hundred leagues. He hears the grass growing on the earth and the wool on sheep, as well as everything else that makes more noise. He has the horn known as Gjallarhorn, and its blast can be heard in all worlds. Heimdall's sword is called a head. It is said:

> Himinbjorg it is called
> and there Heimdall
> rules over sacred places.
> There the watchman of the gods
> drinks in his comfortable lodgings,
> happily, the good mead.
>
> (*The Lay of Grimnir*. 13)

'Further, he himself says in *Heimdall's Chant*:[1]

> "Of nine mothers I am the child,
> of nine sisters I am the son."

28. HOD

'Hod is the name of one of the gods. He is blind and immensely strong. The gods would have wished to avoid mentioning the name of this member of the Æsir, because the work of his hands will long be remembered[1] by gods and men.

29. VIDAR

'One is called Vidar; he is the silent god. He has a thick shoe[1] and is nearly as strong as Thor. The gods rely on him in all difficulties.

30. ALI OR VALI

'Ali or Vali is the name of one god, a son of Odin and Rind. He is bold in battle and a fine shot.

31. ULL

'Ull is the name of one. The son of Sif, he is the stepson of Thor. He is so skilful a bowman and skier that no one can compete with him. He is beautiful to look at, and is an accomplished warrior. He is also a good person to pray to[1] when in single combat.

32. FORSETI

'Forseti is the son of Baldr and Nanna Nep's daughter. His is the hall in heaven called Glitnir. All who come to him with legal difficulties leave reconciled. That hall is the best place of judgment known to gods and men. As it says here:

A hall named Glitnir,
supported by gold pillars
and roofed with silver.
There Forseti
spends most days
and settles all lawsuits.

(*The Lay of Grimnir. 15*)

33. LOKI

'Also counted among the Æsir is one whom some call Slanderer of the Gods, the Source of Deceit, and the Disgrace of All Gods and Men. Named Loki or Lopt, he is the son of the giant Farbauti. His mother is named Laufey or Nal, and his brothers are Byleist and Helblindi. Loki is pleasing, even beautiful to look at, but his nature is evil and he is undependable. More than others, he has the kind of wisdom known as cunning, and is treacherous in all matters. He constantly places the gods in difficulties and often solves their problems with guile. His wife is Sigyn and their son is Nari or Narfi.

34. LOKI'S MONSTROUS CHILDREN

'But Loki had other children. With Angrboda [Sorrow Bringer], an ogress who lived in Giant Land, Loki had three children. One was the Fenriswolf, the second was the Midgard Serpent[1] and the third was Hel. When the gods discovered that these three siblings were being brought up in Giant Land, they learned through prophecies that misfortune and evil were to be expected from these children. All of the gods became aware that harm was on the way, first because of the mother's nature, but even more so because of the father's.

'Then All-Father sent the gods to seize the children and bring them to him. When they appeared before him, he threw the serpent into the deep sea that surrounds all lands. But the serpent grew so large that now, out in the middle of the ocean, it lies coiled around all lands, biting its tail. Hel he threw down into Niflheim and made her ruler over nine worlds. She has the power to dole out lodgings and provisions to those who are sent to her, and they are the people who have died of disease or old age. She has there an enormous dwelling, with walls of immense height and huge gates. Her hall is called Eljudnir [Sprayed with Snowstorms], her dish is Hunger, her knife is Famine, her slave is Lazy, and Slothful is her woman servant. The threshold over which people enter is a pitfall called Fallandaforad [Falling to Peril], her bed is named Kor [Sick Bed], and her bed curtains are named Blikjandabol [Gleaming Disaster]. She is half black and half a lighter flesh colour and is easily recognized. Mostly she is gloomy and cruel.

'The Æsir raised the wolf at home, but only Tyr had the courage to approach it and feed it. But the gods saw how much the wolf grew every day and knew that all the prophecies foretold that it was destined to harm them. Then the Æsir devised a plan to make an especially strong fetter. They named it Laeding and brought it to the wolf, inviting him to test his strength against it. As it seemed to the wolf that this test would not require much strength, he let them do as they wished. The first time the wolf stretched the muscles in his legs, the fetter broke. Thus he freed himself from Laeding.

'Next the gods made a second fetter. Twice as strong, it was called Dromi. Again they asked the wolf to test the fetter, telling him that he would become renowned for his strength if such magnificent forging was unable to hold him. The wolf thought to himself that, even though the fetter was very strong, his strength had grown even more since he had broken Laeding. He also recognized that, to become renowned, he would have to place himself in danger, and so he let them put the fetter on him. When the Æsir were ready, the wolf started to twist and beat the fetter against the ground. He struggled with all his might and, using his legs, he snapped the fetter with such force that the pieces flew into the distance. Thus he escaped from Dromi. Since then, there has been an expression, when a task is extremely difficult, that one frees oneself from Laeding or breaks out from Dromi.

'After this happened, the gods began to fear that they would not succeed in binding the wolf. So All-Father sent Skirnir [Bright One], Frey's messenger, down to Svartalfaheim [World of the Dark Elves], and there he had some dwarves make the fetter called Gleipnir. It was constructed from six elements: the noise of a cat's footsteps, the beard of a woman, the roots of a mountain, the sinews of a bear, the breath of a fish, and the spittle of a bird. Though previously you had no knowledge of these matters, you now can quickly see the proof that you were not deluded. You must have noticed that a woman has no beard, a cat's movement makes no loud noise and mountains have no roots. Truly, I say, all you have been told is equally reliable, even though you have no way to test some things.'

Then Gangleri said, 'I can certainly understand the truth of what you say. I accept the examples you have used. But what did the fetter look like when it was completed?'

High answered, 'That I can easily tell you. The fetter was smooth and soft as a silk ribbon, yet it was reliable and strong, as you will now hear. When the fetter was brought to the Æsir, they heartily thanked the messenger for carrying out his errand. Then the gods travelled out on to a lake called Amsvartnir [Pitch Black] and sent for the wolf to accompany them. They went on to an island named Lyngvi, where they showed the wolf the silky band, offering to let him try to break it. They told him that despite its thinness, it was somewhat stronger than it appeared. Passing it among themselves, each tested the band's strength in his hands. No one could pull it apart. Nevertheless, they said that the wolf would be able to break it.

'Then the wolf answered: "It seems to me that a ribbon like this one, which is so narrow a band, offers no renown even if I break it apart. But if it is made with cunning and treachery, even though it looks unimpressive, then I will not permit this band to be put on my legs."

'The Æsir replied that he would quickly snap such a narrow silky band, as he had already broken powerful iron fetters. "But if you are unable to break free from this band, the gods will have no reason to fear you, and then we will free you."

'The wolf answered: "If you were to bind me in such a way that I was unable to free myself, then you would betray and abandon me, and it would be a long time before I received any help from you. I am unwilling to allow that band to be put on me. Rather than questioning my courage, why not let one of you place his hand in my mouth as a pledge that there is no treachery in this offer?"

'The gods now looked at one another, realizing the seriousness of the problem they faced. No one was willing to hold out his hand until Tyr raised his right hand and laid it in the wolf's mouth. But when the wolf strained against the fetter, the band only hardened, and the more he struggled, the stronger the band became. They all laughed, except Tyr; he lost his hand.

'When the Æsir saw that the wolf was truly bound, they took

the part that hung loose from the fetter. It was called Gelgja, and they threaded the end of it through a huge stone called Gjoll. They fastened the stone deep down in the earth. Then they took an enormous rock called Thviti and drove it even further down into the earth, using it as an anchor post. As the wolf struggled, he opened his mouth. He gaped horribly, trying to bite them, but they slipped a sword into his mouth. The hilt stuck in his lower gums and the blade in the upper gums, wedging his jaw open. As he growled menacingly, saliva drooled from his mouth, forming the river called Van [Hope]. There he remains until Ragnarok.'

Then Gangleri said: 'What gruesome children Loki sired. All these brothers and sisters are in themselves fearsome, but why didn't the Æsir kill the wolf, since they could expect only destruction from him?'

High answered, 'The gods hold their sacred places and sanctuaries in such respect that they chose not to defile them with the wolf's blood, even though prophecies foretold that he would be the death of Odin.'

35. GODDESSES

Then Gangleri asked, 'Who are the goddesses?'

High answered, 'Frigg is the foremost. She owns the dwelling called Fensalir, and it is splendid in all ways.

'A second goddess is Saga. She lives at Sokkvabekk, which is a large dwelling.

'A third is Eir, the best of doctors.

'A fourth is Gefjun. She is a maiden, and women who die as virgins serve her.

'A fifth is Fulla. She, too, is a virgin, and she goes about with her hair falling loose and a gold band around her head. She carries Frigg's ashen box, looks after her footwear, and shares secrets with her.

'Freyja, along with Frigg, is the most noble. She married the man called Od. Their daughter, Hnoss, is so beautiful that from her name comes the word for a treasure that is exceptionally handsome and valuable. Od went travelling on distant paths while Freyja remained behind, crying tears of red gold. Freyja has many names, because she gave herself different names as she travelled among unknown peoples searching for Od. She is called Mardoll and Horn and Gefn and Syr. Freyja owned Brisingamen[1] [Necklace of the Brisings]. She is called the goddess of the Vanir.

'The seventh goddess, Sjofn, is deeply committed to turning the thoughts of both men and women to love. The word for lover, *sjafni*, is derived from her name.

'The eighth goddess is Lofn [Loving]. She is so gentle and so good to invoke that she has permission from All-Father or Frigg to arrange unions between men and women, even if earlier offers have been refused and unions have been banned. From her name comes the word *lof*, meaning permission as well as high praise.

'The ninth is Var [Beloved]. She listens to the oaths and private agreements that are made between men and women. For this reason such agreements are called *várar*. She takes vengeance on those who break trust.

'The tenth, Vor [Careful], is so knowledgeable and inquires so deeply that nothing can be hidden from her. Hence the expression that a woman becomes "aware" [*vor*] of what she learns.

'The eleventh is Syn [Refusal]. She guards the doors in the hall and locks out those who ought not to enter. She is also appointed to defend cases that she wants to see refuted in the courts. From this situation comes the expression that a denial [*syn*] is advanced when something is refused.

'The twelfth, Hlin [Protector], is appointed to guard over people whom Frigg wishes to protect from danger. From her name comes the expression that he who escapes finds *hleinir* [peace and quiet].

'The thirteenth, Snotra, is wise and courtly. From her name comes the custom of calling a clever woman or man *snotr*.

'The fourteenth is Gna. Frigg sends her to different worlds on errands. She has the horse named Hofvarpnir [Hoof Kicker], which rides through the air and on the sea. Once some

Vanir saw her path as she rode through the air, and one of them said:

"What flies there?
What fares there
or moves through the air?"

'She replied:

"I fly not
though I fare
and move through the air
on Hofvarpnir,
the one whom Hamskerpir got
with Gardrofa."

'From Gna's name comes the custom of saying that something *gnaefir* [looms] when it rises up high.

'Sol [Sun] and Bil, whose natures have already been described, are counted among the goddesses.

36. VALKYRIES[1] AND GODDESSES

'There are still others whose duty it is to serve in Valhalla. They bring drink and see to the table and the ale cups. *The Lay of Grimnir* names them in the following way:

Hrist and Mist
I want to bring me the horn.
Skeggjold and Skogul,
Hild and Thrud,
Hlokk and Herfjotur,
Goll and Geirahod,
Randgrid and Radgrid,
and Reginleif –
they bring ale to the Einherjar.

(*The Lay of Grimnir*. 40–41)

'These women are called valkyries. They are sent by Odin to every battle, where they choose which men are to die and they determine who has the victory. Gunn and Rota and the youngest norn, named Skuld, always ride to choose the slain and to decide the outcome of a battle.

'Earth, the mother of Thor, and Rind, the mother of Vali, are counted among the goddesses.

37. THE TALE OF FREY AND THE GIANTESS GERD

'Gymir was the name of a man whose wife, Aurboda, came from the family of the mountain giants. Their daughter was Gerd, the most beautiful of all women. One day Frey entered Hlidskjalf and looked out over all the worlds. When he looked to the north he saw a dwelling with a large splendid house. A woman was walking up to the house. When she raised her arms to unlock the door, the light glanced off her arms, both into the air and on to the sea, and because of her the whole world brightened. For his arrogance of having sat himself in the holy seat, Frey was made to pay, and he went away overcome with sorrow. He was silent when he returned home. He neither slept nor drank, and no one dared to speak to him.

'Then Njord sent for Skirnir, Frey's manservant. He asked Skirnir to go to Frey and ask with whom he was so angry that he would speak to no one. Skirnir said that he would go, although he was not eager to do so, because he expected he would be answered roughly. When Skirnir met with Frey he asked him why he was so downcast and would not speak with anyone. Frey replied that he had seen a beautiful woman and that on her account he was so filled with sorrow that he would not live long if he could not have her.

' "And now you are to go and ask for her hand on my behalf. Bring her back here to my home, whether or not her father agrees. For this service I will pay you well."

'Then Skirnir replied that he would undertake the task. But

in return Frey should give him his sword. The sword was so good that it fought by itself. Frey, however, let nothing stand in the way and gave the sword to Skirnir, who set out and asked for the woman on Frey's behalf. He received her promise that nine nights later she would come to the place called Barey[1] and would marry Frey there. But when Skirnir told Frey the outcome of his mission, Frey replied:

> "Long is one night,
> long is another,
> how will I suffer even three?
> Often for me a month
> much less seemed
> than half this holding time."[2]
>
> (*The Lay of Skirnir*. 42)

'For this reason Frey was without a weapon when he fought with Beli, killing him with a stag's horn.'

Then Gangleri said, 'How very strange that a leader such as Frey would willingly give away his sword when he did not have another equally as good. For him this lack would be a great handicap when he fought with Beli. Truly, he must have regretted this gift.'

High replied, 'It was of little importance when he and Beli met. Frey could have killed him with his hands. The time will come when the sons of Muspell set out on their war journey, and then Frey will find it worse to be without his sword.'

38. THE HIGH ONE SPEAKS OF VALHALLA

Then Gangleri said, 'You say that all men who have fallen in battle from the beginning of the world are now with Odin in Valhalla. With what does he feed them? I should think the crowd there is large.'

High answered: 'It is true as you say. A huge throng is already there, but many more are still to come. Yet even these will be thought too few when the Wolf [Fenrir] comes. Never are there so many in Valhalla that they run out of meat from the boar called Saehrimnir. He is cooked every day but is whole again in the evening. As to your question, few, it seems to me, are so wise that they could answer it correctly. Andhrimnir is the cook and Eldhrimnir is the kettle, as it says here:

Andhrimnir has
Saehrimnir boiled
in Eldhrimnir,
the best of meat.
But few know
on what the Einherjar feed.'

(*The Lay of Grimnir*. 18)

Then Gangleri asked, 'Does Odin eat the same food as the Einherjar?'

High replied, 'He gives the food on his table to his two wolves, Geri and Freki. He himself needs nothing to eat. For him, wine is both drink and food. So it says here:

Geri and Freki
are fed by the battle-skilled
father of armies;
But on wine alone,
weapon glorious
Odin ever lives. (*The Lay of Grimnir*. 19)

'Two ravens sit on Odin's shoulders, and into his ears they tell all the news they see or hear. Their names are Hugin [Thought] and Munin [Mind, Memory]. At sunrise he sends them off to fly throughout the whole world, and they return in time for the first meal. Thus he gathers knowledge about many things that are happening, and so people call him the raven god. As is said:

Hugin and Munin
fly each day
over the wide world.

I fear for Hugin
that he may not return,
though I worry more for Munin.'

(*The Lay of Grimnir*. 20)

39. THE DRINK OF THE EINHERJAR AND WHAT FLOWS FROM VALHALLA

Gangleri then asked, 'What sort of drink do the Einherjar have that lasts them as long as the food? Or is water drunk there?'

High replied, 'That is a strange question. Would All-Father invite kings, jarls [earls] and other men of rank to his hall and give them water to drink? Truly, many who come to Valhalla, having suffered wounds and the pain of death, would think a drink of water dearly bought if no better greeting were available. About that place, I can tell you another story. The goat Heidrun stands on top of Valhalla and eats the leaves from the branches of that most famous tree, Lerad.[1] From her udders streams the mead that daily fills a vat so large that from it all the Einherjar satisfy their thirst.'[2]

Gangleri then said, 'That goat is especially useful to them, and the tree that she eats from must be remarkably good.'

High said, 'Even more notable is the stag Eikthyrnir [Oak Antlers], who stands on top of Valhalla and chews on the branches of that tree. So much moisture drips from his horns that it finds its way down into Hvergelmir. From there flow the rivers Sid, Vid, Sekin, Ekin, Svol, Gunnthro, Fjorm, Fimbulthul, Gipul, Gopul, Gomul and Geirvimul. They flow through the places where the gods live. There are even more rivers called Thyn, Vin, Tholl, Boll, Grad, Gunnthrain, Nyt, Not, Nonn, Hronn, Vina, Vegsvinn and Thjodnuma.'

40. THE DOORS OF VALHALLA

Then Gangleri said, 'Now you tell me such wondrous things, that Valhalla must be a huge house with doorways so crowded that it is difficult to pass through them.'

High answered: 'Why don't you ask how many doors are in Valhalla, or how big they are? When you hear the answers, then you will surely say that it would be remarkable if everyone were unable to pass in and out freely. In truth, it is no harder to find places for people inside the hall than it is to enter it. Listen to *The Lay of Grimnir*:

> Five hundred doors[1]
> and still forty more,
> I believe, are at Valhalla.
> Eight hundred Einherjar
> will go together out each door
> when they go to fight the wolf.'
>
> (*The Lay of Grimnir*. 23)

41. THE DAILY BATTLE AT VALHALLA

Gangleri then spoke: 'Large crowds of people are at Valhalla. It is my belief that Odin must be a powerful lord, because he controls so large an army. But how do the Einherjar amuse themselves when they are not drinking?'

High replied, 'Every day, after they dress, they put on their war gear. Then they go out to the courtyard and battle, the one attacking the other. Such is their sport. When it comes time to eat, they ride home to Valhalla and sit down to drink, as is said here:

> All the Einherjar
> in Odin's home fields
> fight among themselves each day.
> The slain they select[1]

then ride from the battlefield;
reconciled, they sit again together.

(*The Lay of Vafthrudnir.* 41)

'It is true, as you say, that Odin is powerful. Many examples of his power are evident. Here are the words of the Æsir themselves:

The ash Yggdrasil
is foremost of trees,
and Skidbladnir of ships,
Odin of the Æsir,
and of stallions, Sleipnir,
Bifrost of bridges,
and Bragi of skalds,
Habrok of hawks,[2]
and of hounds, Garm.'

(*The Lay of Grimnir.* 44)

42. THE MASTER BUILDER FROM GIANT LAND AND THE BIRTH OF SLEIPNIR

Then Gangleri asked, 'Who owns the horse Sleipnir? What is there to tell about him?'

High replied, 'You know little about Sleipnir and are ignorant of the events that led to his birth, so you will find it a tale well worth hearing. It happened right at the beginning, when the gods were settling. After they had established Midgard and built Valhalla, a smith arrived. He offered to construct in three seasons a fortress so solid and trustworthy that it would be safe against mountain trolls and frost giants even if they entered Midgard. As his payment he asked for Freyja in marriage, but he also wanted the sun and the moon.

'Then the Æsir, consulting among themselves, arrived at their decision. Their agreement with the builder was that he should have what he requested, if he completed the fortress in one winter. But if any part of the fortress was unfinished on the first day of summer, he would lose his part of the bargain. No other man was to help him in this work. When stating these conditions they agreed to let him have the use of his horse, called Svadilfari. Loki was the one who made this decision after the matter was placed before him.

'On the first day of winter the builder began to erect the fortress, and during the night he used his horse to haul in stones. The Æsir were amazed at the size of the boulders the horse could drag; the horse's feat of strength was twice that of the builder's. But good witnesses and many oaths had sealed the bargain, because the giant did not think it safe to be without a truce among the Æsir if Thor should return. At that time Thor was away in the east hammering on trolls.[1] As the winter passed, the building of the fortification steadily advanced, until it became so high and so strong that it was unassailable. With only three days left before summer, the work had progressed right up to the stronghold's entrance.

'Then the gods sat on their thrones of fate and sought a solution. They asked one another who had been responsible for the decision to marry Freyja into Giant Land and to destroy the sky and the heavens by taking the sun and moon and giving them to the giant. And it became clear, as in most other things, that the one who had advised in this matter was Loki, son of Laufey, the one who counsels badly in most matters. They told him that he could expect a bad death if he failed to devise a plan for the builder to lose his wager. They attacked Loki, and when he became frightened he swore oaths that, whatever it cost him, he would find a way to keep the builder from completing his part of the bargain.

'That same evening, as the builder drove out with his stallion Svadilfari to gather stones, a mare leaped from a forest and, neighing, ran up to the horse. When the stallion recognized what manner of horse this was, he became frantic and broke free from his harness. He galloped towards the mare but she raced ahead of him into the forest. Behind them came the builder, trying to grab hold of his horse. Because the horses ran all that evening and night, the work was delayed.

'The next day there was less work done than previously. When the builder saw that the work would not be finished, he flew into a giant's rage. Once the Æsir realized for certain that they were facing a mountain giant, they no longer respected their oaths. They called upon Thor, who came immediately, and the next thing to happen was that the hammer Mjollnir was in the air. In this way Thor paid the builder his wages, but not the sun and the moon. Rather, Thor put an end to the giant's life in Jotunheim. He struck the first blow in such a way that the giant's skull broke into small pieces, and so Thor sent him down to Niflhel. But Loki's relations with Svadilfari were such that a while later he gave birth to a colt. It was grey and had eight feet, and this is the best horse among gods and men.

'*The Sibyl's Prophecy* has this to say:

> Then all the powerful gods went
> to their thrones of fate,
> the gods most sacred,
> and questioned themselves,
> who had infused
> all the air with treachery
> and to the race of giants
> given Od's maid.[2]
>
> Broken were oaths,
> the words and pledges,
> all the powerful agreements
> that had passed between them.
> Thor alone killed,
> bursting with fury.
> He seldom sits still
> when he hears such things.'

(*The Sibyl's Prophecy*. 25–26)

43. THE SHIP SKIDBLADNIR

Then Gangleri asked, 'What can be said about Skidbladnir, since it is the best of ships? Is there no ship its equal or none as large?'

High said, 'Skidbladnir is the best of ships and it was built with the finest craftsmanship. But Naglfar, the largest ship, is owned by Muspell. Dwarves, the sons of Ivaldi, built Skidbladnir and gave it to Frey. That ship is so large that it can accommodate all the Æsir, along with their weapons and their war gear, and a good wind blows whenever the sail is raised, no matter where it is headed. The ship is made of so many different pieces and with so much cunning that, when it is not being used to travel on the sea, it can be folded up like a piece of cloth and placed in a pouch.'

44. THOR ANd LOKI BEGIN THEIR JOURNEY TO GIANT LAND

Then Gangleri said, 'Skidbladnir is a fine ship, and powerful magic must be called upon before something like it is crafted. Tell me, has Thor never been in a situation where he encountered so much strength and power that he was overwhelmed by might or magic superior to his own?'

High replied, 'I expect that there are few others who could answer your question, even though many situations have seemed difficult to Thor. Although some things, because of their power or their strength, have prevented Thor from being victorious, there is no need to tell about them, not least because everybody ought to keep in mind that there are so many examples where Thor is the mightiest.'[1]

Then Gangleri said, 'It seems to me that this time I have asked something that no one can answer.'

Just-as-High replied, 'We have heard reports that seem unreliable to us, yet here, close by, sits the man who can give a true account. You can trust what he says because he has never spoken falsely, and he will not start now.'

Then Gangleri responded: 'I will stand here and listen for a solution. Otherwise I call you beaten, because you are unable to answer my question.'

Third then spoke, 'It is obvious that he wants to know these tales, even though we take no pleasure in telling them. You, however, must now keep quiet.

'It started when Thor the Charioteer was travelling with his goats, accompanied by the god called Loki. Towards dusk they came to the house of a farmer and arranged lodging for the night. In the evening Thor took his goats and slaughtered them both. They were then flayed and carried to the pot. After they had been cooked, Thor and his companions sat down to their evening meal. Thor invited the farmer and his wife and children to join him. The farmer's son was named Thjalfi and his daughter was Roskva. Next Thor spread out the goatskins away from the fire and said that the farmer and his household should throw the bones on to the skins. Thjalfi, the farmer's son, took the thigh bone of one of the goats and, wedging in his knife, broke the bone to reach the marrow.

'Thor stayed the night, and just before dawn he got up and dressed. He reached for his hammer Mjollnir and, lifting it up, consecrated the goatskins. The goats stood up, but one of them was lame in its hind leg. Thor noticed this and suspected that the farmer or one of his household had mistreated the goat's bones. Then he realized that its thigh bone was broken, and there is no need to make a long story of it. Everybody can imagine how frightened the farmer became as he watched Thor's eyebrows sink down low over his eyes. The small part of Thor's eyes that was visible was a sight that alone could have killed. Thor's hands clenched the shaft of the hammer until his knuckles whitened. As might be expected, the farmer and all his household began to wail. Begging for mercy, they offered in return everything they owned. When Thor saw their fear, his anger passed. Calming down, he took from them their children, Thjalfi and Roskva, as compensation. They became Thor's bond servants and follow him ever since.

45. THOR ENCOUNTERS SKRYMIR IN THE FOREST

'Thor left the goats behind and began the trip east into Giant Land, all the way to the sea. From there he continued out over the deep ocean. When he came to land he went ashore, and with him were Loki, Thjalfi and Roskva. After they had travelled a little while they came to a large forest. They continued walking that whole day until dark. Thjalfi, who was faster than anybody else, carried Thor's food bag. They were low on supplies.

'When it became dark they looked for a place to spend the night and came across a very large hall. At one end was a door as wide as the hall itself, where they sought quarters for the evening. But in the middle of the night there was a powerful earthquake; the ground heaved under them and the house shook. Thor stood up and called to his companions. They searched and found a side room on the right, towards the middle of the hall, and they went in. Thor placed himself in the doorway, and the others, who were scared, stayed behind him further inside. Thor held the hammer by its handle, intending to defend himself. Then they heard a loud noise and a roaring din.

'At sunrise, Thor went outside and saw a man lying in the forest a short distance from him. The man snored heavily as he slept, and he was not little. Thor then thought he understood the noise he had heard during the night. He put on his belt of strength, and divine power began to swell in him. But just at that moment the man awoke and quickly stood up. It is said that for once Thor was too startled to strike with the hammer.[1] Instead he asked the man his name, and the other called himself Skrymir.[2]

' "And I do not need," he said, "to ask your name. I know you are Thor of the Æsir. But, have you dragged away my glove?"[3]

'Skrymir then reached out and picked up his glove. Thor now saw that during the night he had mistaken this glove for a hall. As for the side room, that was the glove's thumb. Skrymir asked if Thor wanted to have his company on the journey, and Thor said yes. Then Skrymir took his food bag, untied it, and started to eat his breakfast. Thor and his companions did the same thing elsewhere. Skrymir next suggested that they pool their provisions, and Thor agreed. Skrymir tied together all their provisions in one bag and threw it over his shoulder. He went ahead during the day, taking rather large strides. Later, towards evening, Skrymir found them a place for the night under a great oak tree. Skrymir then told Thor that he wanted to lie down to sleep – "but you take the food bag and prepare your evening meal."

'Next Skrymir fell asleep, snoring loudly, and Thor took the food bag, intending to untie it. There is this to tell, which may seem unbelievable, but Thor could not untie a single knot, nor was he able to loosen any of the straps. None was any looser than when he started. When Thor realized that his effort was being wasted, he became angry. Gripping the hammer Mjollnir with both hands, he strode with one foot out in front to where Skrymir lay and struck him on his head. But Skrymir awoke and asked whether a leaf from the tree had fallen on his head and whether they had eaten and were preparing to bed down. Thor replied that they were getting ready to go to sleep. They then moved to a place under another oak, and it can truly be said that it was not possible to sleep without fear.

'In the middle of the night Thor could hear that Skrymir was sleeping soundly, the forest thundering with the sound of his snoring. Thor stood up and went over to him. Quickly he raised the hammer and with a hard blow struck Skrymir at the midpoint of his skull. He felt the hammer sink deeply into the head. But at that instant Skrymir awoke and said: "What now? Has some acorn fallen on my head? What's new with you, Thor?"

'Thor quickly moved back and said that he had just awakened, adding that it was the middle of the night and there was still time to sleep. Then Thor resolved that, if he could get close enough to strike a third blow, he would arrange matters so that this meeting would be their last one.

'Thor now lay awake watching for Skrymir to fall asleep. A

little before dawn, hearing that Skrymir was sleeping, Thor stood up and, running towards Skrymir, raised his hammer and, with all his might, struck Skrymir on the temple. The hammer sank up to its shaft, but then Skrymir sat up, brushed off the side of his head, and asked:

'"Are there some birds sitting in the tree above me? It seemed to me as I awoke that some leaves or twigs[4] from the branches had fallen on my head. Are you awake, Thor? It is time to get up and get dressed. You don't have a long way to go to reach the stronghold, which is called Utgard. I have heard you whispering among yourselves that I am no small man, and you will see still larger men if you go to Utgard. Now I will give you some good advice: do not act arrogantly. The retainers of Utgarda-Loki will not tolerate bragging from such small fry as you. Your other choice is to turn back, and in my opinion that would be the best thing for you to do. But if you intend to continue, then head for the east. My path now leads me northward to those mountains that you can now see."

'Skrymir took the food bag and threw it on to his back. He turned sharply and headed north into the forest, leaving the others. In this parting, there is no report that the Æsir mentioned they were looking forward to meeting him again.

46. THOR REACHES THE STRONGHOLD OF UTGARDA-LOKI

'Thor and his companions continued on their journey, travelling until midday. Then they saw a fortress standing on a plain, and it was so big that in order to see over it they had to bend their necks all the way back. They approached the fortress, but the front entrance gate was shut. Thor went to the gate and tried to open it, but after struggling to open the stronghold, they finally had to squeeze between the bars. Entering in this way, they saw a large hall and approached it. The door was open, and inside they saw many people sitting on two benches; most of them were rather large.

'They went before the king, Utgarda-Loki, and greeted him, but he took his time in noticing them. Then he said, grinning through his teeth: "News travels slowly from distant parts, but am I wrong in thinking that this little fellow is Thor the Charioteer? Surely there is more to you than meets the eye. Tell me, companions, in what skills do you think you are capable of competing? No one can stay here with us who does not have some skill or knowledge greater than other men."

'Then he who stood at the back of the group, the one called Loki, spoke up: "I have a skill in which I am ready to be tested. No one here in the hall will prove quicker than I at eating his food."

'Utgarda-Loki answered, "That would be an accomplishment, if you are up to it, and feats such as that will be put to the test." Next he called out to the end of the bench to the one who was called Logi [Fire] and told him to come forward on to the floor and pit himself against Loki. Then a trough filled with meat was brought in and set on the hall floor. Loki placed himself at one end and Logi at the other. Each began to eat as fast as he could, and they met in the middle of the trough. Loki had eaten all the meat from the bones, but Logi had eaten not only the meat but also the bones and even the trough. To everyone it seemed that Loki had lost the contest.

'Then Utgarda-Loki asked in what the youngster could compete. Thjalfi replied that he would run a race against whomever Utgarda-Loki chose. Utgarda-Loki called that a fine sport, but said that Thjalfi would have to be very quick if he intended to win. Utgarda-Loki made it clear that the matter would quickly be put to the test. Next Utgarda-Loki stood up and went outside where there was a good running course over the flat plain. He called a little fellow named Hugi to come to him and ordered him to run a race with Thjalfi. They ran the first race, and Hugi was so far in the lead that he turned around at the end and faced his opponent.

'Then Utgarda-Loki said, "Thjalfi, you will need to exert yourself more if you are to win the contest. Yet it is true that no one else has come here who seemed to me faster on his feet than you."

'Then they began to race for a second time. When Hugi came

to the end of the course he turned around, but Thjalfi was behind him by the distance of a long bow shot.

'Utgarda-Loki then said: "I think Thjalfi knows how to run a good race, but I have no faith that he will win. Now comes the test; let them run the third race." When Hugi reached the end of the race and turned around, Thjalfi had not even reached the midpoint of the course. Everyone then said that the contest was over.

'Utgarda-Loki asked Thor what feat he wanted to show them, as so many tales were told about his exploits. Thor answered that he would most like to pit himself against someone in drinking. Utgarda-Loki said that this contest could easily be arranged. He went into the hall and called to his cupbearer, telling him to bring the feasting horn from which his retainers usually drank. The cupbearer quickly brought the horn and placed it in Thor's hand.

'Then Utgarda-Loki said, "It is thought that drinking from this horn is well done if it is emptied in one drink. Some drain it in two, but no one is such a small-time drinker that he cannot finish it in three."

'Thor eyed the horn, and it did not seem to be very large, although it was rather long. He was quite thirsty and began to drink, swallowing hugely and thinking that it would not be necessary to bend himself over the horn more than once. When he had drunk as much as he could, he bent back from the horn and looked in to see how much drink remained. It seemed to him that the level in the horn was only slightly lower than it had been before.

'Utgarda-Loki then said, "Good drinking, although not all that much. I would not have believed it if I had been told that Thor of the Æsir would not have drunk more, but I know that you will drain it in a second drink."

'Thor gave no reply but put the horn to his mouth and resolved to take a larger drink. He struggled with it as long as he could hold his breath and noticed that he could not lift up the bottom end of the horn as much as he would have liked. When he lowered the horn from his mouth and looked in, it seemed to him that the level had gone down even less than it had in the first try, although there was now enough space at the top of the horn above the liquid to carry the drink without spilling it.

'Utgarda-Loki asked, "What now, Thor? Are you going to be so brave that you will take one sip more than is good for you? It seems to me that if you want to take a third drink from the horn, then it will have to be the biggest. But among us here, you will not be known as great a man as the Æsir call you, unless you give a better account of yourself in other contests than it seems to me you are doing in this one."

'Then Thor grew angry. Placing the horn to his mouth, he drank with all his might, continuing as long as he could. When he looked into the horn he could see at least some difference. Then he gave the horn back and would drink no more.

'Utgarda-Loki said, "Clearly your strength is not as great as we thought, but will you still try your hand in other contests? It is obvious that you are not going to succeed here."

'Thor replied: "I will make a try at still another game. But when I was home among the Æsir, I would have found it strange if such drinks were called little. What sort of contest will you offer me now?"

'Utgarda-Loki replied, "Here among us, little boys do something that is thought a rather small matter: they lift my cat off the ground. But I would not have thought it possible to propose such a thing to Thor of the Æsir if I had not already seen that your strength is much less than I had thought."

'Now a grey cat, and rather a large one, jumped out on to the floor of the hall. Thor approached it, and, placing his hand under the middle of the belly, started to lift up the cat. But as much as Thor raised his hand the cat arched its back. When Thor had reached as high as he could, one of the cat's paws was lifted off the ground. Beyond this effort, Thor could do no more.

'Then Utgarda-Loki said, "This contest has gone as I expected it would. The cat is rather large, whereas Thor is short and small compared with the larger men among us here."

'Thor replied, "Although you call me little, let someone come forward and wrestle with me! Now I am angry!"

'Utgarda-Loki looked over the benches and replied, "Here

inside, I do not see any man who would find it dignified to wrestle with you." Then he went on, "But wait, first let us see. Call my nurse, the old woman Elli, to come here, and let Thor wrestle with her, if he wants to. She has thrown to the ground men who seemed to me to be no less strong than Thor."

'Next an old woman walked into the hall. Utgarda-Loki said she should wrestle with Thor of the Æsir. The story is not long to tell. The match went this way: the more Thor threw his strength into the grappling, the more steadfastly she stood her ground. Then the old crone showed her skill. Thor lost his footing and the contest grew fiercer. It was not long before Thor fell to one knee. Then Utgarda-Loki intervened. He told them to stop the contest, saying that there was no need for Thor to challenge others to wrestle in his hall. By then it was late at night. Utgarda-Loki showed Thor and his companions to places on the benches, and there they were treated well for the rest of the night.

47. UTGARDA-LOKI REVEALS THAT THOR WAS DECEIVED

'In the morning, at first light, Thor and his companions stood up, dressed and prepared to leave. Utgarda-Loki then came in and had a table set for them. There was no lack of hospitality as to food or drink. When they finished eating they turned to leave. Utgarda-Loki stayed with them, accompanying them as they left the fortress. At their parting, Utgarda-Loki asked Thor how he thought the trip had gone and whether Thor had ever met a man more powerful. Thor replied that he could not deny that he had been seriously dishonoured in their encounter: "Moreover, I know that you will say that I am a person of little account and that galls me."

'And Utgarda-Loki replied, "Now that you are out of the fortress, I will tell you the truth, for, if I live and am the one to decide, you will never enter it again. On my word, I can assure you, that you would never have been allowed to enter if I had known in advance that you had so much power in you, because you nearly brought disaster upon us. I have tricked you with magical shape-changings, as I did that first time when I found you in the forest. I am the one you met there. And when you tried to untie the food bag, you were unable to find where to undo it, because I had fastened it with iron wire.[1] When you next struck me three times with the hammer, the first was the least, yet it was so powerful that it would have killed me had it found its mark. But when you saw a flat-topped mountain near my hall with three square-shaped valleys in it, one deeper than the others, these were the marks of your hammer. I had moved this flat-topped mountain in front of your blows, but you did not see me doing it. It was the same when your companions contested with my retainers. And so it was in the first contest undertaken by Loki. He was very hungry and he ate quickly. But the one called Logi was wildfire itself, and he burned the trough no less quickly than the meat. When Thjalfi ran against the one called Hugi, that was my mind, and Thjalfi could not be expected to compete with its speed. When you drank from the horn, you thought it slow going, but on my word that was a miracle I would never have believed could happen. The other end of the horn, which you could not see, was out in the ocean. When you come to the ocean you will see how much your drinking lowered it. This is now known as the tides."

'Utgarda-Loki had still more to say: "I thought it no less a feat when you lifted the cat. Truly all those who saw you raise one of the cat's paws off the ground grew fearful, because that cat was not what it seemed to be. It was the Midgard Serpent, which encircles all lands, and from head to tail its length is just enough to round the earth. But you pulled him up so high that he almost reached the sky.

'"It, too, was a real wonder that you remained on your feet for so long during the wrestling. You fell no more than on to one knee, as you struggled with the crone Elli [Old Age], and no one accomplishes that after reaching the point where old age beckons, because no one overcomes Old Age. As we part, I can truthfully say that it would be better for us both if you never come again to meet me. Next time I will defend my stronghold with similar or other trickery, so that you will not get me into your power."

'When Thor heard this account, he gripped his hammer and raised it into the air. But, when he was ready to strike, Utgarda-Loki was nowhere to be seen. Then Thor returned to the fortress, intending to destroy it. There he saw a broad, beautiful plain, but no stronghold. Then, turning back, he journeyed until he came once again to Thrudvangar. In truth, it can be said that from then on he was determined to find a way to confront the Midgard Serpent, and later on that happened.

'Now I believe that no one else could have given you a truer account of this journey by Thor.'

48. THOR AND THE GIANT HYMIR GO FISHING

Gangleri then said: 'Utgarda-Loki is very powerful, and he uses many tricks and much magic. Nevertheless, it is evident that he is a force to be reckoned with, because his retainers have so much strength. But didn't Thor take vengeance in return?'

High answered, 'Even those who are not men of learning know that Thor made amends[1] for the journey just recounted. He was not home for long before he prepared to set out again. He went so quickly that he took with him neither chariot nor goats nor companions. Leaving Midgard disguised as a young boy, he arrived one evening at the house of a giant, the one called Hymir. Thor stayed there that night. At daybreak Hymir got up, dressed and prepared to go fishing in the sea. Thor jumped up, quickly got himself ready and asked Hymir to let him row out to sea with him. But Hymir said he could expect little help from the boy because he was so young and so small. "And you will freeze if you stay as long and as far out as I am accustomed to doing."

'Thor told Hymir that he would not stop him from rowing far out from land, and he added that it was not clear who would be the first one wanting to row back in. Thor grew so enraged at the giant that he almost let the hammer slam into him. Yet he let the matter pass because he had set his mind on testing his strength elsewhere. He asked Hymir what sort of bait they should use, but Hymir told him to get his own. Thor then went off looking until he saw a herd of oxen belonging to Hymir. He took the biggest ox, called Himinhrjot, ripped off its head, and took it with him down to the sea.

'Hymir had already launched the boat. Thor got in and sat down towards the stern. He took two oars and started rowing, and Hymir noticed that he was making some progress. Hymir rowed from forward in the bow, and the boat moved quickly. Hymir then said that they had come to the waters where he usually trawled for flatfish, but Thor said he wanted to row much further, and they started another bout of fast rowing. Hymir then warned that they had come so far out that to go further was dangerous because of the Midgard Serpent. But Thor replied that he wanted to keep on rowing, and so he did. Hymir was by then most unhappy.

'Finally Thor pulled up his oars and set about preparing his line, which was very strong, with a hook that was neither weaker nor less firm.[2] Thor baited the hook with the ox head and cast it overboard, where it sank to the bottom. And it can be said in truth that this time Thor tricked the Midgard Serpent no less than Utgarda-Loki had tricked Thor into lifting the Midgard Serpent with his arm.

'The Midgard Serpent opened its mouth and swallowed the ox head. The hook dug into the gums of its mouth, and when the serpent felt this, he snapped back so hard that both of Thor's fists slammed against the gunwale. Thor now became angry and, taking on his divine strength, he strained so hard that both his feet pushed through the bottom of the boat. Using the sea floor to brace himself, he began pulling the serpent up on board. It can be said that no one has seen a more terrifying sight than this: Thor, narrowing his eyes at the serpent, while the serpent spits out poison and stares straight back from below. It is told that the giant Hymir changed colour. He grew pale and feared for his life when he saw the serpent and also the sea rushing in and out of the boat.

'Just at that instant, as Thor grabbed the hammer and raised it into the air, the giant, fumbling with the bait knife, cut Thor's line where it lay across the edge of the boat, and the serpent sank back into the sea. But Thor threw his hammer after it, and people say that down on the bottom he struck the serpent's head off. But I think the opposite is true: the Midgard Serpent still lives and lies in the surrounding sea. Using his fist, Thor punched Hymir behind the ear so that he fell head over heels overboard. With this Thor waded back to land.'

49. THE DEATH OF BALDR AND HERMOD'S RIDE TO HEL

Then Gangleri asked: 'Is there still more to be told about the Æsir? Thor accomplished a great feat on that journey.'

High replied: 'One could tell of an event that the Æsir themselves thought more important. The origin of this saga was that Baldr the Good had a series of ominous dreams; he saw his life threatened. When he told the Æsir about his dreams, they took council and decided to seek a truce for Baldr, protecting him from all dangers. Frigg took oaths that Baldr would not be harmed by fire and water, iron and all kinds of metal, stones, the earth, trees, diseases, animals, birds, poisons and snakes. When this was done and became known, Baldr and the Æsir took to amusing themselves by having Baldr stand in front of all the others at the assembly while some would shoot at him, some would strike blows, and some would hit him with stones. Whatever was done caused him no injury, and all thought this remarkable.

'But when Loki, son of Laufey, saw this, it angered him that Baldr was uninjured. After changing himself into the likeness of a woman, he went to Frigg at Fensalir. Frigg asked this woman if she knew what the Æsir were doing at the assembly. The woman replied that everyone was shooting at Baldr, yet he suffered no injury.

'Then Frigg said, "Neither weapons nor wood will harm Baldr. I have received oaths from all of them."

'Then the woman asked, "Have all things given their oath not to harm Baldr?"

'Frigg answered, "A shoot of wood grows to the west of Valhalla. It is called mistletoe, and it seemed too young for me to demand its oath." Immediately afterwards, the woman disappeared.

'Loki got hold of the mistletoe. He broke it off and went to the assembly.

'Hod, because he was blind, stood at the edge of the circle of people. Loki spoke to him, asking: "Why aren't you shooting at Baldr?"

'Hod replied, "Because I can't see where Baldr is, and also I have no weapon."

'Then Loki said, "You should be behaving like the others, honouring Baldr as they do. I will direct you to where he is standing. Shoot this twig at him."

'Hod took the mistletoe and, following Loki's directions, shot at Baldr. The shot went right through Baldr, who fell to the ground dead. This misfortune was the worst that had been worked against the gods and men. Baldr's death left the gods speechless and so weak that they were unable to muster the strength to lift him up in their arms. They all looked at one another, and all were of a single mind against the one who had done the killing. But no one could take vengeance because the place was deeply revered as a sanctuary. When the Æsir first tried to speak, all they could do was weep, and no one could form words to tell the others of his grief. Odin suffered most from this misfortune. This was because he understood most clearly how grievous was the loss, and that the death of Baldr was ruin for the Æsir.[1]

'When the gods returned to their senses, Frigg asked who among the Æsir wished to gain all her love and favour by agreeing to ride the Road to Hel to see if he could find Baldr. He was to offer Hel a ransom if she would let Baldr return home to Asgard. Hermod the Bold, Odin's son, was the one who agreed to undertake the journey. They caught Odin's horse Sleipnir and led it forward. Hermod mounted and galloped off.

'The Æsir took Baldr's body and carried it to the sea. Baldr's ship was called Ringhorn and it was the greatest of all ships. The gods wanted to launch it and use it for Baldr's funeral pyre, but the ship would not budge. Then they sent to Giant Land for the giantess called Hyrrokkin. She came riding a wolf, using a poisonous snake for reins. When she jumped off her mount, Odin called to four berserkers. He told them to watch that mount, but they were unable to hold it and they struck it down. Hyrrokkin approached the prow of the ship. On her first try, she pushed so hard that the log rollers underneath the keel[2] of the ship caught fire, and the whole land shook. This angered Thor, who gripped his hammer. He would have crushed her head had not all the gods asked that she be left in peace.

'Baldr's body was carried out on to the ship, and when his wife, Nanna Nep's daughter, saw this, her heart burst from sorrow and she died. She too was carried on to the funeral pyre, which was then set on fire. Next Thor stood up and blessed the pyre with Mjollnir. A dwarf named Lit ran in front of his feet. Thor kicked the dwarf with his foot; it landed in the fire and burned to death.

'Many kinds of beings came to this cremation. First to be mentioned is Odin. Frigg was with him, as were the valkyries and his ravens. Frey rode in his chariot. It was drawn by the boar called Gold Bristle or Sheathed Tooth. Heimdall rode the horse Golden Forelock, and Freyja drove her harnessed cats. Many from among the frost giants and the mountain giants also came. Odin laid the gold ring Draupnir[3] [Dripper] on the pyre. It had the characteristic afterwards that, every ninth night, eight gold rings of equal weight dripped from it. Baldr's horse, with all its riding gear, was led onto the pyre.

'But about Hermod the following is told. For nine nights he rode through valleys so deep and dark that he saw nothing before he reached the river Gjoll and rode on to the Gjoll Bridge.[4] The bridge was roofed with shining gold, and the maiden guarding it was named Modgud. She asked Hermod about his name and family and said that the previous day five troops of dead men had ridden across the bridge, "yet the bridge echoed more under you alone, and you lack the colour of the dead. Why do you ride here on the Road to Hel?"

'He answered, saying, "I ride to Hel in search of Baldr. But have you seen anything of Baldr on the Hel Road?"

'She replied that Baldr had ridden across the Gjoll Bridge, "and down and to the north lies the Road to Hel."

'Hermod rode on until he came to the Gates of Hel. He dismounted from his horse and tightened the girth. Then he remounted and spurred the horse, which sprang forward, jumping with such force that it cleared the top of the gate without even coming near it. Then Hermod rode up to the hall. He dismounted and went inside. He saw that his brother Baldr was sitting in the seat of honour. He then stayed there through the night. In the morning Hermod asked Hel to let Baldr ride home with him, telling her of the deep sorrow and the wailing of the Æsir.

'But Hel answered that a test would be made to see whether Baldr was as well loved as some say: "If all things in the world, alive or dead,[5] weep for him, then he will be allowed to return to the Æsir. If anyone speaks against him or refuses to cry, then he will remain with Hel."

'Thereupon Hermod stood up. Baldr led him out of the hall, and, taking the ring Draupnir, he sent it to Odin as a token. Along with other gifts, Nanna sent to Frigg a linen robe. To Fulla she sent a gold finger ring. Hermod then retraced his path, riding into Asgard where he recounted all that had happened: what he had seen and heard.

'Next the Æsir sent messengers throughout the world, asking that Baldr be wept out of Hel. All did so, people and animals, the earth, the stones, the trees and all metals in the way that you have seen these things weep when they come out of the freezing cold and into warmth. As the messengers, having accomplished their task, were returning home, they found a giantess sitting in a cave. She said her name was Thokk [Gratitude]. When they asked her to weep Baldr out of Hel, she said:

"Thokk will weep
dry tears at
Baldr's funeral pyre.
Alive or dead the old man's [Odin's]
son gave me no joy.
Let Hel hold what she has."[6]

'People believe that the giantess was Loki, the son of Laufey, the one who did the most harm to the Æsir.'

50. LOKI IS CAUGHT AND THE ÆSIR TAKE VENGEANCE

Then Gangleri said, 'Loki was the cause of many things. First he caused Baldr's death, and then managed to have Baldr retained in Hel. But was no vengeance taken for this?'

High replied, 'He was repaid in a way that he will long feel. With the gods as angry at him as might be expected, he ran away and hid on a mountain. There he built a house with four doors, so that he could look out from the house in all directions. During the day he often changed himself into a salmon and hid in a place called Franang's Falls. He set his mind to discovering what sort of ploy the Æsir might devise to catch him in the waterfall. Sitting in the house, he took some linen yarn and looped it into a mesh in the way that nets have been made ever since. A fire was burning in front of him. Suddenly he saw that the Æsir were only a short distance away – Odin having discovered Loki's whereabouts from Hlidskjalf. Loki jumped up and threw the net into the fire, as he dashed out to the river.

'When the Æsir reached the house, the first to enter was Kvasir, the wisest of all. He looked into the fire, and when he saw the outline of the net in the ashes, he realized that it was a device for catching fish. He told the Æsir, and they set to work. They made a net for themselves, copying from Loki what they had seen in the ashes.

'With the net ready, the Æsir went to the river and cast it into the waterfall. Thor held one end and all the Æsir held the other, and together they dragged the net. But Loki moved ahead of them and, diving deep, he placed himself between two boulders. As the Æsir pulled the net over him, they realized that something alive was there. They went back up to the waterfall and again cast the net. This time they weighed it down so heavily that nothing could slip under it. Again Loki stayed ahead of the net, but when he saw it was only a short distance to the sea, he jumped up over the top of the net and swam back up to the falls. The Æsir, now seeing where he was going, returned to the falls. They divided themselves between the two banks, while Thor waded in the middle of the river, and then they worked their way down towards the sea.

'Loki realized that he had two options. He could leap out to the sea, which meant putting his life in danger, or he could once again jump over the net. He chose the latter, jumping as fast as he could over the net. Thor reached out and succeeded in grabbing him, but still the salmon slipped through his hands. Thor finally got a firm hold on it near its tail, and for this reason salmon are narrow towards the rear.

'Loki was now captured, and with no thought of mercy he was taken to a cave. They [the Æsir] took three flat stones and, setting them on their edges, broke a hole through each of them. Then they caught Loki's sons, Vali and Nari or Narfi. The Æsir changed Vali into a wolf, and he ripped apart his brother Narfi. Next the Æsir took his guts, and with them they bound Loki on to the top of the three stones – one under his shoulders, a second under his loins and the third under his knees. The fetters became iron.

'Then Skadi took a poisonous snake and fastened it above Loki so that its poison drips on to his face. But Sigyn, his wife, placed herself beside him from where she holds a bowl to catch the drops of venom. When the bowl becomes full, she leaves to pour out the poison, and at that moment the poison drips on to Loki's face. He convulses so violently that the whole earth shakes – it is what is known as an earthquake. He will lie bound there until Ragnarok.'

51. THE HIGH ONE REVEALS THE EVENTS OF RAGNAROK

Then Gangleri asked, 'What is to be said about Ragnarok? I have not heard it spoken of before.'

High replied: 'There are many important things to be said about it. First will come the winter called Fimbulvetr [Extreme Winter]. Snow will drive in from all directions; the cold will be severe and the winds will be fierce. The sun will be of no use. Three of these winters will come, one after the other, with no summer in between. But before that there will have been another three winters with great battles taking place throughout the world. Brothers will kill brothers for the sake of greed, and neither father nor son will be spared in the killings and the collapse of kinship.[1] So it is said in *The Sibyl's Prophecy*:

> Brothers will fight,
> bringing death to each other.
> Sons of sisters
> will split their kin bonds.
> Hard times for men,
> rampant depravity,
> age of axes, age of swords,
> shields split,
> wind age, wolf age,
> until the world falls into ruin.
>
> (*The Sibyl's Prophecy*. 45)

'Next will come an event thought to be of much importance. The wolf will swallow the sun, and mankind will think it has suffered a terrible disaster. Then the other wolf will catch the moon, and he too will cause much ruin. The stars will disappear from the heavens.

'So, also, there is this to be told: the whole earth, together with the mountains, will start to shake so that the trees will loosen from the ground, the mountains will fall, and all fetters and bonds will sever and break. Then the Fenriswolf will break free. The sea will surge on to the land as the Midgard Serpent writhes in giant fury and advances up on the land. Then it also will happen that the ship Naglfar loosens from its moorings. It is made from the nails of dead men, and for this reason it is worth considering the warning that if a person dies with untrimmed nails he contributes crucial material to Naglfar, a ship that both gods and men would prefer not to see built. On the flooding sea, Naglfar comes floating. The giant steering Naglfar is named Hrym. Meanwhile, the Fenriswolf advances with its mouth gaping: its upper jaw reaches to the heavens and the lower one drops down to the earth. He would open it still wider, if only there were room. Flames shoot out of his eyes and nostrils. The Midgard Serpent spews out so much venom that it spatters throughout the air and into the sea. He is terrible and will be on one side of the wolf.

'Amid this din the sky splits apart and in ride the sons of Muspell. Surt comes first, riding with fires burning both before and behind him. His sword is magnificent, and the glare from it is brighter than that from the sun. As they ride across Bifrost, it will break, as was told earlier. Muspell's sons advance until they reach the plain called Vigrid [Battle Plain]. The Fenriswolf and the Midgard Serpent also go there. Then Loki arrives and also Hrym. The latter is accompanied by all the frost giants, while all of Hel's own follow Loki. The sons of Muspell have their own battle troop, and it shines brilliantly. The field Vigrid lies a hundred leagues in each direction.[2]

'As these events occur, Heimdall stands up and blows the Gjallarhorn with all his strength. He wakens all the gods, who then hold an assembly. Odin now rides to Mimir's Well, seeking Mimir's counsel for both himself and his followers. The ash Yggdrasil shakes, and nothing, whether in heaven or on earth, is without fear.

'The Æsir and all the Einherjar dress for war and advance on to the field. Odin rides in front of them. He wears a gold helmet and a magnificent coat of mail, and he carries his spear called Gungnir. He goes against the Fenriswolf with Thor advancing at his side. Thor will be unable to assist Odin because he will have his hands full fighting the Midgard Serpent. Frey will fight against Surt, and it will be a fierce exchange before Frey falls. His death will come about because he lacks the good sword, the one that he gave to Skirnir. By now the hound Garm, who was bound in front of Gnipahellir,[3] will also have broken free. He, the worst of monsters, will fight against Tyr. They will be each other's death.

'Thor will kill the Midgard Serpent, and then he will step back nine feet. Because of the poison the serpent spits on him, he will fall to the earth, dead. The wolf will swallow Odin, and that will be his death. But immediately afterwards Vidar will stride forward and thrust one of his feet into the lower jaw of the wolf. He wears on that foot the shoe that has been assembled through the ages by collecting the extra pieces that people cut away from the toes and heels when fashioning their shoes. Thus those who want to help the Æsir should throw these extra pieces away. With one hand he takes hold of the wolf's upper jaw and rips apart its mouth, and this will be the wolf's death. Loki will battle with Heimdall, and they will be the death of each other. Next Surt will throw fire over the earth and burn the whole world. So says *The Sibyl's Prophecy*:

Heimdall blows loudly
his horn in the air.
Odin speaks
to Mimir's head.
The ash of Yggdrasil trembles
as it stands,
the old tree groans
and the giant breaks free.[4]

What of the Æsir?
What of the elves?
All Giant Land groans.
The Æsir meet in assembly.
The dwarves moan
before their doors of stone,
they who know the cliffs.
Do you know now or what?

Hrym drives from the east,
holding his shield before him;
Jormungand thrashes
in giant wrath.
The serpent lashes the waves;
the eagle screeches,
Nidfol, rips apart corpses.[5]
Naglfar breaks loose.

A ship sails from the east,
Muspell's followers are coming
across the sea,
and Loki is steering.
There with the Wolf[6]
are all the giant sons.
With them on the voyage
is Byleist's brother [Loki].

Surt comes from the south
with the fiery destruction of branches.
The sun shines from the sword
of the gods of the slain.
Stone cliffs tumble
and troll witches stumble.
Men tread the Road to Hel
as the sky splits apart.[7]

Then comes to Hlin [Frigg]
her second sorrow
when Odin goes
to fight with the wolf,
and Beli's bright bane [Frey]
advances against Surt.
There Frigg's beloved [Odin]
will fall.

Odin's son goes
to fight with the wolf,
Vidar on the way
to the carrion beast;
he lets his sword
hew to the heart
of Hvedrung's son [the wolf Fenrir].
Thus the father is avenged.

Steps back the renowned
son of Earth[8] [Thor]
doomed from the serpent,
fearing no shame.
All men will
abandon their world
when Midgard's protector
strikes in rage.

The sun grows black,
the earth sinks into the sea.
The bright stars
vanish from the heavens.
Steam surges up
and the fire rages.[9]
Heat reaches high
against heaven itself.

(*The Sibyl's Prophecy*. 46–57)

'Here it is also said:

Vigrid is the plain's name
where Surt and the dear gods
meet in battle.
One hundred leagues
it extends in each direction.
That field is destined for them.'

(*The Lay of Vafthrudnir*. 18)

52. AFTER RAGNAROK

Then Gangleri asked, 'What will be after heaven and earth and the whole world are burned? All the gods will be dead, together with the Einherjar and the whole of mankind. Didn't you say earlier that each person will live in some world throughout all ages?'

And Third replied, 'There will be, at that time, many good places to live. So also there will be many evil ones. It is best to be in Gimle in heaven. For those who take pleasure in good drink, plenty will be found in the hall called Brimir.[1] It stands at the place Okolnir [Never Cold]. There is likewise a splendid hall standing on Nidafjoll [Dark Mountains]. It is made of red gold and is called Sindri [Sparkling]. In this hall, good and virtuous men will live. On Nastrandir [Corpse Strands][2] there is a large, foul hall whose doors look to the north. It is constructed from the spines of snakes like a house with walls woven from branches.[3] The heads of all the snakes turn into the house, spitting venom so that a river of poison runs through the hall, and down it must wade those who are oath breakers and murderers. As it says here:

I know a hall, standing
far from the sun
on Corpse Strand.
The doors face north.
Poison drips in
through the smoke hole.
Walls of that hall are
woven from snakes' spines.
There oath breakers
and murderers wade
through heavy streams.

(*The Sibyl's Prophecy*. 38–39)

'But the worst place is in Hvergelmir.

There Nidhogg torments
the corpses of the dead.'
(*The Sibyl's Prophecy*. 39)

53. THE HIGH ONE DESCRIBES THE REBIRTH OF THE WORLD

Then Gangleri asked, 'Will any of the gods be living then? Or will there be anything of the earth or the sky?'

High said, 'The earth will shoot up from the sea, and it will be green and beautiful. Self-sown acres of crops will then grow. Vidar and Vali survive, as neither the flood nor Surt's fire destroyed them, and they will inhabit Idavoll, the place where Asgard was earlier. To there will come Thor's sons Modi and Magni, and they will have Mjollnir with them. Next Baldr and Hod will arrive from Hel. They will all sit together and talk among themselves, remembering mysteries and speaking of what had been, of the Midgard Serpent and the Fenriswolf. Then they will find in the grass the gold playing pieces which the Æsir had owned. So it is said:

Vidar and Vali will live
in the sanctuaries of the gods
when Surt's fire goes dark.
Modi and Magni
will have Mjollnir
at Vingnir's[1] [Thor's] end of battle.
(*The Sibyl's Prophecy*. 51)

'In the place called Hoddmimir's Wood, two people will have hidden themselves from Surt's fire. Called Lif [Life] and Leifthrasir [Life Yearner], they have the morning dew for their food. From these will come so many descendants that the whole world will be inhabited. So it says here:

Lif and Leifthrasir
will hide themselves
in Hoddmimir's Holt.[2]
The morning dew
they have for food,
from them springs mankind.

(*The Lay of Vafthrudnir.* 45)

'There is something else that you will find amazing. The sun will have had a daughter no less beautiful than she, and this daughter will follow the path of her mother. As it says here:

One daughter
is born to Alfrodul [Sun]
before Fenrir destroys her.
When the gods die
this maid shall ride
her mother's paths.

(*The Lay of Vafthrudnir.* 47)

'If you know how to ask questions reaching still further into the future, then I do not know the source of your questions, because I have never heard of anyone who could tell events of the world further into the future. And may you find use in what you have learned.'

54. GANGLERI RETURNS HOME TO TELL THE TALES

Next Gangleri heard loud noises coming at him from all directions. He looked to one side and, when he looked back again, he was standing outside on a level plain, where he saw neither the hall nor the fortress. He left and travelled back home to his kingdom, where he told of the events that he had seen and what he had heard. And after him, people passed these stories down from one to the other.

55. THE EPILOGUE TO *GYLFAGINNING*[1]

As for the Æsir, they sat down to discuss and take counsel. They recalled all the stories they had told him [Gangleri]. Then they gave the same names, mentioned above, to people and places there, so that, after much time had passed, people would not doubt that all were one and the same, that is, those Æsir who have been spoken about and the ones who now were assigned the very same names. Someone there was then called by the name Thor, and he was taken to be the old Thor of the Æsir and Thor the Charioteer. To him they attributed the great deeds that Thor or Ector [Hector] accomplished in Troy. Thus people believed that it was the Turks who told stories about Ulixes [Ulysses] and it is they who called him Loki, because the Turks were his worst enemy.

SKALDSKAPARMAL (POETIC DICTION)

The following translation from *Skaldskaparmal* is divided into two sections. The first, *Mythic and Legendary Tales from Skaldskaparmal*, contains the major prose stories about the gods and heroes. The second section, *Poetic References from Skaldskaparmal*, tells how to refer to gods, people and things.

MYTHIC AND LEGENDARY TALES FROM *SKALDSKAPARMAL*

I
Bragi Tells Ægir Stories of the Gods

A man was named Ægir or Hler. He lived on the island now called Hlesey, and was greatly skilled in magic. He set off on a trip to Asgard. The Æsir knew he was coming and they received him well, but much of what they showed him was fashioned through spells and shape-changings. In the evening when it was time to drink, Odin had swords brought into the hall. These shone so brightly that no other light was used while they sat at the drinking. The Æsir then went to their feast, and the twelve Æsir who were to be judges sat in their high seats. They were named Thor, Njord, Frey, Tyr, Heimdall, Bragi, Vidar, Vali, Ull, Hoenir, Forseti and Loki. The goddesses, who did likewise, were Frigg, Freyja, Gefjun, Idunn, Gerd, Sigyn, Fulla and Nanna. To Ægir it seemed that everything he saw around him was noble. Magnificent shields hung on all the wallboards. Strong mead was served and the drinking was heavy. Next to

Ægir sat Bragi.[1] They drank together and exchanged stories. Bragi told Ægir about the many things that had happened to the Æsir.

The Theft of Idunn and Her Apples

Bragi began his storytelling by saying that three of the Æsir – Odin, Loki and Hoenir – were once travelling from home and crossed mountains and deserts, where they found little food. When coming down into a valley they saw a herd of oxen and, taking one, they began to cook it. When they thought the meat was ready, they broke open the cooking pit, but found the ox was not cooked. A while later, when for the second time they broke open the cooking pit, the meat was still raw. As they began asking each other what could be the cause, they heard a voice coming from above in an oak tree under which they were standing. The one who was sitting up in the tree said that he was causing the food to remain uncooked in the oven. Looking up they saw an eagle sitting there, and it was not small.

The eagle said, 'If you are willing to give me my fill of the ox, the pit will cook.'

They agreed to this. Then the eagle glided down from the tree and landed on the pit. The first thing it did was to eat the ox's two thighs and both of its shoulders. This angered Loki, who picked up a large stick and, swinging with all his might, struck the eagle. Recoiling from the blow the eagle started to fly, but one end of the pole was stuck fast to the eagle's body, with Loki hanging on to the other end.

The eagle flew so low that Loki's feet were dragged on the ground, striking stones, gravel and trees, and he thought his arms would be pulled from their sockets. He called out, begging the eagle for mercy, but the bird answered that Loki would not be saved unless he swore an oath that he would find a way to lure Idunn, with her apples [of youth], out of Asgard. When Loki agreed, he was set free and returned to his companions. Nothing else is said to have occurred during that trip before they reached home. At the time agreed upon, Loki tricked Idunn into leaving Asgard and going into the forest with him. He told her that he had found apples that she would find to be of great worth and asked her to bring along her apples so that she might compare them. Just then the giant Thjazi arrived in the shape of an eagle and, seizing Idunn, he flew off with her to his home in Thrymheim.

Idunn's disappearance badly affected the Æsir, and they soon began to grow old and grey. The Æsir gathered together in an assembly and asked one another the news of Idunn. They realized that she had last been seen leaving Asgard with Loki. Then Loki was seized and brought to the assembly, where he was threatened with torture or death. When he grew frightened, he said he would go into Giant Land to find Idunn if Freyja would lend him her falcon shape.[2]

Loki Retrieves Idunn from the Giant Thjazi

When Loki got hold of the falcon shape, he flew north into Giant Land. He arrived at Thjazi's on a day when the giant had rowed out to sea, so Idunn was home alone. Loki changed her into the shape of a nut and, holding her in his claws, flew away as fast as he could. When Thjazi returned home and found Idunn missing, he put on his eagle shape and flew after Loki, the air booming with the sound of the eagle's flight. When the Æsir saw the falcon flying with the nut and the eagle in pursuit, they went outside to the walls of Asgard, carrying piles of wood shavings. As the falcon flew in over the fortress, it dived down alongside the fortress wall, and at that moment the Æsir set fire to the wood shavings. But the eagle, having just missed the falcon, was unable to stop himself before his feathers caught fire, and he fell from the air. The Æsir who were nearby killed the giant Thjazi inside the gate of Asgard, and this slaying is very famous.

Skadi Seeks Vengeance for Her Father

Now Skadi, daughter of the giant Thjazi, put on her helmet and coat of mail and, taking all her weapons of war, set out for Asgard to avenge her father. But the Æsir offered to reconcile and proposed compensation. First she should choose a husband for herself from among the Æsir, but she might choose only from the feet of the man, seeing nothing else. She saw that the feet of one man were especially beautiful and said 'I choose that one; few things on Baldr will be ugly.' But that was Njord[3] from Noatun.

Another condition of her settlement was that the Æsir must do something she thought they could not do: make her laugh. Then Loki tied one end of a cord to the beard of a goat and tied the other end around his own testicles. The goat and Loki started pulling back and forth, each squealing loudly until finally Loki fell into Skadi's lap, and then she laughed. With this, the Æsir concluded their part of the settlement with her.

It is said that Odin, to compensate her further, took Thjazi's eyes and cast them up into the heavens, where he made from them two stars.

The Inheritance of the Giants

Then Ægir said, 'Thjazi seems to me to have been exceptionally powerful, but what are his origins?'

Bragi answered, 'Olvaldi was the name of Thjazi's father, and if I were to tell you about him, you would find it a remarkable story. He had great wealth in gold, and when he died his sons were to divide the inheritance. In dividing the gold, they measured their shares by each taking the same number of mouthfuls in turn. One of them was Thjazi, the second Idi, and the third was Gang. From this story comes the expression whereby gold is referred to as the mouth count of these giants. We conceal this reference to gold in cryptic speech or poetic allusions by referring to it as the speech or the words or the count of these giants.'

Then Ægir said, 'It seems to me that this story is well hidden in secret lore.'

2
Kvasir and the Mead of Poetry

Ægir continued, 'What is the origin of the accomplishment you call poetry?'

Bragi replied, 'It originated when the gods were at war with that people called the Vanir, and the two sides agreed to hold a peace meeting. They reconciled their differences by the following procedure: both sides went to a vat and spat into it. At their parting, the gods, not wanting to lose this mark of the truce, took the spittle and from it they created a man called Kvasir. He was so wise that no one could ask him a question that he could not answer.

'Kvasir travelled throughout the world, teaching men knowledge. Once he came as a guest to the dwarves Fjalar and Galar. They asked him for a word in private, but instead they killed him, letting his blood flow into two vats called Son and Bodn, and into a kettle named Odrerir. The dwarves blended honey with the blood and from this mixture came the mead that makes whoever drinks it a poet or a scholar. They told the Æsir that Kvasir had choked on his own knowledge because there was no one there learned enough to ask him questions.

'The dwarves then invited the giant Gilling and his wife to come and visit them. They asked Gilling to row out to sea with them, and while travelling down the coast the dwarves rowed the boat on to some rocks just under the surface, overturning it. Gilling could not swim and was lost, but the dwarves righted their ship and rowed back to land. When they told Gilling's wife what had happened, she took the news badly and cried loudly. Fjalar asked her if it would lighten her spirits to look out to sea to the spot where Gilling had drowned, and she wanted to do so. Then Fjalar told his brother Galar to climb up over the door and, as she went out, to drop a millstone on to her head. Fjalar said that he was tired of her wailing, so Galar did this.

'When Suttung, Gilling's son,[1] learned what had happened, he travelled there and seized the dwarves. He ferried them out to sea and stranded them on some rocks that would be covered at high tide. The dwarves begged Suttung for their lives. They offered him the valuable mead as compensation for his father, and that offer became the basis of their agreement. Suttung took the mead home with him. For safekeeping, he put it in the place called Hnitbjorg and set his daughter Gunnlod to watch over it.

'For this reason we call poetry Kvasir's blood, the drink or intoxication of the dwarves, or some kind of liquid of Odrerir, Bodn or Son. The mead is also called the ship of the dwarves because it provided the ransom that floated them off the rocks. It is also called Suttung's mead or Hnitbjorg's liquid.'

Then Ægir said, 'It seems to me that calling poetry by these names obscures the truth. But how did the Æsir get Suttung's mead?'

Odin Seeks the Mead

Bragi replied, 'The story is that Odin travelled from home and came to a place where nine slaves were cutting hay. He asked if they wanted him to sharpen their scythes. They agreed. Then he took a whetstone from his belt and sharpened the scythes. To them it seemed that the scythes now cut much better, and they wanted to buy the whetstone. Odin set this price on the stone: he asked that whoever wanted to buy it should give what he thought was reasonable. They all said they wanted it and each asked to buy it, but instead he threw it into the air. They all scrambled to catch it with the result that they slit each other's throats with their scythes.[2]

'Odin sought lodgings for the night with the giant named Baugi, Suttung's brother. Baugi complained that his wealth had decreased, saying that nine of his slaves had been killed and that he had no hope of finding other workmen. But Odin, who went under the name Bolverk, offered to undertake for Baugi the work of nine men. As payment, he asked for a drink of Suttung's mead. Baugi said that he had no control over the mead, because Suttung wanted it all for himself. Baugi added, however, that he would go with Bolverk to see if together they could get the mead. That summer Bolverk did the work of nine men for Baugi.

'Towards the beginning of winter, Bolverk asked Baugi for his wages. Then they went together to Suttung's, where Baugi told his brother of his agreement with Bolverk. But Suttung flatly refused to give away a single drop of the mead. Then Bolverk said to Baugi that they should try a few tricks to see if they could get hold of the mead. Baugi was agreeable, and Bolverk brought out the auger called Rati and told Baugi that, if the auger would drill, he should bore a hole through the mountain. So he did. When Baugi said that he had bored through the mountain, Bolverk blew into the hole made by the auger, but chips came flying back at him. Realizing that Baugi wanted to betray him, Bolverk told Baugi to continue drilling until he had bored through the mountain. Baugi started to bore again, and when Bolverk blew for the second time, the chips flew inward. Then Bolverk changed himself into the shape of a snake and crawled into the auger hole. Baugi struck at him with the auger from behind, but missed him.

'Bolverk moved forward until he came to the place where Gunnlod was. He lay with her three nights, and she then allowed him three drinks of the mead. With his first drink he emptied Odrerir. With the second, he drained Bodn. His third emptied Son, and now he possessed all the mead. Then, changing himself into the shape of an eagle, he flew away as fast as he could. When Suttung saw the eagle's flight, he too put on his eagle shape and flew after him.

'When the Æsir saw Odin flying, they placed their vats in the courtyard, and when Odin entered Asgard he spat the mead into the vats. It was such a close call, with Suttung almost catching him, that he blew some of the mead out of his rear. No one paid attention to this part, and whoever wanted it took it; we call this the bad poets' portion. Odin gave Suttung's mead to the Æsir and to those men who know how to make poetry. For this reason we call poetry Odin's catch, find, drink or gift, as well as the drink of the Æsir.'

3
The Giant Hrungnir

Bragi told Ægir, 'Once, when Thor had gone into the east to fight trolls, Odin rode Sleipnir into Giant Land and came to the giant called Hrungnir. Hrungnir asked who it was that wore a golden helmet and rode through the sky and over the sea on such a fine horse. Odin said he would wager his head that no horse in Giant Land was its equal. Hrungnir answered that Sleipnir was a good horse but let on that he himself had a horse that took far bigger strides, and "this horse is named Gullfaxi [Golden Mane]".

'Losing his temper, Hrungnir jumped on to his horse and raced after Odin, hoping to repay him for his bragging. Odin galloped so fast that he stayed ahead of the giant, always just over a hill. But Hrungnir was in such a giant fury that he had passed through the gate of Asgard before he realized it.

'When he arrived at the hall doors, the Æsir invited him to drink. Walking into the hall, he demanded the drink. Then Thor's usual drinking bowls were brought out, and Hrungnir drained them all. When he became drunk, there was no end to his boasting.[1] He said he would lift up Valhalla and take it to Giant Land, bury Asgard, and kill all the gods except Freyja and Sif, whom he wanted to take home with him. When Freyja went to serve him, he vowed that he would drink all of the Æsir's ale.

Thor Duels with Hrungnir

'When the Æsir grew tired of Hrungnir's boasting they called on Thor, who quickly entered the hall, his hammer raised in the air. Enraged, he asked who had allowed the cunning giant to drink there. Who had granted Hrungnir permission to be at Valhalla, and why should Freyja be serving him as though he were feasting among the Æsir? Then Hrungnir answered, his eyes showing no friendship for Thor. He said that Odin had invited him to drink and that he was there on Odin's safe conduct. Thor said Hrungnir would regret that invitation before he left. Hrungnir replied to Thor of the Æsir that there was little renown in killing him weaponless, but Thor would find it a greater test of courage if he dared to fight him on the border at Grjotunagardar [Courtyards of Rocky Fields].

' "It was very foolish of me," said Hrungnir, "that I left my shield and whetstone at home. If I had my weapons here, we would now be testing each other in a duel; as matters stand, however, I lay on you a charge of cowardly betrayal if you choose to kill me when I am weaponless." Thor wanted on no account to miss the opportunity to take part in a duel, because no one had ever challenged him before.

'Hrungnir now went back the way he had come, galloping as fast as he could until he reached Giant Land. There among the giants his trip became famous, not least because a contest had been arranged between him and Thor. The giants felt that there was much at stake in who would gain the victory, for it seemed to them that they would have little hope against Thor if Hrungnir was killed, since he was their strongest.

'The giants then fashioned a man from clay at Grjotunagardar. He was nine leagues high and three leagues wide under the arms. They could not find a heart that was suitably large for him until they took one from a mare, but this heart became unsteady as soon as Thor arrived. Hrungnir had a heart that was famous. It was made of hard stone with three sharp-pointed corners just like the carved symbol called Hrungnishjarta [Hrungnir's Heart]. His head was also made of stone, as was his shield, which was wide and thick. Holding his shield in front of him, he stood waiting at Grjotunagardar for Thor. He had a whetstone for a weapon, and it rested ready on his shoulder. He was not a welcoming sight. Standing terrified at Hrungnir's side was the clay giant, called Mokkurkalfi. It is said that, on seeing Thor, he wet himself.[2]

'Thor, accompanied by Thjalfi, went to the duelling ground. Thjalfi ran ahead to where Hrungnir stood and said to him: "You stand unprepared, giant, holding your shield in front of you. Thor has seen you. He is travelling underneath in the earth and will come at you from below."

'Hrungnir then shoved his shield under his feet and stood on top of it, grasping the whetstone with both hands. He saw flashes of lightning and heard enormous claps of thunder. Then he saw Thor in his divine rage. Thor was rushing towards him, but when still at a long distance away, he raised his hammer and threw it at Hrungnir. The giant, using both hands, lifted his whetstone and threw it towards Thor. The whetstone struck the hammer in mid flight and broke into two. One part fell to the earth, and from it come all whetstones. The other part pierced Thor's head so that he fell to the earth. But the hammer Mjollnir landed right in the middle of Hrungnir's head. It smashed his skull into small pieces, and he fell forward, landing on top of Thor with his leg lying across Thor's neck. Meanwhile Thjalfi attacked Mokkurkalfi, who fell in such a way that it is hardly worth a story.

'Thjalfi then went to Thor, intending to lift Hrungnir's leg off him, but he could not move it. When they learned that Thor had fallen, all the Æsir came and tried to lift the leg, but they could not budge it. Then Magni, the son of Thor and Jarnsaxa, arrived; he was three years old[3] at the time. He flung Hrungnir's leg off Thor and said, "It is a great shame, Father, that I came so late. I imagine that with my fist I would have killed this giant, had I met him."

'Thor stood up and, greeting his son warmly, declared that he would become powerful. "And," he said, "I want to give you the horse Gullfaxi", which Hrungnir had owned.

'Then Odin spoke. He said that Thor was wrong to give so fine a horse to the son of a giantess, instead of to Thor's own father.

'Thor returned home to Thrudvangar, and the whetstone remained stuck in his head. Then the seeress called Groa arrived, the wife of Aurvandil the Bold. She sang her spells over Thor until the whetstone began to loosen. When Thor felt that, he expected the whetstone would soon be removed. Wanting to please and reward Groa for her healing, he told the story of his return from the north, and how he had waded across the river Elivagar, carrying Aurvandil southwards from Giant Land on his back in a basket. He recounted that one of Aurvandil's toes had stuck out from the basket and had frozen. Thor broke it off and threw it up into the heavens as a token, making from it the star called Aurvandil's Toe.[4] Thor added that it would not be long before Aurvandil returned home. Then Groa became so happy that she couldn't remember any of her magic, and the whetstone got no looser but remained lodged in Thor's head. And it is offered as a warning that one should not throw a whetstone across a floor, because then the whetstone in Thor's head moves. Thjodolf of Hvin tells this story in his poem *Haustlong*.'

4
Thor Journeys to Geirrod's Courts

Then Ægir said, 'To me Hrungnir seems to have been extremely powerful. Did Thor work any other great feats in his dealings with the trolls?'

Bragi replied, 'The story of Thor's journey to Geirrod's courts is well worth the telling. Loki was with him on the journey and, because of Loki, Thor did not have the hammer Mjollnir, his belt of strength or his iron gloves. This was because of what had happened to Loki earlier when, in order to amuse himself, he put on Frigg's falcon shape, and then, driven by curiosity, he flew into Geirrod's courts. Seeing there a great hall, he landed and looked in through a window. But Geirrod looked in his direction, and then commanded that the bird be seized and brought to him. The henchman charged with doing so, however, had trouble climbing up the wall of the hall because it was so high. Loki was amused to see so much effort expended in getting to him, so he delayed flying away until the man had almost finished the difficult climb.

'Just as the man rushed at him, Loki finally started to fly. He beat his wings but discovered that his feet were stuck fast. So Loki was seized and brought to the giant Geirrod. When Geirrod looked into the bird's eyes he suspected that it was a person, and he demanded that it answer him. But Loki remained silent. Then Geirrod locked Loki in a chest, starving him there for three months. This time, when Geirrod lifted him out and asked him to speak, Loki told him who he was. As ransom for his life he swore to Geirrod an oath that he would devise a way to bring Thor to Geirrod's courts and that Thor would have neither his hammer nor his belt of strength.

'Thor came to stay with the giantess named Grid as a guest for the night; she was the mother of Vidar the Silent. She told Thor the truth about Geirrod: that he was a cunning giant and that there was much danger in dealing with him. She lent Thor a belt of strength and iron gloves which she owned. She also lent him her staff, Gridarvol [Grid's Staff].

'Thor then travelled to the river Vimur; a great waterway.

He buckled on the belt of strength and supported himself against the current by placing Grid's pole on the downstream side while Loki held on to the belt of power. But when Thor got to the middle of the river, the water had risen so high that it reached to his shoulders. Then Thor spoke this verse:

> "Rise not, Vimur,
> as I want to wade you,
> crossing to the giant's courts.
> Beware. If you grow,
> divine might will grow in me
> as high as heaven!"

'Thor looked up and saw in a certain cleft Gjalp, the daughter of Geirrod, straddling the river with one leg on either side, and it was she who was causing the river to rise. Thor took a large stone from the river and threw it at her, saying: "At the source will a river be stemmed!" He did not miss his target.

'Just then he was swept towards the shore, where he was able to grab hold of some rowan branches,[1] and so was able to climb up from the river. This event is the origin of the expression that rowan trees are Thor's salvation.

'When Thor arrived at Geirrod's, he and his companions were first directed to a goat shed as their lodgings. There was only one chair, and Thor sat on it. But he soon noticed that the chair under him was rising towards the roof. He stuck Grid's pole up into the rafters and pushed down hard on the chair. Then came the sound of a loud crack, followed by a loud scream. Geirrod's daughters, Gjalp and Greip, had been under the chair, and he had broken both their backs.

'Then Geirrod had Thor called into the hall for contests. Large fires were burning down the length of the hall, and Thor approached until he stood opposite Geirrod. With his tongs, Geirrod grabbed a glowing piece of iron and threw it at Thor. Thor caught the red-hot piece in the iron gloves and, lifting it into the air, he threw it back at Geirrod, who ran behind an iron pillar to save himself. But the lump of glowing metal was thrown in such a way that it pierced the pillar and then Geirrod himself, before crashing through the wall and landing on the ground outside.'

5
The Dwarves Make Treasures for the Gods

'Why is gold called Sif's hair?'

'As a prank, Loki, son of Laufey, cut off all Sif's hair. When Thor learned of this, he grabbed hold of Loki and would have broken every bone in his body had Loki not sworn to find a way to get the dark elves to make hair from gold for Sif, which would grow like any other hair. Then Loki went to those dwarves called the sons of Ivaldi, and they made the hair, Skidbladnir, and Odin's spear, called Gungnir.

'Loki then wagered his head with the dwarf named Brokk that Eitri, Brokk's brother, could not make three treasures equally as good. When they entered the smithy, Eitri placed a pigskin in the forge. He told Brokk to work the bellows and not let up until Eitri had removed from the forge what he had put into it. But as soon as Eitri left the smithy and the other began to pump the air, a fly landed on Brokk's hand and bit him. Brokk continued, nevertheless, to work the bellows as before, and kept on until the smith pulled the work from the forge. It was a boar with bristles of gold.

'Next Eitri put gold in the forge. He asked the other to work the bellows and not to stop pumping until he returned. Then he left. The fly returned and settled on Brokk's neck, and this time it bit twice as hard. Still Brokk continued to pump until the smith took from the forge a gold ring, the one called Draupnir.

'Then the smith placed iron in the forge, telling the other to pump air with the bellows. He said that his work would be ruined if the bellows failed. This time the fly landed between Brokk's eyes, biting his eyelids. Finally, with blood flowing into his eyes, he was unable to see. So, as quickly as he could, he took his hand from the bellows on the down stroke and swatted the fly away. At that moment the smith returned and said that everything in the forge had just barely escaped ruin. Then he took a hammer from the forge, and, entrusting all the treasures to his brother Brokk, he asked him to go to Asgard to settle the wager.

'When Brokk and Loki arrived and displayed their treasures, the Æsir took their places on their thrones of fate. Odin, Thor and Frey were to be the judges, thus settling the matter. Loki gave to Odin the spear Gungnir; to Thor, the hair for Sif; and to Frey, Skidbladnir. He then described the characteristics of each of the treasures: the spear always pierced cleanly through, never stopping during the thrust; the hair would grow fast to the skin as soon as it came on to Sif's head; and Skidbladnir would receive a fair wind whenever its sail was raised, no matter where it was going. It could also be folded up like a cloth and put into one's pouch if so desired.

'Brokk then brought out his treasures. He gave the ring to Odin, saying that every ninth night eight rings of equal weight would drip from it. To Frey he gave the boar, remarking that night or day it could race across the sky and over the sea better than any other mount. Furthermore, night would never be so murky nor the worlds of darkness so shadowy that the boar would not provide light wherever it went, so bright was the shining of its bristles. Then he gave the hammer to Thor, and said that with it Thor would be able to strike whatever came before him with as mighty a blow as he wished, because the hammer would never break. And if he decided to throw the hammer, it would never miss its mark, nor could it ever be thrown so far that it would not find its way back home to his hand. It was also so small that, if he wished, he could keep it inside his shirt. There was, however, one defect: the handle was rather short. It was their judgment that the hammer was the best of all the treasures, and that it provided the best protection against the frost giants. Therefore they decided that the dwarf had won the wager.

'Loki then asked to be allowed to ransom his head, but the dwarf replied that there was no hope of that. "Catch me then," said Loki. But when the dwarf tried to grab hold of him, Loki was already far away.

'Loki had shoes that allowed him to race through the air and over the sea. The dwarf told Thor that he should catch Loki, and Thor did so. The dwarf wanted to cut off Loki's head, but Loki said that the dwarf had a right to his head but not to the neck. The dwarf then took a narrow strip of leather and a knife. He intended to cut holes in Loki's lips and to sew his mouth shut, but the knife would not cut. The dwarf said that it would be better if his brother Awl were there. No sooner had he mentioned it than the awl was there, and it punched holes through the lips.[1] He then stitched the lips together before ripping away the outer edges. The thong sewing shut Loki's mouth is called Vartari.'

6
Ægir's Feast

'Why is gold called the fire of Ægir?'

'The story is that Ægir, as mentioned previously, came as a guest to Asgard, and when he was ready to return home he invited Odin and all the gods to visit him in three months. Odin, Njord, Frey, Tyr, Bragi, Vidar and Loki went on this journey, and with them were the goddesses Frigg, Freyja, Gefjun, Skadi, Idunn and Sif. Thor was not among them. He had gone to the east to kill trolls. When the gods had taken their seats, Ægir commanded that gleaming gold be brought in and placed on the floor of the hall. It lit up the hall, shining like fire, and was used for light at his feast in the manner that swords replaced fires for light in Valhalla. Then Loki exchanged insults with all the gods, and he killed Fimafeng, Ægir's slave. Another of Ægir's slaves was called Eldir. Ran was the name of Ægir's wife and they had nine daughters. At this feast everything, the food, the ale and all the necessary tableware, served itself. Then the Æsir became aware that Ran had a net and with it she caught all men who came into the sea. This story explains why gold is called the fire or the light or the brightness of Ægir, Ran or Ægir's daughters.'

7
Otter's Ransom: The Rhinegold and Sigurd the Dragon Slayer

'Why is gold called Otter's ransom?'[1]

'It is said that once when the Æsir, Odin, Loki and Hoenir, were travelling to find out about the wide world, they came to a river and walked along its bank until they arrived at a waterfall. Beside it was an otter who had caught a salmon in the falls and was dozing as he ate it. Loki picked up a stone and, throwing it at the otter, struck its head. Loki was pleased with his catch, having with one blow caught both an otter and a salmon.

'The gods, taking both the salmon and the otter with them, continued on until they came to a house and went in. The farmer living there was named Hreidmar; he was a powerful man and very skilled in magic. The Æsir asked to stay there for the night. They said that they had with them enough food and showed the master of the house their catch. But when Hreidmar saw the otter he called his sons, Fafnir and Regin, to tell them that their brother Otter had been killed, and who was responsible.

'The father and sons now attacked the Æsir, seizing and binding them. They told the Æsir about Otter, saying that he was Hreidmar's son. The Æsir offered to ransom their lives with as much wealth as Hreidmar himself would demand, and these terms, bound by oaths, became the basis of their agreement. Then the otter was flayed. Hreidmar took the otter skin, shaped like a bag, and commanded them to fill the skin with red gold and also to cover the outside completely. This would be the terms of the reconciliation between them.

'Odin then sent Loki into Svartalfaheim, and there he found the dwarf called Andvari. He was a fish in water, and Loki caught him, demanding as ransom all the gold that the dwarf had in his home of stone. Then they entered into the rock, and the dwarf brought forward all his gold. It was a huge treasure. But the dwarf hid in his hand a little gold ring. Loki saw him do this and told him to hand over the ring. The dwarf begged Loki not to take the ring. He confided that if the ring remained in his possession, he would be able to make more wealth for himself. Loki said that not one coin[2] was to remain with Andvari and, taking the ring from the dwarf, he left. The dwarf called after him, saying that the ring would be the death of whoever possessed it. Loki replied that was fine with him. He said that this foretelling would hold, because he would bring these words of warning to the ears of those who would get the ring.

'Loki then returned to Hreidmar's and showed Odin the gold. When Odin saw the ring, he found it beautiful and removed it from the treasure, paying Hreidmar the rest of the gold. Then Hreidmar stuffed the otter skin with as much of the treasure as he could and set it upright when it was full. Odin then came forward and started to cover the skin with the gold, as he was required to do. He then told Hreidmar to come and see whether the skin was completely covered. Hreidmar looked carefully. When he saw that one whisker stuck out, he asked that it be covered; otherwise, their agreement would be broken. Odin then brought out the ring and with it he covered the whisker, saying that they were now free from the otter's ransom.

'When Odin had taken his spear and Loki his shoes, so that they no longer had anything to fear, Loki recounted Andvari's words, saying that the ring and the gold would be the death of anyone who owned it. And so it happened ever afterwards.

'Now it has been told why gold is called Otter's ransom, the forced payment of the Æsir or the metal of strife.'

The Curse on the Gold Begins to Work

'What more is there to tell about the gold?'

'Hreidmar took the gold as compensation for his son, but Fafnir and Regin asked for part of it as payment for their brother. Hreidmar, however, would not grant them a single gold coin, and the tragic response of these brothers was that they killed their father for that gold. Then Regin asked Fafnir to divide the gold equally between them. Fafnir replied that there was little hope of his sharing the gold with his brother after he had killed his own father for it. He told Regin to leave, otherwise he would follow the same path as Hreidmar. Fafnir had by then taken Hreidmar's helmet and placed it on his head.

It was called the Ægis-Helm [the Helm of Dread], and it brought fear to all living things when they saw it. Also he took the sword called Hrotti, whereas Regin had the sword called Refil. Regin now fled, and Fafnir went up on to Gnita-Heath. There he made for himself a lair, and, changing himself into the likeness of a serpent, he lay down on the gold.

Sigurd the Volsung

'Regin then went to King Hjalprek in Thjod and became his smith. He took Sigurd, the son of Sigmund, who was the son of Volsung, as his foster son. Sigurd's mother was Hjordis, the daughter of Eylimi. Sigurd was the finest of all warrior kings because of his family, his strength and his courage. Regin told him where Fafnir lay on the gold and urged him to seek the treasure.

'Regin then forged the sword called Gram. It was so sharp that when Sigurd lowered it into running water it sliced through a tuft of wool carried by the current against the sword's edge. Next Sigurd used the sword to cut Regin's anvil in two, starting from its top down to the log on which it rested.

'Sigurd and Regin next travelled together to Gnita-Heath. Sigurd dug a pit in the path used by Fafnir and lowered himself into it. As Fafnir crawled to the water he passed over the pit, and at that instant Sigurd thrust his sword through him. That was his death. Regin then came forward and said that Sigurd had killed his brother. As settlement between him and Sigurd, he asked Sigurd to take Fafnir's heart and roast it on the fire. Regin then lay down, drank Fafnir's blood and went to sleep.

'Sigurd roasted the heart, and when he thought it was cooked, he touched it with his finger to find out if it was still raw. The boiling juice from the heart ran on to his finger, scalding it, and he stuck his finger into his mouth. When the heart's blood ran on to his tongue, he suddenly understood the speech of birds. He heard nuthatches speaking as they sat in the trees. One of them said:

"There sits Sigurd
spattered with blood, as
Fafnir's heart
he roasts, on the fire.
Wise would seem
the breaker of rings,
if he would eat
the gleaming heart."

'Another said:

"There lies Regin,
making his plans,
intending to betray the boy
who trusts him.
Moved by anger,
he gathers evil thoughts;
the forger of trouble wants
vengeance for his brother."

'Then Sigurd went up to Regin and killed him. Afterwards, he mounted his horse Grani and rode until he came to Fafnir's lair. There Sigurd gathered up the gold and put it into sacks. These he placed on Grani's back, and then climbed up himself and rode on his way.

'Now the story has been told why gold is called the lair or the home of Fafnir, the metal of Gnita-Heath, or Grani's burden.

The Valkyrie Brynhild and the Gjukungs

'Sigurd rode until he came to a house up on a mountain. Inside a woman was sleeping; she wore a helmet and a mail coat. He drew his sword and cut the mail coat from her. She then awakened and said that her name was Hild but that she was called Brynhild and was a valkyrie.

'Sigurd rode away until he came to a king named Gjuki and his wife named Grimhild. Their children were Gunnar, Hogni, Gudrun and Gudny. Gothorm was Gjuki's stepson. After staying there for a long time, Sigurd married Gjuki's daughter,

Gudrun. With Gunnar and Hogni, Sigurd swore oaths of brotherhood.

'Next Sigurd and the sons of Gjuki travelled together to ask Atli [Attila the Hun], the son of Budli, to give his sister Brynhild as a wife to Gunnar. She was living on the mountain called Hindafell, and around her hall burned a wavering flame. She had taken an oath to marry only that man who dared ride through the wavering flame. Sigurd and the Gjukungs, also called the Niflungs,[3] rode up the mountain with Gunnar intending to ride through the wavering flame. Gunnar's horse, named Goti, would not jump into the fire. Then Sigurd and Gunnar exchanged their shapes and their names because Grani refused to be ridden by any man other than Sigurd. Springing on to Grani's back, Sigurd rode through the wavering flame.

'That evening Sigurd wed Brynhild. But when they got into the bed, he drew the sword Gram from its sheath and placed it between them. In the morning, after he got up and had dressed, he gave to Brynhild, as the linen fee,[4] the gold ring that Loki had taken from Andvari. In return, he took from her another ring as a remembrance. Sigurd then jumped on to his horse and rode to his companions. He and Gunnar then returned to their own shapes. Together with Brynhild, they returned to Gjuki. Sigurd had two children with Gudrun, Sigmund and Svanhild.

Brynhild and Gudrun Quarrel

'It happened once that Brynhild and Gudrun went down to the water to wash their hair. When they reached the river, Brynhild waded out from the shore. She said that she did not want water on her head which had already rinsed through Gudrun's hair, because hers was the more courageous husband. Then Gudrun followed her out into the river, saying that it was her privilege to wash her hair higher up in the river, because she was married to a man braver than Gunnar or anyone else in the world, and it was he who had killed Fafnir and Regin and taken both their inheritances.

'Brynhild replied: "Greater was the feat when Gunnar rode through the wavering flame while Sigurd would not dare."

'Then Gudrun laughed and said, "Do you think it was

Gunnar who rode through the wavering flame? This I know: the one who came into your bed was the one who gave me this gold ring. Further, the gold ring you have on your hand, which you received as the morning gift, is called Andvaranaut [Andvari's Gift], and I do not believe that Gunnar was the one who won it at Gnita-Heath."

'Brynhild then grew silent and returned home.

'From then on she urged Gunnar and Hogni to kill Sigurd. But because they had sworn oaths to Sigurd, they urged their brother Gothorm to kill Sigurd, which he did by thrusting a sword through Sigurd while he slept. When Sigurd felt the wound, he threw his sword Gram at Gothorm, slicing the man in half at the middle. Sigurd died there together with his three-year-old son Sigmund, whom they also killed. Brynhild then thrust a sword into herself, and she was burned with Sigurd. As for Gunnar and Hogni, they took Fafnir's wealth and the ring Andvari's Gift and ruled over the lands.

The Rhinegold, King Atli's Greed and Queen Gudrun's Vengeance

'Brynhild's brother King Atli, the son of Budli, then married Gudrun, Sigurd's former wife, and together they had children. King Atli invited Gunnar and Hogni to come for a visit, and they accepted the invitation. Before setting out from home they hid the gold, Fafnir's inheritance, in the Rhine. That gold has never been found.

'King Atli was waiting for them with his men, and he fought with Gunnar and Hogni, seizing them in the end. King Atli had Hogni's heart cut out while he was alive, and that was his death. Atli had Gunnar thrown into the snake pit, but Gunnar secretly was given a harp. Because his hands were bound he played it with his toes; all the snakes fell asleep, except for one adder. This one glided towards him and struck just below his breastbone so that she buried her head into his flesh, grabbing hold of his liver until he died.

'Gunnar and Hogni are called Niflungs and Gjukungs, and for this reason the gold is called the treasure or the inheritance of the Niflungs.

'Shortly after that Gudrun killed her two sons, and she had goblets made from their skulls, using gold and silver. Then a funeral feast was held for the Niflungs at which Gudrun had King Atli served mead in these cups, mixed with the blood of the boys. She also had their hearts roasted and given to the king to eat. She then confronted Atli and, with foul words, told him what she had done. There was no lack of strong mead at the feast and most people fell asleep where they were sitting. Later in the night, Gudrun, accompanied by Hogni's son, approached the king as he slept and struck him his death blow. Then they spread fire in the hall, and the people inside burned to death.

Gudrun's Third Marriage

'After that Gudrun went down to the shore and jumped into the sea, wanting to drown herself. But she was carried across the fjord and came to the land ruled by King Jonak. When he saw her, he took her as his own and married her. They had three sons:[5] Sorli, Hamdir and Erp. Their hair was black as a raven's, as was the hair of Gunnar and Hogni and of the other Niflungs.

'Svanhild, the daughter of Sigurd in his youth, was raised there and became the most beautiful of women. King Jormunrek the Powerful,[6] learning of her beauty, sent his son Randver to ask for her hand on his behalf. After Randver's arrival at Jonak's, Svanhild was entrusted to his keeping, as he was the one who was to take her to Jormunrek. Then Bikki[7] [the king's adviser] spoke. He suggested that it would be better if Randver took Svanhild for himself, because the two were young, whereas Jormunrek was an old man. The idea appealed to the young people, but the next thing Bikki did was to tell the king what had happened.

King Jormunrek's Tragedy

'King Jormunrek had his son seized and led to the gallows. Randver grabbed hold of his hawk and plucked out its feathers, asking that it be sent to his father. Then Randver was hanged. When King Jormunrek saw the hawk, he realized that, like it, now featherless and unable to fly, his kingdom also was disabled as he was old and had no son.

'Later King Jormunrek was returning from a hunt with his retainers. Riding from the forest, he saw Queen Svanhild sitting outside, washing her hair. He and his men rode her down, trampling her to death under the feet of their horses.

'When Gudrun learned about this, she incited her sons to seek vengeance for Svanhild. As they prepared their trip, she gave them mail coats and helmets so strong that iron would not pierce them. Her advice to her sons was that when they reached King Jormunrek they should attack him at night while he slept. Sorli and Hamdir should cut off his arms and legs, and Erp the head. As they travelled, the brothers asked Erp what assistance they could expect from him, should they actually get to King Jormunrek. He answered that he would help them just as the hand helps the foot. They said that the foot was not supported at all by the hand.

'Their mother had taunted the sons as they set out, and that made them so angry with her that they wanted to do whatever would hurt her the most. So they killed Erp, because she loved him the most. A little while later, as Sorli was walking, one of his legs slipped under him, and he supported himself with his hand. Then he said: "The hand now has helped the foot. It would have been better if Erp had lived!"

'It was night when they reached King Jormunrek's sleeping quarters. He awoke as they struck off his hands and legs, and he called out to his men, commanding them to rise.

'Then Hamdir said: "The head would now have been off, if Erp had lived!"

'The king's men rose and attacked the brothers, but they could not harm them with weapons. Finally Jormunrek called to his men, telling them to stone them. They did so and Sorli and Hamdir both fell. Now the house of Gjuki and all his descendants were dead.

'From his youth, Sigurd was survived by a daughter named Aslaug.[8] She had been born at the home of Heimir in Hlymdales, and from her great families are descended.

'It is said that Sigmund, the son of Volsung, was so tough that he could drink poison and not be harmed. Also that his son Sinfjotli, as well as Sigurd,[9] had skin so hard that poison caused them no harm even if it came on to their bare flesh.'

8
Frodi's Mill and His Peace

'Why is gold called Frodi's flour?'

'There is a tale about this: Skjold was a son of Odin, the one from whom the Skjoldungs are descended. He had a court and ruled over lands that are now called Denmark but were known at that time as Gotland. Skjold had a son named Fridleif, who ruled over lands after him. Fridleif's son was named Frodi, and he took the kingdom after his father in the period when Emperor Augustus was pacifying the whole world; this was when Christ was born. Because Frodi was the most powerful king in the northern countries, his name became connected with the peace which reigned throughout all the lands speaking the Danish tongue.[1] The Norwegians called it Frodi's peace. No man harmed another, even if he came upon the killer of his father or of his brother, whether they were free or bondsmen. There were neither thieves nor robbers and for a long time a gold ring lay untouched on Jalangr's Heath.[2]

'King Frodi went on a visit to Sweden as guest of the king named Fjolnir. He bought there two slavewomen. They were called Fenja and Menja and were huge and strong. At that time there were in Denmark two millstones so large that no one was strong enough to get them turning. The nature of these stones was that they ground out whatever the miller commanded to be ground. The mill was called Grotti, and Hang Jaw was the name of the one who gave the mill to King Frodi.

'King Frodi had the slavewomen taken to the mill and commanded them to grind gold, peace and prosperity for Frodi. He gave them no more time to rest or to sleep than a cuckoo takes to remain silent or a person to sing a verse. It is said that then they chanted the lay called *Grotti's Song*. And before they had finished their singing, they ground out an army to oppose Frodi. That very same night the sea king named Mysing arrived there and killed Frodi, taking much plunder. With that, Frodi's peace ended.

'Mysing took Grotti and also Fenja and Menja away with him and told them to grind salt. Towards the middle of the night, they asked Mysing if he was not growing tired of salt. He told them to keep on grinding, but they continued for only a short time before the ship sank. From that time on there has been a whirlpool in the ocean where the sea flows down into the eye of the millstone. It was then that the sea became salty.'

9
Kraki's Seed and King Hrolf Kraki of Denmark

'Why is gold called Kraki's seed?'

'There was a king in Denmark named Hrolf Kraki. He was the most renowned of the old kings, chiefly because of his generosity, valour and humility. A mark of his humility, and one that is often repeated in stories, is that a little poor boy named Vogg came into King Hrolf's hall. At the time, the king was young and slender in build.

'Vogg went before Hrolf and stared up at him. Then the king said: "What do you want to say, boy, since you are staring at me?"

'Vogg replied: "When I was at home I heard it said that King Hrolf at Hleidra was the greatest man in the northern lands, but now there sits before me on the throne a thin pole[1] [*kraki*] of a man; and you call him your king!"

'In reply the king said, "You, boy, have given me a name. I shall be called Hrolf Kraki, and it is the custom that a gift shall accompany the name giving. I can see, however, that at this naming you have no gift for me which I would find acceptable. So the one who has will give to the other." And he took a gold ring from his arm and gave it to the boy.

'Then Vogg said, "May your giving be blessed above all kings, and I swear an oath to be the death of the man who kills you."

'The king laughed as he replied, "It takes little to please Vogg."[2]

King Hrolf and King Adils of Sweden

'Another story that illustrates King Hrolf's valour has to do with a king named Adils, who ruled over Uppsala[3] and who was married to Yrsa,[4] Hrolf Kraki's mother. Adils was at war with the king called Ali, who ruled Norway. They arranged to meet in battle on the ice of the lake named Vaeni, and King Adils sent a request to his stepson Hrolf Kraki to come to his assistance. He promised to pay Hrolf's whole army while it was away from home, and King Hrolf was to choose for himself three of Sweden's treasures. As King Hrolf was unable to undertake the trip because of his conflict with the Saxons, he sent to Adils his twelve berserkers. Bodvar Bjarki was among them, and so also was Hjalti the Courageous, Hvitserk the Bold, Vott, Veseti and the brothers Svipdag and Beigud. In that battle King Ali fell, along with a large part of his army. Then King Adils took the helmet called Battle Pig from Ali's dead body and the horse Raven.

'Then Hrolf Kraki's berserkers asked that each of them should be paid three pounds of gold for their services. Furthermore, they asked to take back to Hrolf Kraki the treasures that they would choose for him: the helmet Hildigolt [Battle Boar] and the mail shirt Finnsleif [Finn's Legacy], which weapons could not pierce, and the gold ring called Sviagris[5] [the Swedes' Pig], which had been in the possession of Adils' ancient ancestors. But the king refused to give up any of these treasures, and he would not even pay them their wages.

'Little pleased with their lot, the berserkers left. They reported the outcome to Hrolf Kraki, who immediately set out for Uppsala. After first guiding his ships up the river Fyri,[6] Hrolf rode to Uppsala accompanied by his twelve berserkers, all of them without safe conduct. Hrolf's mother Yrsa welcomed him. She showed him to his lodgings, though not to the king's hall. Large fires were lit for them, and they were supplied with ale. Next, King Adils' men entered. They heaped logs on to the fires, making them burn so hot that the clothes were burned off King Hrolf and his men.

'Adils' men asked: "Is it true that Hrolf Kraki and his berserkers flee neither fire nor iron?"

'Then Hrolf Kraki and all his men jumped to their feet, and Hrolf answered: "Let's further increase the fires in Adils' house", and, grabbing his shield, he threw it into the blaze. As the shield burned, he jumped over the flames and said, "He does not flee fire who leaps over it." Now, each of his men, one after the other, did the same thing. And as they did so, they took hold of those who had been feeding the fire and threw them into the blaze.

'Yrsa now arrived and gave Hrolf Kraki an animal's horn filled with gold, including the ring Sviagris. She advised them to ride back to their army, and they leapt on to their horses and rode down to the Fyri Plains. It was then that they saw King Adils riding after them. His army was with him, dressed for war and intending to kill. With his right hand, King Hrolf Kraki reached into the horn and, taking hold of the gold, he sowed it like seed all along the road. When the Swedes saw him doing that, they leapt from their saddles, each trying to grab as much gold as he could. King Adils commanded his men to continue riding, and he himself galloped as hard as he could. His horse, named Slungnir, was the fastest of mounts.

'When Hrolf Kraki saw King Adils coming up fast behind him, he took the ring Sviagris and threw it in front of Adils, inviting him to take it as a gift. King Adils rode up to where the ring lay and reached for it with his spear, letting the ring slide on to the blade all the way to the socket. Hrolf Kraki now looked back and, seeing Adils bent over, he said: "I made the most powerful of the Swedes grovel like a pig." Then they parted.

'From this story, gold is called the seed of Kraki or the seed of the Fyri Plains.'

10
The Never-ending Battle

Battle is called the weather or the storm of the Hjadnings, and weapons are known as the fires or the wands of the Hjadnings. There is a story behind these names.

A king named Hogni had a daughter called Hild [Battle]. While King Hogni was away at a kings' assembly, King Hedin Hjarrandason abducted Hild, taking her as a prize of war. When Hogni heard that his kingdom had been raided and his daughter had been taken captive, he set out with his men to search for Hedin. He learned that Hedin had sailed north, following the coastline. But when King Hogni arrived in Norway, he heard that Hedin had sailed west over the sea.[1] Hogni then sailed after him all the way to the Orkney Isles. When he reached the place called Haey [Hoy or High Island], Hedin was there, waiting with his men.

Then Hild went to meet her father. As a sign of reconciliation from Hedin, she offered him the gift of a necklace. She informed him that otherwise Hedin was prepared to fight, and, if he did, there would be no hope of his showing Hogni any mercy. Hogni's response to his daughter was harsh. When she returned to Hedin, she told him that Hogni did not want to reconcile and advised him to prepare for battle. Both sides now went to the island, the two sides drawing up in battle order. Hedin then called to Hogni, his father-in-law, offering to settle with him. He proposed to pay a large compensation in gold.

Hogni replied, 'It is too late for you to want to settle and make such an offer, because I have now drawn Dainsleif [Dain's Legacy] from its sheath. The dwarves made it and it must be the death of a man each time it is unsheathed. Its stroke never fails and its wounds do not heal.'

Then Hedin replied, 'You boast about your sword but not about victory. Still, I call good whatever serves its master well.'

The battle named the Fight of the Hjadnings then began, and they fought all through that day. At dusk the kings returned to their ships. But during the night Hild went to the slain, and through magic she awakened all those who were dead. On the second day the kings went to the battlefield, as did all those who had fallen on the previous day. In this manner the battle continued day after day. All who fell were turned to stone, together with all the weapons and shields lying on the field. But at the dawn of the new day, all the dead men stood up and began to fight again, while all their weapons became like new.

It says in the poetry that in this way the Hjadnings await Ragnarok. Concerning this tale, the poet Bragi composed a passage in his formal poem about Ragnar Lodbrok [*Ragnarsdrapa*].

POETIC REFERENCES FROM *SKALDSKAPARMAL*

Translated by Russell Poole

In addition to the myths and legends above, *Skaldskaparmal* contains many specific examples of kennings and other instructional information about the language of skaldic verse. These passages, of which the following is an appreciable sampling, teach, in a schoolmasterly tone, how to refer to the gods and goddesses as well as to people, places and things. At times the passages offer us otherwise unknown mythological, legendary and genealogical information. As with the Heimdall story, translated below, many of these passages are short and sketchy. Luckily a good number of the stories that are mentioned in this section are told more fully elsewhere in the *Edda*.

An Explanation of Kenning Structure

Then Ægir said, 'In how many ways do you vary the diction in poetry, and how many types of poetry are there?'

Bragi replied, 'All poetry belongs to one or another of two types.'

Ægir asked, 'Which two?'

Bragi said, 'We classify poetry according to diction and metre.'

'What kind of diction is used in poetry?'

'There are three categories.'

'What are those?'

'I'll tell you. One, to name things by their ordinary names. Two, to substitute alternative names. Three, to use what are called kennings. To understand this third type of diction, suppose that in a poem I use the name Odin or Thor or Tyr, or some other name identifying one of the Æsir or the elves, but add to it a characteristic or attribute that properly belongs to another god or elf. Then it is this other personage that is referenced in the kenning and not the one actually named. For instance, I might say Tyr of victory or Tyr of the hanged man or Tyr of the cargo, and then in each case I am adding a piece of diction that relates to Odin. The phrase as a whole then refers to Odin, not to Tyr. We call that a "name with identifying attribute" [*kent heiti*]. An example is Tyr of the wagon, referring to Odin.'

Kennings for Gods

'How should Thor be referred to?'

'By calling him the son of Odin and Earth, the father of Magni, Modi and Thrud, the husband of Sif, the stepfather of Ull, the wielder or possessor of the hammer Mjollnir, of the mighty girdle and of the hall Bilskirnir, the defender of Asgard and Midgard, the foe and killer of giants and troll women, the adversary of Hrungnir, Geirrod and Thrivaldi, the lord of Thjalfi and Roskva, the enemy of the Midgard Serpent and the foster son of Vingnir and Hlora.'

'How should Baldr be referred to?'

'By calling him the son of Odin and Frigg, the husband of Nanna, the father of Forseti, the possessor of the ship Hringhorni and the ring Draupnir, the adversary of Hod, the comrade of Hel and the god of laments.'

'How should Njord be referred to?'

'By calling him the god of wagons, the descendant of the Vanir, one of the Vanir, the father of Frey and Freyja or the god of gift-giving.'

'How should Frey be referred to?'

'By calling him the son of Njord, the brother of Freyja, the god of the Vanir, the descendant of the Vanir and one of the Vanir, the god of a good year, and the giver of wealth . . . He is called the foe of Beli . . . and the possessor of the boat Skidbladnir and the boar Gullinbursti . . . The boar is also called Slidrugtanni.'

'How should Heimdall be referred to?'

'He can be called the son of nine mothers, the watchman of the gods, as stated previously, the white one of the Æsir, Loki's foe, or the seeker of Freyja's ring. The phrase "Heimdall's head" is a way of referring to a sword. The story goes that Heimdall was struck through by a man's head, and there is a poem about him called *Heimdall's Chant*. As a consequence a head can be referred to as the undoing of Heimdall, just as a sword can be called a man's undoing. Heimdall is the owner of the horse Gulltopp. He is also the voyager to Vagasker and Singastein; it was on that occasion that he and Loki came to blows over the ring of the Brisings. The skald Ulf Uggason devotes a lengthy passage to that story in his poem *Husdrapa*, and it is stated there that Heimdall and Loki took on the shape of seals. Another name for Heimdall is Vindhler. He can also be called son of Odin.'

'How should Tyr be referred to?'

'By calling him the one-handed god, the foster-father of the wolf, the god of battles and the son of Odin.'

'How should Bragi be referred to?'

'By calling him the husband of Idunn, the first maker of poetry, the son of Odin and the long-bearded god. Hence anyone who sports a big beard is called a bearded Bragi.'

'How should Vidar be referred to?'

'He can be called the silent god, the possessor of the iron shoe, the foe and slayer of the wolf Fenrir, the avenger of the gods, the god who lives on his father's house site, the son of Odin, and the brother of the Æsir.'

'How should Vali be referred to?'

'By calling him the son of Odin and Rind, the stepson of Frigg, the brother of the Æsir, the god who avenged Baldr, the foe and slayer of Hod and the resident on his father's house site.'

'How should Hod be referred to?'

'By calling him the blind Æsir, the killer of Baldr, the shooter of the mistletoe, the son of Odin, the comrade of Hel and the foe of Vali.'

'How should Ull be referred to?'

'By calling him the son of Sif, the stepson of Thor, the god with skis, the god with a bow, the hunting god and the god with a shield.'

'How should Hoenir be referred to?'

'By calling him the seat mate, comrade, or trusted companion of Odin, the fast-moving god, the long leg or the king of clay.'

'How should Loki be referred to?'

'By calling him the son of Farbauti and Laufey or Nal, the brother of Byleist and Helblindi, the father of the spewer of the river Van, who is the wolf Fenrir, the father of Jormungand, who is the Midgard Serpent, the father of Hel and Nari, the kinsman and father's brother of Ali, the comrade and bench mate of Odin and the Æsir, the guest of Geirrod, the adornment of Geirrod's wooden chest, one who steals from giants, the thief of the goat, of Idunn's apples, and of the ring of the Brisings, the kinsman of Sleipnir, the husband of Sigyn, the foe of the gods, the wrecker of Sif's hair, the author of woes, the sly god, the one who slanders and betrays the gods, the one who engineered Baldr's death, the bound one and the vexing litigant against Heimdall and Skadi.'

References to Goddesses

'How should Frigg be referred to?'

'By calling her the daughter of Fjorgyn, the wife of Odin, the mother of Baldr, the rival paramour of Earth, Rind, Gunnlod and Gerd, the mother-in-law of Nanna, or the queen of the gods and goddesses, of Fulla, of the falcon's feather cloak and of the halls of Fensalir.'

'How should Freyja be referred to?'

'By calling her the daughter of Njord, the sister of Frey, the wife of Od, the mother of Hnoss, the possessor of those fallen in battle, of the hall Sessrumnir, of male cats and of the ring of the Brisings, the god of the Vanir, the household deity of the Vanir and the god whose weeping is beautiful. Any goddess can be referenced in kennings by associating her characteristic possessions, activities or family members with the name of another goddess.'

'How should Sif be referred to?'

'By calling her the wife of Thor, the mother of Ull, the goddess with beautiful hair, the rival concubine of Jarnsaxa or the mother of Thrud.'

'How should Idunn be referred to?'

'Call her the wife of Bragi and the guardian of the apples, these apples being a remedy for old age used by the Æsir. She is also the plunder taken by the giant Thjazi, since he abducted her from the Æsir, as previously stated.'

References to Sky, Earth and Natural Phenomena

'How should one refer to the sky?'

'By calling it Ymir's head and hence the giant's skull, the burden or heavy load on the dwarves, the helmet of the dwarves West, East, South and North, the land of the sun, moon, heavenly bodies, constellations and winds, or the helmet or house of the air, of the earth and of the sun.'

'How should the earth be referred to?'

'Call it the flesh of Ymir, the mother of Thor, the daughter of Onar, the bride of Odin, the rival concubine of Frigg, Rind and Gunnlod, the mother-in-law of Sif, the floor or footing of the hall of the winds, the sea trodden on by animals, the daughter of Night or the sister of Aud and Day.'

'How should the sea be referred to?'

'By calling it the blood of Ymir, the visitor to the gods, the husband of Ran, the father of the daughters of Ægir whose names are Himinglaeva, Dufa, Blodughadda, Hefring, Udr, Hronn, Bylgja, Bara and Kolga, by calling it the land of Ran, and of the daughters of Ægir, and of ships or of the names of sea-going vessels, and of the keel, and of the prow, and of planks and seams, and of fish and of ice, and calling it the way and routes taken by sea kings, likewise the ring of the islands, house of sands and seaweed and rocky islets, or the land of fishing gear, sea birds and the following wind.'

'How should the sun be referred to?'

'By calling it the daughter of Mundilfoeri, the sister of the Moon, the wife of Glen and the fire of the heavens and the air.'

'How should the wind be referred to?'

'By calling it the son of Fornjot, the brother of Ægir and of fire, the breaker of timber, and the enemy, destroyer, hound, or wolf of timber, of the sail or of rigging for the sail.'

'How should fire be referred to?'

'By calling it the brother of the wind and of Ægir, the ruination and destroyer of timber and of houses, the undoing of Half and the sun of houses.'

'How should winter be referred to?'

'By calling it the son of Vindsval, the mortal foe of snakes and the season of blizzards.'

'How should summer be referred to?'

'By calling it the son of Svasud, respite for snakes and growing time for men.'

References to Men

'How should a man be referred to?'

'He should be referred to in terms of his work, what he supplies or receives or does. He can also be referred to in terms of his possessions, both those he owns and those he gives away. Likewise in terms of the families he is descended from and those who are descended from him.

'How should we make up a kenning for him based on these features? It is done by calling him the performer or advancer of his journeys, doings, fights, voyages, hunting expeditions, weapons or ships. Thus he is the prover [*reynir*] of weapons and the maker of war – the word "maker" being equivalent to "performer" [*vidr*]. Now the word *reynir* also means rowan tree and the word *vidr* means timber in general. With these words as a point of departure, poets have called men ash, maple, or grove or used other masculine gender words for types of tree, adding identifying attributes such as those of battles, of ships, or of property. It is also correct to refer to a man by using all the different names of the gods. Giants' names can be used as well, but that is mostly for purposes of mockery or satire. It is considered appropriate to use the names of the elves.

References to Women

'A woman should be referred to in terms of all the types of female attire, gold and precious stones, and ale, wine and other beverages that she pours or serves; likewise in terms of receptacles for ale and all the things that it is fitting for her to do or provide. It is correct to refer to her by calling her the giver [*selja*] or disposer [*log*] of the thing that she shares. These words, *selja* and *log*, also denote trees, willow [*selja*] and log respectively, from which it follows that a woman can be referred to in kennings with all the feminine gender words for types of tree. The use of words for precious stones and pieces of glass to refer to a woman arises from an item of jewellery women used to wear around their necks called a stone necklace. That has now been taken up in kennings, so that a woman is referred to by using the word stone or all the names of specific types of stone. A woman can also be referred to by using the names of all the goddesses, valkyries, norns and female guardian deities. It is also correct to refer to a woman in terms of all her activities, possessions or family.'

References to Gold

'How should gold be referred to?'

'It can be called the fire of Ægir, the leaf of Glasir, the hair of Sif, the headband of Fulla, the tears of Freyja, the utterance, voice, or words of the giants, the drops of Draupnir, the rain or shower from Draupnir or from Freyja's eyes, recompense for the otter, repayment for the blow struck by the gods, the seed of the plains of Fyri, the covering of Holgi's burial mound or the fire of all expressions for water and hands, also the boulder, rocky islet or lustre of the hands.

'It has now become customary for gold to be called "fire of the sea", and all the words for sea, on the basis that Ægir and Ran's names denote the sea. Hence gold is now called the fire of lakes or rivers and all the specific names of rivers. Indeed, the range of these words has been further extended, just as with other poetic diction and kennings, so that more recent poets have composed their verses by expanding on the instances of this diction found in the work of their predecessors. They have included words that in their opinions corresponded to diction already in use: for example, lake is similar to sea, river is similar to lake, and creek is similar to river. For this reason we apply the term *nygerving* [new coinage] to all such extensions of a given type of diction. They are regarded favourably when there is a natural and unstrained resemblance between the concepts.'

'Why is gold called the foliage or leaf of Glasir?'

'In front of the doors of Valhalla in Asgard is a grove called Glasir, whose foliage consists entirely of red gold. This is the most beautiful woodland known to gods and humans.'

References to Battle, Weapons and Armour

'How should battle be referred to?'

'By calling it the wind, tumult and din of weapons, and of shields, and of Odin, and of the Valkyrie and of invading kings.'

'Weapons and armour can be named with reference to battle, to Odin, to valkyries and invading kings. Helmets can be referred to as helm, hat and headdress; mailcoats as shirt or tunic; shields as awning; and shield formations as hall, roof, wall and floor. Shields can also be called sun, moon, leaf, lustre, or fence of the ship, using ship as the other component in the kenning. Another possibility is to call the shield the ship of Ull or to allude to Hrungnir's feet, since he used a shield to stand on. On old shields it was the practice to decorate the rim, which was called the ring, and this ring becomes another way of identifying shields in kennings. Cutting weapons, such as axes and swords, are called the fires of blood or wounds. Swords are referred to as the fires of Odin. In kennings for axes the name of a troll woman is used, combined with an expression for blood, wound, forest or wood. Thrusting weapons can appropriately be referred to as snakes or fish. Thrown weapons are frequently referred to as hail, snowfall or rainstorm. There are numerous variations on all these kenning types because so much poetic composition is in the form of praise poems, which make particularly heavy use of such kennings.'

References to Ships

'How should a ship be referred to?'

'By calling it the horse, animal or ski of sea kings, the sea, rigging or wind.'

References to Christ

'How should Christ be referred to?'

'By calling him the creator of heaven, earth, angels and the sun; the ruler of the world, the heavenly kingdom and the angels; the king of the heavens, the sun, angels, Jerusalem, Jordan and Greece and the counsellor of the apostles and saints. Early poets associated him with the wellspring of the norns and with Rome, as for instance in the verse from Eilif Gudrunarson:

They say he sits on a mount in the south and by the wellspring of the norns. In this way the mighty king of Rome has strengthened his realm with the lands of the heathen gods.'

The Reckoning of Time

Harvest month is the name for the last month before winter. The first month in winter is called culling month, followed by frost month, ram month, Thorri, Goi, single month, cuckoo month and seed time, hatching time and lambing time, sun month and upcountry pasture month, haymaking and finally corn-reaping month.

The Story of Halfdan the Old and Distinguished Names

There was a king called Halfdan the Old, who was the greatest of all kings. He organized a big sacrifice at midwinter, intending to secure the destiny of living in his kingdom for three hundred years, but he received the answer that he would live no longer than a very protracted single lifetime. On the other hand, for three hundred years his lineage would contain no women and no lowly ranked men. He was a great man for raiding expeditions and made extensive forays in the eastern regions. There, in single combat, he felled a king called Sigtrygg. Then he took a woman in marriage called Alvig the Wise, daughter of King Emund the Mighty of Novgorod. They had eighteen sons, of whom nine were born at the same time. These were their names: one was Thengil [Prince], known as Thengil of men; the next Raesir [Leader of the Onslaught]; the third Gram [Fearsome King]; the fourth Gylfi; the fifth Hilmir; the sixth Jofur [Wild Boar]; the seventh Tiggi [Noble]; the eighth Skyli or Skuli [Protector]; and the ninth Harri or Herra [Lord]. These nine brothers had such prowess in raiding that in all subsequent traditions their names rate as distinguished titles, fitting for kings and earls. They had no children and all of them died in battle.

Halfdan the Old and Distinguished Lineages

Halfdan and his wife had another nine sons, whose names are as follows. The first was Hildir, founder of the dynasty of Hildings. The second was Nefir, founder of the Niflungs. The third was Audi, founder of the Odlings. The fourth was Yngvi, founder of the Ynglings. The fifth was Dag, founder of the Daglings. The sixth was Bragi, founder of the Bragnings (of which clan Halfdan the Magnanimous is a member). The seventh was Budli, founder of the Budlungs (Atli and Brynhild are members of that clan). The eighth was Lofdi; he was a great warrior king with a following called the Lofdar; he founded the dynasty of Lofdungs. To that lineage belongs Eylimi, the maternal grandfather of Sigurd who slew the serpent Fafnir. The ninth was Sigar, founder of the Siklingar. To that lineage belongs Siggeir, the kinsman by marriage of Volsung, and the Sigar who hanged Hagbard. From the Hilding lineage came Harald of the Red Moustache, maternal grandfather of Halfdan the Black. From the Niflung lineage came Gjuki. From the Odling lineage came Kjar. From the Ylfing lineage came Eirik the Eloquent. The following are also distinguished royal lineages. Yngvi founded the dynasty of Ynglings; Skjold, in Denmark, the Skjoldungs; and Volsung, in France, the Volsungs. Skelfir was a warrior king whose lineage is called the Skilfings, who hold sway in the eastern regions. The lineages listed above are all mentioned in poetry as names of great distinction.

References to Poets

Poets are called *greppar* and it is appropriate in poetry, if one wishes, to refer to any kind of man with that word. The men who formed King Half's warband were called *rekkar*. From that name warriors can be called *rekkar*, and in poetry it is appropriate to use that name for all types of men. Another general word in poetry for men is *lofdar*, as previously noted. The men in the warband of King Skati the Generous were called *skatnar*, and from his name any man who is generous can be called *skati*. The men in the warband of King Bragi the Old were called *bragnar*. The men who adjudicate on legal cases are called *virdar*. Men responsible for the defence of the land are called *fyrdar*, *firar* and *verar*. The warbands on board ships are called vikings and *flotnar*. Men in the warband of King Beimuni are called *beimar*. The leaders of a band of men are called *gumnar* or *gumar*, similar to the *gumi* or groom in a bridal party. The name *gotnar* comes from a king called Goti, after whom Gotland is named. His name is one of the names applied to Odin, and it derives from Gaut, since both Gotland and Gautland get their names from names for Odin. Similarly Sweden, which comes from the name Svidur, is yet another name for Odin. At that time the whole of the mainland in his possession was called Reidgotaland and the offshore islands were called Eygotaland. These are now called Denmark and Sweden. Young men who have not yet taken possession of a farm are called *drengir* while they build up their resources and reputations. If they travel from country to country, they are called *fardrengir* [travelling lads]. If they serve kings they are called the king's *drengir*, and the same designation is used for men who serve magnates and property holders and for men who are ambitious and manly.

Appendix 1

The Norse Cosmos and the World Tree*

In describing different places in the cosmos, the *Edda* often employs the imprecise word *heimr*, meaning 'home', 'world' or 'land', and we must guess at the locations of many of the described areas. In addition to the realms of gods, men and giants, the *Edda*, speaks of geographically disparate regions such as Ginnungagap in the north, an empty place filled with ice, and Muspell, a burning place of intense heat to the south. So also there are several heavens; one is called Andlang and another, 'further up', is where light elves live.

Many elements in Norse cosmology, however, as described in the *Edda*, fit into a coherent picture derived from the main stories. One is the World Tree, whose trunk remains consistently at the centre of the Norse universe. Another is the heavenly vault which the gods made from the skull of the giant Ymir, and which gives a shape to the upper part of the universe. Four dwarves, one under each of the compass points, hold up this vault. At the skull's upper reaches shine the heavenly bodies, and some of them – the ones that appear to the naked eye to remain steady – were thought to be furthest up in the heavens, while the heavenly bodies that were visibly moving were thought to be lower in the sky. The sun and the moon were clearly the most important of these moving bodies, and chariots pulled them daily across the sky, just ahead of pursuing hungry wolves. In the sky there is also a giant who, in the guise of an eagle, beats its wings and blows winds across the world.

Rising up into the heavens, the World Tree is a living entity,

* For illustration, see Introduction, p. xxvi.

whose branches spread majestically over all lands. This *axis mundi* or cosmic pillar at the centre of the world is described as a giant ash, binding together the disparate places of the universe, and it serves as a symbol for a dynamic cosmos.

The concept of a World Tree exists in many mythologies. In the case of the Scandinavian World Tree, the idea may reach back thousands of years and may have an Indo-European origin. Although people in Old Scandinavia probably interpreted the tree in different ways, the name Yggdrasil, a compound word with several layers of meaning, perhaps gives us a clue as to how the tree was understood in symbolic terms. One possible interpretation is that the first part of the name, *Ygg*, meaning the 'terrible one' and one of Odin's many names, is connected to the aspect of Odin's persona as god of the hanged. *Drasill* is an ancient term for 'horse'. Hence Yggdrasil (*Ygg-drasill*) means Ygg's (or Odin's) horse and is a metaphor for a gallows tree. This view assumes that the ancient Scandinavians saw a similarity between how people ride horses and how a hanged person bobs as he 'rides' the gallows. The gallows tree was an emotionally significant site for the passage between life and death, and is a fitting symbol for the World Tree as the causeway connecting the heavens and the underworld.

Three roots, spread far apart, support the ash tree. Each root extends into a different world, and each is nourished by a well. Through these wells, the tree draws its life force from the waters of three worlds: those of the gods, the giants and the dead. The root that reaches the highest goes to Asgard, where the Æsir live in different halls. Asgard is located close enough to the branches of the tree for the goat that stands on the roof of Valhalla to eat its leaves. Under the root leading to Asgard is the Well of Urd, near which the Æsir daily hold court and make their decisions. Beside the well live three norns – Urd (Fate), Verdandi (Becoming) and Skuld (Obligation) – who are similar to the weirds or prophetic women of Old English tradition and the witches found in *Macbeth*.

Asgard is connected to the world below, called Midgard (Middle Enclosure or Middle Earth), by the rainbow bridge, Bifrost. This middle world is conceived as a landmass inhabited by humans, who live towards the centre, and giants, who live at the periphery in the region called Utgard. Midgard does not have a root or a well, but under the root that leads to the frost giants in Utgard is the Well of Mimir. A mysterious figure, Mimir owns the well in which wisdom and intelligence are hidden. Odin went to Mimir's Well and asked for one drink, but his request was denied until he pledged one of his eyes, plucking it out and placing it in the well. Because of this, Odin became known as the one-eyed god. The poem *The Sibyl's Prophecy* tells that each day Mimir drinks 'mead', a beverage of inspiration from the well containing Odin's pledged eye.

Midgard's geographical relationship to Utgard and its threatening giants is somewhat unclear, in part because the *Edda* refers to Midgard both as the earth itself and as a central fortress. The lack of clarity is heightened because the *Edda* also gives several descriptions of the placement of the sea, and it is not clear whether the ocean surrounds Midgard and Utgard together or lies between these two regions. One passage suggests that the 'earth's girdle', as the sea was called, lies at Utgard's outer edge. Another concept of the placement of the sea, which may not be fully contradictory, is gleaned from the story about Thor's route on his way to visit the giant Utgarda-Loki. This story leaves Midgard in the centre. Since Thor, however, has to cross water after leaving Midgard and before arriving in Utgard, it implies that the sea, or at least an inlet, lies between Midgard and Utgard. Perhaps the discrepancy is mostly a question of emphasis, because a passage describing the Midgard Serpent tells that the outer sea surrounds all the land, and the huge serpent lies in this outer sea, biting its tail.

Yggdrasil's third root goes to the underworld, a region guarded by the great hound Garm, and into the dark world called Niflheim and Niflhel. The *Edda* tells us that the well of the underworld, Hvergelmir, is a seething cauldron of waters that unleash a torrent of underworld rivers. The eddic poem *The Lay of Grimnir* (*Grímnismál*, Grimnir being Odin) also speaks of Hvergelmir, saying that all the rivers of the world spring from this well. In the underworld is the huge serpent Nidhogg, lying among smaller, gnawing snakes too numerous to count. Nidhogg is not isolated in its dark home, because a squirrel named Ratatosk runs up and down the trunk of the tree, carrying insults between the serpent and a great eagle, who sits high up in the airy branches of the tree with a hawk between its eyes.

The lower region also contains Hel, the realm of those who die a natural death, in contrast to the warriors who enter Valhalla. Hel is also the name of the goddess overseeing the World of the Dead, and her unlucky charges enter the underworld by passing through the Gates of Hel and then crossing the Gjoll Bridge. Old Scandinavian Hel was a pre-Christian concept and was understood to be a shadowy region much like the Greek Hades. As the realm of those who die undistinguished deaths, Hel is very different from the boisterous Valhalla.

Despite the tree's inherent strength and the sustenance received from the wells, it faces constant peril from several directions: Nidhogg gnaws its deepest root, and four stags move through its branches, ripping and devouring its foliage. The trunk is also subject to rot, and the great ash would die were it not for the three norns in Asgard who nurture it. To slow the rot, these norns draw water every day from Urd's Well, mix it with the mud lying beside their spring and then coat this potent salve on to the trunk. In the long run, this attempt at healing will be in vain. The *Edda* implies that the tree is threatened at Ragnarok. The great ash trembles and groans at the coming of the final battle, but it is not clear that it is destroyed.

Appendix 2

The Language of the Skalds: Kennings and *Heiti*

The Viking Age was a time when information was transmitted orally. Traditional stories were usually told in verse, with the rhythms of metre and the patterns of poetic phrasing providing aids to memory and transmission. Norse heroic and mythic poetry was also a word game whose intricate language paralleled the style of Viking Age carvings made on wood, stone and metal objects. Both Scandinavian wordsmiths and artisans shunned realistic depictions, and instead intertwined their representations into complex images. In Old Scandinavia, participation of both skald and audience in the game of creating and unravelling poetic diction (*skáldskaparmál*) was a sign of intellect and learning.

Reading the *Edda* with an awareness of the techniques employed by skalds or poets greatly adds to the reader's understanding and enjoyment of this text. The most frequent device used in these word games is the naming of people and things by metaphors called kennings, a word which comes from the verb *at kenna*, which has several meanings, including 'to name and to call'. The other common device is the use of synonyms called *heiti*, a term which means 'name' and derives from the verb *at heita*, 'to name'. *Heiti* were mostly nouns used to replace more common nouns, but *heiti* could also be proper nouns. For instance, skalds referred to Odin as Ygg, a *heiti* meaning 'terrible one'. When referring to Odin's son, Thor, a skald might use the *heiti* Ygg to build the kenning Ygg's child. Such a kenning increased a skald's word choice by paralleling other kennings, which may depend on kinship bonds, but do not employ *heiti*, as, for example: Odin's son, Sif's husband, Modi's father, friend of men, lord of he-goats, relation to Odin, enemy of the wolf, slayer of the serpent, killer of giants and griefmaker of giantesses. All of these allusions are explained in tales gathered in the *Edda*.

Kennings at their simplest are phrases composed of a base noun qualified by a possessive noun. In the kenning 'icicle of blood', meaning sword, 'icicle' is the base word and 'of blood' is the qualifier in the possessive. Other examples are 'horse of the sea' for ship, and 'moons of the forehead' for eyes. The raven became 'swan of blood' because it ate the battlefield dead. Kennings have a logic and require a knowledge of Norse society and mythology to construct them. For example, a chieftain is referred to in the *Edda* as 'breaker' or 'distresser of rings', reflecting the common practice whereby leaders rewarded followers by breaking off pieces from their gold or silver arm rings and giving them as gifts.

Sometimes several kennings were strung together into one complex kenning. For example, a leader could be called 'spurner of the bonfire of the sea'. The spurning refers to the generosity of a leader, whereas 'bonfire of the sea' is a kenning for gold, because there were stories about Ægin, a lord of the sea, whose home fires burned red, like gold beneath the sea. The audience for this poetry expected a good skald not only to replace a commonplace word like gold with a kenning, but also to be able to construct in a creative manner several kennings for the same commonplace word. Another kenning for gold was 'Otter's ransom', an allusion to the gold that Odin had to pay as compensation to the giant Hreidmar for killing his son Otter, who had changed his shape to that of the animal (see *Skaldskaparmal* 7). Kennings appealed to skald and audience, because they awakened a shared understanding of Norse history and lore.

In stanza 3 of his poem *Hattatal*, Snorri offers several examples of kennings, concentrating on those meaning 'earth' or 'land':

The glorious *spurner of the bonfire of the sea* (*giver of gold*)
defends the *woman friend of the adversary of the wolf* (*Earth or land*).
The ship runs up in front of the steep
brows of the lady of the friend of Mimir (*cliffs*).
The mighty lord has the power to retain
the mother of the destroyer of the serpent (*Earth*).
Distresser of rings, may you enjoy (*giver of Rings*)
the mother of the foe of the giantess until old age (*Earth*).[1]

The following stanza from *Gylfaginning* (on p. 10) provides a rich example of a kenning that assumes the audience shared knowledge of specific historical events along with mythology.

On their backs they let shine
hall shingles of Svafnir,
when bombarded with stones,
those resourceful men.

This stanza is employed in the *Edda* for several purposes. First, it reminds the audience that Svafnir is another name for Odin. Second, the kenning for 'shield', 'hall shingles of Svafnir', turns on the understanding that Valhalla was roofed with shields in the manner of wooden shingles. The stanza, however, is older than the *Edda*. Just how old we do not know but it comes from a skaldic poem commemorating the famous victory about the year 870 by Norway's King Harald Fairhair. It is a mocking reference to Harald's enemies, who are resourceful in covering or roofing their backs with their shields as they flee.

Heiti, or synonyms, allowed skalds to replace a common word, such as 'horse', with the more poetic, 'steed'. Most *heiti* (the word is both singular and plural) are more obscure than this example and require a familiarity with Scandinavian myth and legend that the *Edda* provides. Largely because of *heiti*, Norse poetry has its own vocabulary or lexicon, and mastering the art of poetic composition means learning new meanings and names. In *Gylfaginning* High explains that Odin is known by many names:

All-Father in our language, but in Asgard the Old, he has twelve names: one is All-Father, a second is Herran or Herjan, a third is Nikar or Hnikar, a fourth is Nikuz or Hnikud, a fifth is Fjolnir, a sixth Oski, a seventh Omi, an eighth Biflidi or Biflindi, a ninth Svidar, a tenth Svidrir, an eleventh Vidrir and a twelfth Jalg or Jalk. (p. 11)

Heiti fall into several groups. One is ancient words used only in poetry. A good example of this group is the word *gumi*, meaning 'man'. Although *gumi* is found in prose compound words, such as the word for bridegroom (*brudgumi*), as a single word *gumi* is never found outside poetry. Another example of *heiti* from this group is the word *drasill*, meaning horse, as in Yggdrasil (*Yggdrasill*), meaning Odin's horse. Many *heiti* for the gods fall into this group. For example, Hnikar and Fjolnir in the above list of names for Odin are found only in the poetry. Hence they are listed in the *Edda* for aspiring skalds to learn. Another important group consists of words well known in prose but with different meanings in poetry. An example is the word (*brúðr*) bride. In prose it refers to a woman who is about to marry, but in poetic diction *brúðr* had the broader meaning of 'woman'.

NOTE

1. My thanks to Russell Poole for translating this stanza.

Appendix 3

Eddic Poems Used as Sources in *Gylfaginning*

The mythic stories in *Gylfaginning* rely to a large degree on eddic poetry. Some of these poems are now lost. For example, *Gylfaginning*, chapter 27, mentions *Heimdall's Chant* (*Heimdalargaldr*), but this eddic poem no longer exists. Many eddic poems, however, survive in the *Poetic Edda*. Below is a list of the mythological eddic poems cited in *Gylfaginning* which are found in the *Poetic Edda*.

The Lay of Fafnir (*Fáfnismál*)
The Lay of Grimnir (*Grímnismál*)
The Lay of Hyndla (*Hyndluljóð*)
The Lay of Skirnir (*Skírnismál*)
The Lay of Vafthrudnir (*Vafþrúðnismál*)
Loki's Flyting (*Lokasenna*)
The Sayings of the High One (*Hávamál*)
The Shorter Sibyl's Prophecy (*Völuspá in skamma*)
The Sibyl's Prophecy (*Völuspá*)

At times, stanzas found in the *Poetic Edda* vary from their counterparts in the *Prose Edda*. This suggests that the author of the *Edda* may have known the eddic poems orally or in a different written form. In some instances the differences of wording between lines found in the *Prose Edda* and the *Poetic Edda* can be significant, as is often the case with *The Sibyl's Prophecy*. In the *Poetic Edda* the third stanza of *The Sibyl's Prophecy* opens with the line: 'Early of ages, when Ymir dwelled'. Yet the stanza in the *Prose Edda* mentions only a void and not the giant Ymir: 'Early of ages, when nothing was'. This difference in wording changes the picture of the creation. So also the *Edda* and the *Poetic Edda* sometimes employ different terms. The *Edda* calls the final battle at the end of the world by the singular word *Ragnarøkr*, meaning 'Twilight of the Gods' or 'Darkness of the Gods'. With the exception of *Loki's Flyting*, eddic poems employ a different word, *Ragnarök*, meaning 'End of the Gods' or 'Doom of the Gods'.

Genealogical Tables

Ymir and the Sons of Bor

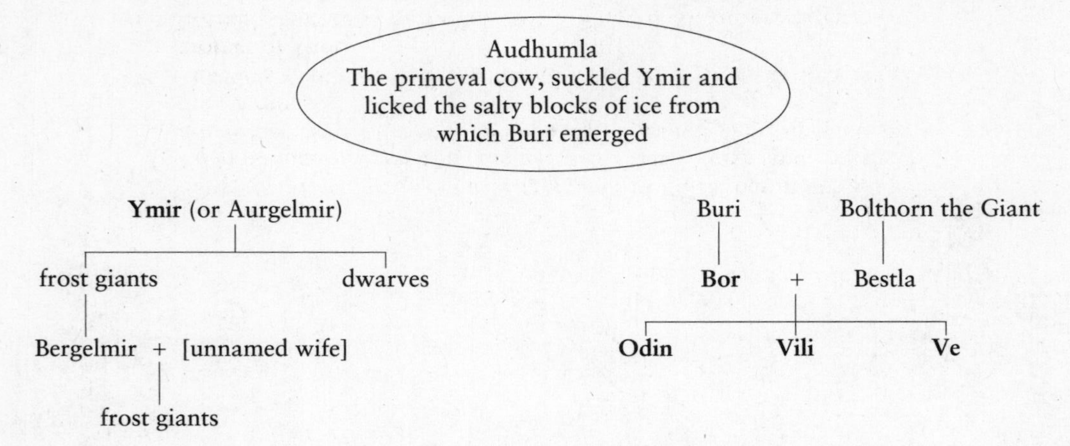

Dwarves and giants developed from the body of the primordial giant, Ymir (also called Aurgelmir by the frost giants). The dwarves grew in Ymir's flesh. The frost giants were created from Ymir's sweat 'under his left arm' while one of his legs 'got a son with the other'. These first generations of giants drowned in Ymir's blood when the sons of Bor killed him. The only survivors were Bergelmir and his wife. From them came a second family of frost giants.

Odin's Consorts and Offspring

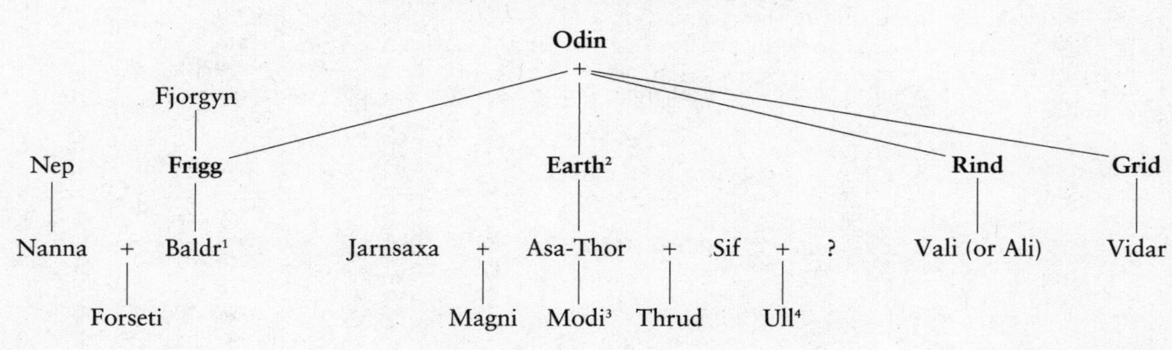

[1] Frigg is not explicitly named the mother of Baldr, but in the *Poetic Edda* this mother–son relationship is clear. Vidar and Hermod are also sons of Odin, but *Gylfaginning* does not name or allude to their mothers.

[2] Earth is said to be both a wife and daughter of Odin, as well as the mother of Thor.

[3] Modi's mother is not given, but Modi and Magni are often mentioned together.

[4] Ull is said to be Thor's stepson.

The Vanir and Njord's Marriages

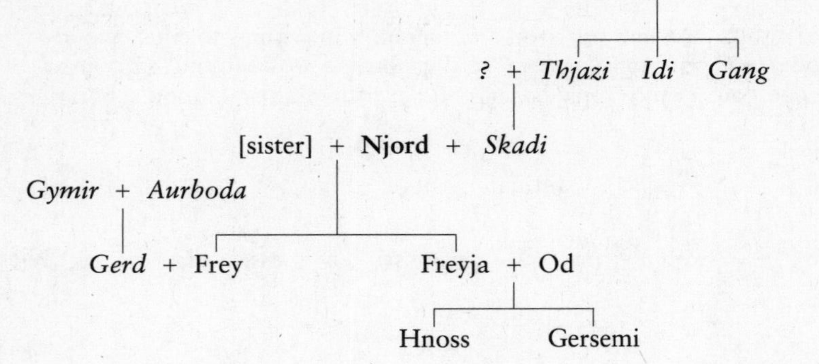

Both Njord and his son Frey marry daughters of giants. (*Italics* denote giants.)

The Families of Loki
Farbauti + Laufey (or Nal)
Byleist
Loki
Helblindi
+
Angrboda
Svadilfari
Sigyn
?
Fenriswolf
Jormundgand
(Midgard Serpent)
Hel
Sleipnir
Nar(f)i
Vali

The Three Marriages of Night

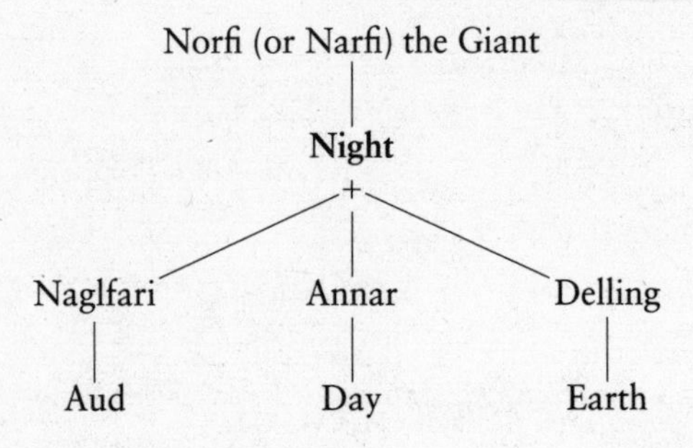

Night first marries Naglfari and then Annar. Finally she marries Delling from the family of the gods.

The Family of Sun and Moon, and Vidfinn's Children

The gods placed the brother and sister Moon and Sun in the heavens. Vidfinn's children, Bil and Hjuki, follow Moon across the sky.

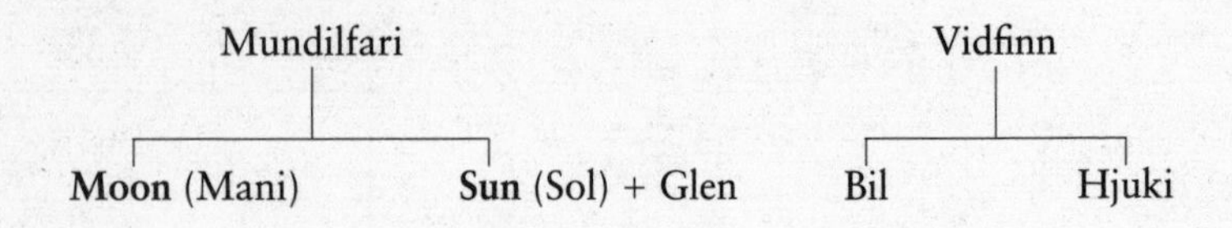

The Practitioners of Magic

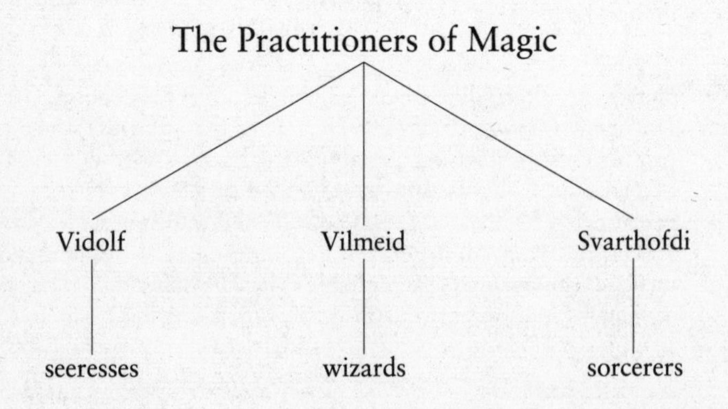

Notes

PROLOGUE

2. THE THREE PARTS OF THE WORLD

1. *the region called Asia*: The concept of Asia included the Middle East as well as the Far East.

3. THE PEOPLE OF TROY AND THOR

1. *all manner of berserkers*: Ferocious and feared warriors, they may have been members of cults connected with Odin in his capacity as god of warriors.
2. *Frigida, we call Frigg*: 'Frigida' may be a play on the Latin word for cold. The introduction of such classical learning is characteristic of the *Prologue*.

5. ODIN'S JOURNEY CONTINUES AND THE ÆSIR SETTLE IN THE NORTH

1. *Sigtun*: An old trading town near modern-day Stockholm.
2. *Haleygjatal*: *Háleygjatal* (*The Helgeland Genealogies*) was a *tal* or poetic list of the jarls of Halogaland, the far northern section of Norway. Composed in the tenth century by the Norwegian poet Eyvind Skaldaspillir, *Haleygjatal* traced the ancestry of Jarl Hakon of Hlade (d. 995) back to distant mythical times. Fragments of the poem are preserved in poetic passages in *Skaldskaparmal* and in different versions of the kings' sagas.

GYLFAGINNING (THE DELUDING OF GYLFI)

1. KING GYLFI AND THE WOMAN GEFJUN

1. *Sjaelland*: The large island in Denmark.
2. *Logrinn [the Lake]*: An old name for Lake Mälar in Sweden.

2. GYLFI ENCOUNTERS THE THREE CHIEFTAINS OF THE ÆSIR

1. *Gylfi Encounters ... Æsir*: The preceding first short story of Gefjun has long been considered to be a later addition to the original manuscript. If this is so, *Gylfaginning* began at this point with chapter 2.
2. *conjured up visual illusions*: The text employs the word *sjónhverfing* (pl. *sjónhverfingar*), with the sense of an optical illusion. In medieval Iceland *sjónhverfing* was understood to be the result of spells, part of a popular form of magic called *galdr*.
3. *Thjodolf of Hvin*: Thjodolf of Hvin or Hvinir was a Norwegian skald in the court of King Harald Fairhair around the year 900. He is credited with composing *Ynglingatal* (*The Counting of the Ynglings*), a poem treating mythological subjects and offering a genealogy of the kings of Sweden.
4. *he was called High . . . was called Third*: High (*Hár*), Just-as-High (*Jafnhár*) and Third (*Þriði*) are names for Odin.

3. THE ALL-FATHER

1. *Hel*: The world of the dead, a pre-Christian concept.
2. *Niflhel*: *Nifl*, an old word, means mist, fog and darkness. At the time the *Edda* was written, the word was already obsolete but remained in many mythological compounds, as here in *Niflhel* (Dark Hel), a place seemingly different from *Hel*, where the worst of men underwent a kind of second death. Some manuscripts confuse Niflhel with Niflheim, the dark world of freezing mists.

4. NIFLHEIM AND MUSPELLSHEIM

1. *Ginnungagap*: The great void before creation.
2. *Muspell*: The text sometimes uses the shortened name *Muspell* for *Muspellsheim* (the world or region of Muspell). The name is related to the Old High German and Old Saxon *muspelli*, *muspille* and *muspelle*. These names are found in Christian poems and carry the meaning of doomsday, that is, the end of the world.
3. *troll witches stumble*: The verb *rata*, translated here as 'stumble', has at least three meanings: to travel, in the sense of moving about or roaming; to find one's way; and to fall or crash. It is unclear which meaning is intended.

5. GINNUNGAGAP AND THE EMERGENCE OF YMIR

1. *seeresses*: *Völur*, sibyls who act as seeresses or prophetesses.
2. *under his left arm*: The Icelandic word is *hönd*, meaning arm or armpit, as well as hand.

7. BERGELMIR AND THE APPEARANCE OF THE SECOND RACE OF FROST GIANTS

1. *wooden box*: The word *lúðr* has several meanings. I translate *lúðr* as wooden box, because the word also means a stand for holding a handmill, that is, the wooden box that surrounds the millstone into which the ground flour falls. This box could function as a vessel. It is also somewhat like a coffin, and the usage of the word in this line carries the imagery both of a boat and of death. Another meaning for *lúðr* is a trumpet.
2. *Countless winters*: The passage of years was counted by winters.

8. THE WORLD IS CREATED FROM YMIR'S BODY

1. *eyelashes*: Related to English 'brow', the Old Norse word *brá* (here in the plural *brár*) means eyelash or the eye itself. Probably the reference is to eyelashes, resembling a fence or wall. Possibly the reference is to all of the eye.
2. *called this stronghold Midgard*: Perhaps the name Midgard refers to the fortress-like wall that surrounds and protects the world of men from the giants.

9. MEN ARE CREATED AND ASGARD IS BUILT

1. *The sons of Bor . . . hearing and sight*: *The Sibyl's Prophecy* stanzas 17–18 tells a similar story but names Odin's companions as Hoenir and Lodur.
2. *Earth was his daughter*: In chapter 36, Jord or Earth is counted among the *ásynjur* or goddesses of the Æsir. In chapter 10, Earth is the daughter of Night and Annar.

12. THE WOLVES

1. *he will swallow the moon*: The word used is *tungl*, which usually means moon, but *tungl* may be a shortening of *himintungl*, meaning heavenly body or bodies. Alone, *tungl* can mean sun. In the verse that follows, *tungl* probably means moon, if one thinks of Managarm (Moon Dog), but it is possible that the reference is to the sun. *The Lay of Vafthrudnir* offers a different version of the destruction of the sun, in which Fenrir swallows it.
2. *In the East the old one lives*: It is not clear to whom 'the old one' (*in aldna*) refers. In the prose preceding the verse she is called the old ogress or giantess (*in gamla gýgr*) and seems to be a creature from the oldest times. Possibly she refers to Angrboda, the mother of Fenrir (see chapter 34).

14. ASGARD AND THE ORIGIN OF THE DWARVES

1. *the middle of the stronghold*: The text uses the word *borg*, which in this context could mean a fortress or a town. The idea seems to be an extensive stronghold and a town within.
2. *goddesses*: Here the goddesses are called *gyðjur* (female gods); elsewhere they are often referred to as *ásynjur* (female Æsir).
3. *the women . . . from Giant Land*: This line corresponds to stanza 8 of *The Sibyl's Prophecy*, which speaks of the coming of three giant maidens from Giant Land. Who these women are is unclear.
4. *from the waves of blood*: The text uses the word *brim*, meaning surf. In *The Sibyl's Prophecy*, Brimir is the name for a giant, possibly Ymir. If the verse is referring to a giant, then the line possibly reads: 'from Ymir's blood'.
5. *live in the ground*: The text uses the word *mold*, meaning the ground, soil or earth. These dwarves live in holes in the earth, that is, in some form of underground houses, perhaps caves.
6. *The Sibyl's Prophecy*: The lists of the dwarves differ significantly between the *Prose Edda* and *The Sibyl's Prophecy*.

15. THE ASH YGGDRASIL, THE NORNS AND THE THREE WELLS

1. *drinks . . . from the Gjallarhorn*: The god Heimdall also has a horn or trumpet named Gjallarhorn. They may be the same. See chapter 27.
2. *Urd . . . Verdandi . . . and Skuld*: Urd (*Urðr*) and Verdandi (*Verðandi*) are names derived from the verb *verða*, meaning 'to become'. They may also be related to the helping verb 'must'. The name *Skuld* is problematic, with numerous possibilities. It may derive from the verbal form *skal*, which corresponds to the English 'shall', conveying the idea of necessity or responsibility, i.e., something in the future that cannot be avoided. *Skuld* may also mean 'obligation', 'debt', 'fault' or 'blame'. Together the names of these norns imply 'to become', 'to have to' and 'to be absolutely required to', and may also signify 'past', 'present' and 'future'.

16. THE CREATURES OF THE ASH TREE YGGDRASIL

1. *devouring the tree's foliage*: This line has often been mistranslated, leading to the wrong assumption that the World Tree was a conifer. The text uses the words *bíta barr*. *Bíta* means to bite, rip with the teeth, or eat. *Barr* means the foliage of a tree, whether leaf or pine needle, although frequently it refers to just pine needles. Together, *bíta barr* means to eat the foliage off a tree, words suitable for both an ash tree and a pine.

20. ODIN THE ALL-FATHER

1. *one of the Æsir called Loki*: In other places Loki is not considered a member of the Æsir.
2. *Hapta-God*: Hapta-God (*Haptaguð*) can mean God of fetters, hence a connection with prisoners. But it could also be 'he who employs fetters' and/or perhaps even 'he who loosens fetters'. *Höpt* can also mean gods, with the possibility that *Haptaguð* refers to 'foremost of the gods'. Further, as a noun *hapt* might mean godly powers. The name could thus mean the god of gods or the 'god who restricts men with his divine laws'.
3. *Helblindi . . . Sann, Svipal*: Helblindi could be a scribal error for Herblindi (Blinder of Armies). Sann and Svipal mean truthful and changing (shifting). Some of the pairs of names in this verse contain similar contrasts.
4. *Truly*: The expression *þat veit trúa mín* means something like 'truly' or 'by my faith'. The expression is not found in the earliest Icelandic texts but becomes common in thirteenth-century romance sagas, many of which derive from French stories translated into Old Norse.

21. THOR

1. *five hundred and forty living spaces*: The usual meaning of the word *gólf* is floor. Here the word most probably refers to divisions in a longhouse building, such as the living spaces set off from each other by pillars holding up the roof. The term 'hun-

dred' probably stood for 120, as was customary (the medieval 'long hundred' was based on the number twelve). Thus the figure of 540 would be larger if the author is using the long hundred.

22. BALDR

1. *One plant . . . Baldr's brow*: The Icelandic plant *Baldrs brá* is *Matricaria maritima*.

23. NJORD AND SKADI

1. *three nights at Noatun*: The *Codex Regius* says 'nine winters . . . and another nine', but the other three main manuscripts, *Codex Upsaliensis*, *Codex Wormianus* and *Codex Trajectinus*, say 'nine nights . . . and another three'.

24. FREY AND FREYJA

1. *She is easily approachable . . . pray to her*: This clause is somewhat unusual in Old Icelandic. A second translation might be: 'She most successfully fulfils the desires of people who pray to her.'
2. *from her name . . . title of honour . . . ladies*: *Fróva*, later *frú*, meaning lady, appears to be a loan word from Low German.

25. TYR

1. *Tyr*: Related to Latin *deus* and Greek *Zeus*, the name Tyr may derive from postulated Old Germanic *tiwaz*, meaning 'god'. In *The Lay of Sigurdrifa* Tyr is the name of a rune that brings victory.

26. BRAGI

1. *wooden box*: *Eski* means a wooden box made of ash and generally used for carrying personal possessions. In chapter 35, the goddess Fulla is said to carry Frigg's *eski*.

27. HEIMDALL

1. *Heimdall's Chant*: *Heimdall's Chant* no longer exists; see Appendix 3 for more details.

28. HOD

1. *work . . . will long be remembered*: See chapter 49.

29. VIDAR

1. *thick shoe*: At Ragnarok, Vidar uses his special shoe to kill the Wolf; see chapter 51.

31. ULL

1. *Ull . . . good person to pray to*: Although not an important figure in the surviving mythology, Ull is often mentioned in skaldic verse, and his cult was widespread throughout the north.

34. LOKI'S MONSTROUS CHILDREN

1. *the Midgard Serpent*: (*Miðgarðsormr*) Also referred to by the name Jormungand (*Jörmungandr*).

35. GODDESSES

1. *Brisingamen*: Several figures, including giants and Heimdall, possessed Brisingamen at different times.

36. VALKYRIES AND GODDESSES

1. *Valkyries*: 'Valkyrie' derives from two words, the noun *valr*, the slain on the battlefield, and the verb *kjósa*, 'to choose'. The compound means 'chooser of the slain' and the Old

Norse *valkyrja* (plural *valkyrjur*) is cognate with Old English *wælcyrge*.

37. THE TALE OF FREY AND THE GIANTESS GERD

1. *the place called Barey*: In some manuscripts *Barey* is spelled *Barrey*. The word has several possible meanings, which has stirred controversy. If a compound, the second part of the word, *ey*, probably means island. One possibility for the first part of the word, *Barr*, is evergreen tree; hence *Barey* would mean wooded or conifer island, perhaps even a forest. *Barr* could also mean barley and, if so, the meaning could be connected with fertility worship. The god of fertility consummating his longing and marriage in a barley field with a young woman who meets him there has cultic possibilities. In *The Lay of Skirnir*, the place is called *Barri*, which seems to be a windless or quiet grove. *Barey* might refer to the Hebridean island Barra, lying off the western coast of Scotland. Barra was occupied by Norsemen and is mentioned in Icelandic writings, including *Grettir's Saga*.
2. *half this holding time*: The term used is *hálf hýnótt*. The *hýnótt* was a waiting period preceding a wedding. The phrase seems to mean half of such a waiting or holding time. Already Frey knows he can barely make it past three nights.

39. THE DRINK OF THE EINHERJAR AND WHAT FLOWS FROM VALHALLA

1. *famous tree, Lerad*: *The Lay of Grimnir* mentions the tree Lerad or Laerad, which seems to be the same as Yggdrasil.
2. *all . . . satisfy their thirst*: The word *fulldrukkinn* (fully drunk) is an ironic usage. It could mean either drink to their satisfaction or become drunk.

40. THE DOORS OF VALHALLA

1. *Five hundred doors*: If the counting is in long hundreds of 120, which is probable, then five hundred doors would be six hundred.

41. THE DAILY BATTLE AT VALHALLA

1. *The slain they select*: This line could have several meanings, among them the following: they determine ahead of time who is to be slain, or they choose from among the slain those who should be taken back to Valhalla.
2. *Habrok of hawks*: Habrok is the hawk of King Hrolf. In *The Saga of King Hrolf Kraki*, Habrok fights for his lord.

42. THE MASTER BUILDER FROM GIANT LAND AND THE BIRTH OF SLEIPNIR

1. *Thor . . . hammering on trolls*: The verb used is *berja*, meaning to strike, to beat, with the idea of hammering on something. The medieval author is humorously playing on words. Rather than fighting with trolls, which requires the verb *berjast* (the '*-st*' ending changing the meaning of the verb to indicate that two or more people are fighting among themselves), Thor, alone, is hammering on the trolls.
2. *Od's maid*: The verses refer to Freyja by the word *mær*, which means maiden or virgin, as well as wife or beloved.

44. THOR AND LOKI BEGIN THEIR JOURNEY TO GIANT LAND

1. *so many examples . . . Thor is the mightiest*: The idea seems to be that even when Thor loses, as he does to Utgarda-Loki, it is because of deception and not through a lack of might.

45. THOR ENCOUNTERS SKRYMIR IN THE FOREST

1. *Thor was too startled . . . with the hammer*: This story about Thor is filled with humour. The wording gives the impression that Thor, who was something of a bungler, rather than being frightened, which is a possible translation, was surprised and

startled, having acted before taking the time to think out the best course of action.

2. *Skrymir*: Different meanings have been proposed for the name Skrymir (*Skrýmir*), among them braggart and big fellow.
3. *dragged away my glove*: Another example of medieval Icelandic humour. The words and the image of dragging away a glove give the impression of the work of a child or small animal like a puppy.
4. *some leaves or twigs*: The word used is *tros*. It means rubbish, including leaves or twigs from a tree gathered and used for fuel.

47. UTGARDA-LOKI REVEALS THAT THOR WAS DECEIVED

1. *iron wire*: *Grésjarn* is some kind of iron fastening, perhaps magical. *Grés* is probably a loan word from Old Irish, where it meant deception and trickery.

48. THOR AND THE GIANT HYMIR GO FISHING

1. *Even those . . . know that Thor made amends*: The myth of Thor fishing for the great serpent that encircles the earth is ancient. It is the subject of the eddic poem *The Lay of Hymir* (*Hymiskviða*), and is mentioned in several ninth- and tenth-century skaldic poems, including *Ragnarsdrapa* and *Husdrapa*. Thor's fishing expedition is also represented on four Viking Age pictorial stones from Altuna (early eleventh century), Hørdum (eighth to eleventh century), Ardre VIII (eighth century) and Gosforth (tenth century).
2. *neither weaker nor less firm*: An ironic understatement that does not translate well into English.

49. THE DEATH OF BALDR AND HERMOD'S RIDE TO HEL

1. *ruin for the Æsir*: Odin, who sees into the future, is apparently thinking of the coming of Ragnarok.
2. *log rollers underneath the keel*: When a ship was hauled up on the shore, logs were placed as rollers under the keel.
3. *the gold ring Draupnir*: Magical rings such as Draupnir had creative powers and play significant roles in Norse myth and legend. *Skaldskaparmal*, *The Saga of the Volsungs* and the Sigurd poems in the *Poetic Edda* speak of a magical ring called Andvaranaut (Andvari's Gift). In his retelling of the tale of Baldr's death, the medieval Danish writer Saxo Grammaticus also refers to a gold ring that made wealth for its owner.
4. *the Gjoll Bridge*: The boundary separating the world of the living from the world of the dead.
5. *all things in the world, alive or dead*: Alive or dead (*kykr ok dauðr*) means things possessed of the quickening of life, as opposed to objects that are dead, that is, inanimate. This has a similar meaning to the biblical phrase the quick and the dead.
6. *Thokk will weep . . . Let Hel hold what she has*: This verse, which is not known elsewhere, may come from a lost poem about Baldr's death.

51. THE HIGH ONE REVEALS THE EVENTS OF RAGNAROK

1. *the collapse of kinship*: *Sifjaslit* means the breaking of kinship bonds, but there is also the connotation of incest.
2. *a hundred leagues in each direction*: If the figure referred to here is the long hundred, then the resulting size of the field is 120 leagues in each direction.
3. *the hound Garm . . . Gnipahellir*: Garm is mentioned in *The Lay of Grimnir* and in *The Sibyl's Prophecy*. *Baldr's Dreams* speaks of a hound in Hel, which might not be Garm. *Hellir* in the name *Gnipahellir* means cave. The whole word could be translated as a jutting or overhanging cave, and *Gnipahellir* is perhaps an entrance to Hel. Garm could be another name for Fenrir.
4. *the giant breaks free*: The giant who breaks free could be the

Fenriswolf, the hound Garm or Loki. All were bound, and all will break free at Ragnarok.

5. *Nidfol rips apart corpses*: If a proper noun, Nidfol (darkly pale) is perhaps the same as Nidhogg, who rips apart corpses at Hvergelmir (chapter 52). Possibly the reference is to Hraesvelg.
6. *There with the Wolf*: The line uses the name Freki, which means a wolf, perhaps also with the connotation of greedy, hence greedy wolf. Freki can be a name for Fenrir and the reference is probably to him.
7. *Surt comes . . . the sky splits apart*: The same verse is found at the end of chapter 4.
8. *Steps back . . . son of Earth*: The first part of this stanza, containing the words *nepr at naðri*, is unclear. The great son of Earth is Thor. Earth, Thor's mother, was also named Hlodyn and the verse uses the kenning 'the son of Hlodyn'. The line foretells Thor's death from the serpent's poison.
9. *the fire rages*: The term used is *aldrnari*, meaning nourisher of life, that is, fire. The line is perhaps ironic, as fire is destroying rather than nourishing.

52. AFTER RAGNAROK

1. *the hall called Brimir*: In *The Sibyl's Prophecy* Brimir is not the hall, but the name of the giant that owns the hall. The name Sindri, a few lines later, is the name of a dwarf.
2. *Nastrandir [Corpse Strands]*: The Old Norse word *nár* had two meanings. It meant corpse, that is, an actual dead body, but the word also had the more general meaning of a deceased person. With the second, more general meaning in mind, the Corpse Strands, that is, the beaches of the dead, might be another realm of the dead. Strand is plural in the prose and singular in the verse immediately following.
3. *walls woven from branches*: The text reads *sem vandahús* (like a wattle house), a building whose walls are made from poles and thin branches covered with mud. Here the wattle is live snakes.

53. THE HIGH ONE DESCRIBES THE REBIRTH OF THE WORLD

1. *Vingnir's*: Vingnir here most probably refers to Thor, who elsewhere is called Vingnir's foster son. Vingnir is also one of Odin's names as well as the name of a giant.
2. *Hoddmimir's Holt*: It is not clear who Hoddmimir is; *hodd* can be a hoard, but also has the meaning of holy place, temple or sanctuary where precious things are hoarded. 'Hoddmimir' could be translated as Hoard Mimir. The word *holt* means woods, but could be a tree. Hence Hoddmimir's Holt (the wood or tree of Mimir) is perhaps Yggdrasil, the World Tree.

55. THE EPILOGUE TO *GYLFAGINNING*

1. *Epilogue to Gylfaginning*: Because this short concluding paragraph is so different from the main body of *Gylfaginning* in style, subject matter, sentence structure and word choice, scholars have often treated it as an epilogue added by a later scribe.

SKALDSKAPARMAL (POETIC DICTION)

I

Bragi Tells Ægir Stories of The Gods

1. *Ægir ... Bragi*: Both Ægir and Bragi have their own histories. Ægir is either a giant or a god of the sea. The *Edda* calls Bragi a god, but he may originally have been Bragi Boddason the Old, a famous ninth-century court poet perhaps elevated to the rank of a god.
2. *her falcon shape*: This object, a falcon skin or cloak (*valshamr*), gave the possessor the ability to change shape into a falcon.
3. *I choose ... Njord*: She meant to choose Baldr, assuming that his feet would be the most beautiful. Instead she chose Njord, the god of the sea, because his feet were clean. The story of their marriage is told in *Gylfaginning*, chapter 23.

2
Kvasir and the Mead of Poetry

1. *Suttung, Gilling's son*: Although some manuscripts call Suttung the son of Gilling's brother (*bróðurson*), that is, his nephew, son makes more sense.
2. *they slit each other's throats . . . scythes*: Rather than fighting among themselves, which is a possibility, the wording gives the impression that these workers, probably giants, were so clumsy that they ended up killing each other as they jostled about.

3
The Giant Hrungnir

1. *no end to his boasting*: Describing Hrungnir's boasts, the text uses the term *stór orð,* meaning 'big words', and the scene has the flavour of depicting ritual drinking oaths.
2. *Mokkurkalfi . . . wet himself*: 'Mokkurkalfi' (*Mökkurkálfi*) has sometimes been translated as Mist Calf. However, the first part of the word, *mökkur*, most probably means earth or dirt such as clay. There has been confusion because *kálfi*, which specifically means the calf muscle of the leg, resembles the word *kálfr*, meaning a newborn cow. Given the story, it would make sense if the meaning of this name were something like 'clay foot', indicating the weakness of this clay creature, especially when wet.
3. *three years old*: Some manuscripts say three nights rather than winters (years).
4. *the star called Aurvandil's Toe*: *Aurvandilstá* is a star or perhaps a planet. Aurvandil is Earendel in Old English and may be the Morning Star.

4
Thor Journeys to Geirrod's Courts

1. *rowan branches*: The rowan tree, thought to be holy, was associated with Thor.

5
The Dwarves Make Treasures for the Gods

1. *awl . . . punched holes through the lips*: An awl is a sharp pointed tool, usually of iron, for making holes in wood or leather.

7
Otter's Ransom

1. *Why . . . gold called Otter's ransom*: The story recounted here agrees in the main with the material found in both the eddic poems and *The Saga of the Volsungs*.
2. *coin*: The Old Norse word is *penningr*, a coin.
3. *Gjukungs, also called the Niflungs*: King Gjuki's sons, the Gjukungs, were also called Niflungs, a name related to the Nibelungs of the South German epic the *Nibelungenlied*.
4. *linen fee*: The linen fee (*línfé*) was a gift paid by the bridegroom to the bride on the morning after the marriage was consummated.
5. *Gudrun . . . King Jonak . . . three sons*: This part of the story is also known from *The Lay of Hamdir* and *Gudrun's Incitement*, as well as from *The Saga of the Volsungs*. Skaldic verses by the poet Bragi Boddason also allude to the events.
6. *King Jormunrek the Powerful*: The Gothic King Jormunrek is based on a historical figure, known to the Romans as Ermanaric, Hermanaric or Ermenrichus. In the fourth century, this king ruled a vast Ostrogothic empire of horsemen north of the Black Sea on the steppes of what is today Ukraine. The contemporary Roman historian Ammianus Marcellinus, in his *History*, claims that Ermenrichus (d. 375) killed himself rather than face attack by the Huns. The sixth-century Gothic historian Jordanes relates in his *History of the Goths* an old story about the killing of a woman, Sunilda, which is remarkably close to the Norse version. Jordanes' story includes the vengeance of the woman's brothers Sarus and Ammius. The legend of Ermanaric was known throughout the northern lands and his tragedy is mentioned in the Old English poem *Widsith*.
7. *Bikki*: According to *The Saga of the Volsungs* Bikki is King Jormunrek's adviser.
8. *Aslaug*: *The Saga of the Volsungs* tells that Aslaug is the daughter of Sigurd and Brynhild.
9. *Sinfjotli . . . Sigurd*: Sigurd and Sinfjotli are half-brothers, both the sons of Sigmund, the son of Volsung. In *The Saga of the*

Volsungs, Sinfjotli is said to be Sigmund's son by an incestuous union with his sister Signy, and Sigmund and Sinfjotli live in the forest as wolves while seeking vengeance for the killing of Volsung.

8

Frodi's Mill and His Peace

1. *the Danish tongue*: Scandinavians in the Viking Age tended to call their common language the Danish tongue (*Dönsk tunga*). Just when and why they used this term is unclear, but it may be because Denmark became a powerful royal state earlier than the other regions of the north. At times Danish kings controlled large parts of Scandinavia.
2. *Jalangr's Heath*: A heath on Jutland near Jelling, the ancient royal seat of the Danish kingdom.

9

Kraki's Seed and King Hrolf Kraki of Denmark

1. *a thin pole*: Acccording to the Danish historian Saxo Grammaticus, writing about 1200, *kraki* refers to a tree trunk trimmed so that it can be used as a ladder. The place Hleidra (*Hleiðra,* modern Danish Lejre) on Sjaelland was an ancient seat of Danish chieftains where archaeological remains of large halls and burial mounds have been found, dating at least from the fifth and sixth centuries.
2. *It takes little to please Vogg*: An expression still in use in modern Icelandic, used when indicating that someone is easily pleased.
3. *Uppsala*: Just north of modern-day Stockholm, Uppsala was the seat of the ancient Swedish kings and a centre of religious observance.
4. *Yrsa*: Queen Yrsa's marital relationships and the enmity between King Hrolf of Denmark and King Adils of Sweden are major themes in *The Saga of King Hrolf Kraki*. In *Beowulf*, Adils appears as Eadgils.
5. *helmet Hildigolt . . . mail shirt Finnsleif . . . ring called Sviagris*: The gold ring called Swedes' Pig, or Sviagris, was one of the great treasures of the Uppsala dynasty. The helmet Battle Boar, or Hildigolt, is probably the same as Battle Pig, or Hildisvin, mentioned a few lines earlier. Finn's Legacy, or Finnsleif, is perhaps the work of a dwarf.

6. *river Fyri*: Runs through Uppsala; the Plains of Fyri lie just outside Uppsala.

10

The Never-ending Battle

1. *west over the sea*: This expression refers to the British Isles, especially Scotland, Orkney, the Hebrides and Ireland.

Glossary of Names

This glossary, which also serves as an index, lists the names of individuals (divine, otherworldly and human), groups, places, animals and objects. Entries are alphabetized in anglicized form, followed by the Old Icelandic within parentheses. Where meanings of names are given, they reflect the understanding of the thirteenth century. The citation numbers for *The Deluding of Gylfi* (*Gylfaginning*) refer to chapters. Items from *Skaldskaparmal* are preceded by the letter 'S', followed by the number of the story, hence 'S1' cites *Skaldskaparmal*, the first story. References to the *Prologue* are marked by the letter 'P', followed by the number of the section within the Prologue.

Adam (*Adam*): P1, is created by God
Adils (*Aðils*), legendary king of Sweden: S9
Ægir or **Hler** (*Ægir* or *Hlér*): S1, visits the Æsir in Asgard; S2; S3; S4; S6, Gold called fire of Ægir, the gods visit him, wife Ran, nine daughters
Ægis-Helm (*Œgishjálmr*; Helm of Dread): S7
Æsir (*Æsir*; the gods, sing. *Áss*): 1, Gefjun is from the family of Æsir; 2, Gylfi encounters three of their chieftains; 9, live in Old Asgard; 15, one of Yggdrasil's roots is among them, a list of their horses; 20, twelve are of divine nature; 21; 22; 23; 25; 27; 28; 33; 34, bind Fenrir; 41; 42, make a deal with the master builder; 43; 45, meet Skrymir; 46, put to tests by Utgarda-Loki; 49, the killing of Baldr; 50, the chaining of Loki; 51, fight the monsters at Ragnarok; 53; 55, give themselves names after hearing Gylfi's tale; S1, entertain Ægir, the killing of Thjazi; S2, make Kvasir, acquire the mead of poetry; S3; S5, judge the treasures brought by Loki; S7, pay the Otter's ransom; P5, Gylfi goes to meet them
Africa (*Affrica*): P2
Ai (*Ái*), dwarf: 14

Alf (*Álfr*), dwarf: 14
Alfheim (*Álfheimr*; Elf World, World of the Elves), World of the Light Elves: 17
Alfrodul (*Álfröðul*; Elf Beam), a name for the sun: 53, in a verse
Ali (*Áli*), legendary king of Norway: S9
Ali (*Áli*). *See* ***Vali***
All-Father (*Alföðr*): 3, one of the twelve names of Odin, description of; 9, sees everything; 10; 14; 15, pledges his eye to Mimir; 17; 20; 34, deals with Loki's children; 35; 39. *See* ***Odin***
Alsvinn (*Alsviðr*; All Swift), one of Sun's horses: 11
Althjolf (*Alþjólfr, Alþjófr*), dwarf: 14
Amsvartnir (*Ámsvartnir*; Pitch Black), lake to which Fenrir is taken: 34
Andhrimnir (*Andhrímnir*), cook in Valhalla: 38
Andlang (*Andlangr*; Long and Wide), one of three heavens: 17
Andvaranaut (*Andvaranautr*). *See* ***Andvari's Gift***
Andvari (*Andvari*; Careful One), dwarf: 14; S7, Odin sends Loki to the dwarf Andvari
Andvari's Gift (*Andvaranautr*), magical gold ring which Loki took from Andvari: S7
Angrboda (*Angrboða*; Sorrow Bringer), ogress/giantess: 34, her children by Loki. *See* ***Old One***
Annar (*Annarr*; Second, Other), Night's second husband, Earth's father: 10; P3
Arvak (*Árvakr*; Early Riser), one of Sun's horses: 11
Asa-Thor (*Ásaþórr*; Thor of the Æsir). *See* ***Thor***
Asbru (*Ásbrú*; Bridge of the Æsir): 15. *See* ***Bifrost***
Asgard (*Ásgarðr*; Realm of the Æsir): 2, Gylfi, king of Sweden, journeys there; 9, is built by the sons of Bor; 14, description of the twelve seats; 49; 53, with reference to the place where Asgard was earlier; S1, is visited by Ægir; S2; S3; S5; S6. *See* ***Asgard, the Old***
Asgard, the Old (*Ásgarðr inn forni*): 3, in Asgard the Old, Odin has twelve names; 9, stronghold in the middle of the world built by the sons of Bor, called a name for Troy. *See* ***Asgard***
Ash, the or the Ash Tree (*Askrinn*). *See* ***Yggdrasil***
Asia (*Asia*), one of the three parts of the world, Æsir were called men of Asia (*Asiamenn*): P2; P5
Ask (*Askr*; Ash Tree), first man: 9, formed out of a log by the sons of Bor
Aslaug (*Áslaug*), Sigurd's daughter: S7
Athra (*Athra*), a name for Annar, son of Bedvig: P3

Atli Budlason (*Atli Buðlason*), Attila the Hun, Brynhild's brother, Gudrun's second husband: S7
Atrid (*Atríðr*), name of Odin: 20
Aud (*Auðr*; Wealth, Rich One), one of Night's sons: 10, son of Naglfari
Audhumla (*Auðhumla*), primeval cow: 6, licks Buri out of a block of ice
Augustus, Emperor (*Augustus keisari*): S8
Aurboda (*Aurboða*), giantess, Gymir's wife, Gerd's mother: 37
Aurgelmir (*Aurgelmir*; Mud Bellower), the name given to Ymir by the frost giants: 5
Aurvandil the Bold (*Aurvandill inn frækni*), the husband of the Sibyl Groa, his toe becomes a star: S3
Aurvandil's Toe (*Aurvandilstá*), star or planet: S3
Aurvangar (*Aurvangar*; Mudfields): 14
Austri (*Austri*). *See East*
Awl (*Alr*; Awl), brother of the dwarf Brokk, S5
Bafur (*Báfurr*), dwarf: 14
Baldr (*Baldr*; see note 1, chapter 22), Odin's son: 15, his horse is burned with him; 22, a description of; 32; 49, his death; 50; 53, will come from Hel after Ragnarok; S1; P4
Baleyg (*Báleygr*; Flame Eyed), name of Odin: 20
Barey (*Barey* or *Barrey*), place where Frey marries Gerd: 37, note 1
Battle Boar (*Hildigöltr*), helmet: S9
Battle Pig (*Hildisvín*), helmet: S9
Baugi (*Baugi*), brother of Suttung: S2
Bedvig (*Beðvig*), son of Seskef: P3
Beigud (*Beiguðr*), one of Hrolf Kraki's berserkers: S9
Beldegg (*Beldegg*), name for Baldr, Odin's son that ruled over Westphalia: P4
Beli (*Beli*; Bellower), giant: 37, killed by Frey; 51, in a verse
Belt of Strength (*Megingjörð* or *Megingjarðar*), belts in the possession of Thor and Grid: 21; 45; S4
Bergelmir (*Bergelmir*), a frost giant: 7, survives the flood after Ymir is slain by the sons of Bor, the tribe of frost giants is formed from him
Bestla (*Bestla*), Odin's mother, giantess: 6
Biaf (*Biaf*), a name for Bjar, son of Skjaldun: P3
Biflidi or **Biflindi** (*Bifliði* or *Biflindi*; Spear Shaker, or Shield Shaker, or One with a Painted Shield/Spear?): 3, one of the twelve names of Odin
Bifrost (*Bifröst*; Trembling or Quivering Way, Multicoloured Way), bridge to Asgard: 13, is built by the gods, will break; 15, the gods ride over it daily on their way to their court of justice; 27, Heimdall lives beside it; 41, in a verse; 51, will break at Ragnarok

Bifur (*Bifurr*), dwarf: 14
Bikki (*Bikki*), Jormunrek's adviser: S7
Bil (*Bil*), Moon's follower: 11, taken along with Hjuki by Mani; 35, counted among the goddesses
Bileyg (*Bileygr*; One Whose Eye Fails, One Eyed?), name of Odin: 20
Bilskirnir (*Bilskirnir*), Thor's hall: 21
Blain (*Bláinn*; Dark One), possibly a name for Ymir: 14, in a verse
Blikjandabol (*Blíkjandaböl*; Gleaming Disaster), Hel's bed curtains: 34
Blindi (*Blindi*; Blind One), name of Odin: 20
Bodn (*Boðn*), one of the vats holding the mead of poetry: S2
Bodvar Bjarki (*Böðvarr Bjarki*), *bjarki* means Little Bear, Hrolf Kraki's warrior: S9
Boll (*Böll* or *Höll*), a river: 39
Bolthorn (*Bölþorn*; Thorn of Bad Luck), father of Bestla, giant: 6
Bolverk (*Bölverkr*): 20, name of Odin; S2, offers to work for Baugi for a drink of Suttung's mead
Bombor (*Bömbörr*), dwarf: 14
Bor (*Borr*), Buri's son, Odin's father: 6; 7, Bor's sons kill Ymir, drowning the frost giants; 8, his sons create the world out of Ymir's body; 9, his sons create man
Bragi (*Bragi*), god of poetry: 26, a description of; 41, in a verse; S1; S2; S3; S4; S6, visits Ægir
Bragi the Old (*Bragi inn gamli*), poet: 1, a verse from him; S10, composed a poem on Ragnar Lodbrok
Brand (*Brandr*), son of Beldegg: P4
Breidablik (*Breiðablik*; Gleaming Far and Wide), Baldr's home: 17; 22
Brimir (*Brimir*), a hall in heaven: 52, after Ragnarok, a hall with plenty of good drink
Brisingamen (*Brísingamen*; Necklace of the Brisings): 35, owned by Freyja
Brokk (*Brokkr*), dwarf, brother of the smith Eitri: S5
Brynhild (*Brynhildr*): S7, called Hild and is a valkyrie, marries Gunnar, has Sigurd killed and commits suicide
Budli (*Buðli*), father of Atli and Brynhild: S7
Buri (*Búri*), Odin's grandfather, primogenitor: 6, licked out of ice by Audhumla
Byleist (*Býleistr*), Loki's brother: 33; 51, in a verse
Byrgir (*Byrgir*; Hider of Something), well: 11
Christ (*Kristr*): S8
Dain (*Dáinn*), dwarf: 14

Dain (*Dáinn*), stag feeding in the branches of Yggdrasil: 16
Dain's Legacy (*Dáinsleif*), sword made by the dwarves: S10
Dark Elves (*Dökkálfar* and *Svartálfar*): 17, description of; 34, Skirnir goes to the World of the Dark Elves; S5, Loki promises to get the dark elves to make gold hair for Sif; S7, Loki travels to the World of the Dark Elves. *See **Elves***
Day (*Dagr*), son of Night and Delling: 10, rides the sky in a chariot drawn by the horse Skinfaxi
Delling (*Dellingr*; Shining One), Day's father: 10, Night's third husband
Denmark (*Danmörk*): 1, in a verse; S8; S9; P5, is ruled by the Skjoldungs, the language of the men of Asia is brought to Denmark
Dolgthvari (*Dólgþvari*), dwarf: 14
Dori (*Dóri*), dwarf: 14
Drapa of Ragnar Lodbrok (*Ragnars drápa loðbrókar*): S10
Draupnir (*Draupnir*), dwarf: 14
Draupnir (*Draupnir*; Dripper), a magical ring: 49, is laid by Odin on Baldr's funeral pyre and brought back from Hel by Hermod; S5, forged
Dromi (*Drómi*), fetter: 34
Duf (*Dúfr*), dwarf: 14
Duneyr (*Duneyrr*), stag feeding in the branches of Yggdrasil: 16
Durathror (*Duraþrór*), stag feeding in the branches of Yggdrasil: 16
Durin (*Durinn*; Doorkeeper? Drowsy?), dwarf: 14
Dvalin (*Dvalinn*), dwarf : 14; 15, daughters of
Dvalin (*Dvalinn*), stag feeding in the branches of Yggdrasil: 16
Dwarves (*Dvergar*, plural, *Dvergr*, sing.): 14, their origins and names; 15, some norns descended from them; 34, make Gleipnir; 35, said to have made the necklace of the Brisings; 43, makers of Skidbladnir; 51, in a verse concerning Ragnarok; S2, make the mead of poetry; S5, make treasures for the gods; S7, Loki takes a ring from the dwarf Andvari; S10, dwarves said to have made Dain's Legacy. *See **Dark Elves***
Earth (*Jörð*), mother of Thor: 9, daughter and wife of Odin; 10, daughter of Night and Annar; 36; 51, in a verse
East (*Austri*), dwarf: 8, holding up a corner of the sky formed out of Ymir's skull; 14
Ector (*Ector*), Hector or Thor at Troy: 55
Eikinskjaldi (*Eikinskjaldi*; Oaken Shield), dwarf: 14
Eikthyrnir (*Eikþyrnir*; Oak Antlers), stag from whose horns moisture drips down to Hvergelmir: 39
Einherjar (*Einherjar*; Those Who Fight Alone, Good Warrior?), Odin's

warriors in Valhalla: 20; 36, in a verse; 38, with reference to their feeding in Valhalla; 39, on their drinking in Valhalla; 40, number that can pass through the doors of Valhalla; 41, with reference to their amusements in Valhalla; 51, at Ragnarok will fight on the side of the Æsir; 52

Einridi (*Einriði*), son of Loridi: P3

Eir (*Eir*; Merciful?), goddess: 35

Eitri (*Eitri*; Venomous), smith among the dwarves: S5

Ekin (*Ekin* or *Eikin*; Raging), river flowing from Hvergelmir: 39

Eldhrimnir (*Eldhrímnir*), kettle used to feed Odin's champions in Valhalla: 38

Eldir (*Eldir*), slave of Ægir: S6.

Elivagar (*Élivágar*; Storm Waves), the rivers flowing from Hvergelmir: 5, in a verse; S3

Eljudnir (*Eljúðnir* or *Éljúðnir*; Sprayed with Snowstorms, Damp with Sleet or Rain), Hel's hall: 34

Elli (*Elli*; Old Age), Utgarda-Loki's foster mother: 46, her wrestling contest with Thor; 47, her identity is revealed to Thor

Elves (*Álfar*, plural, *Álfr*, sing.; Light Elves [*Ljósálfar*], Dark Elves [*Dökkálfar* and *Svartálfar*]): 15, some norns descended from them; 17, difference between dark and light elves; 34, Skirnir goes to the World of the Dark Elves; 51, in a verse concerning Ragnarok; S5, Loki promises to get the dark elves to make gold hair for Sif and the dwarves make treasures for the gods; S7, Loki travels to the World of the Dark Elves

Embla (*Embla*; Vine or some kind of tree), first woman: 9, is formed out of a log by the sons of Bor

England (*England*): P5, its ancient place names are derived from a different language

Ermanaric or **Ermenrichus**. *See* ***Jormunrek***

Erp (*Erpr*), son of Gudrun and Jonak, brother of Hamdir and Sorli: S7

Europe or **Enea** (*Evropa* or *Enea*), one of the three parts of the world: P2

Eve (*Eva*): P1

Eylimi (*Eylimi*), father of Hjordis, Sigurd Fafnisbani's grandfather: S7

Fafnir (*Fáfnir*), shape-shifter, dragon who sits on the treasure: S7, is killed by Sigurd

Fal (*Falr*), dwarf: 14

Falhofnir (*Falhófnir*; Yellow Hoofed or Hairy Hoofed), horse: 15

Falling to Peril (*Fallandaforað*; Falling to Peril, Pitfall), Hel's threshold or doorstep: 34

Famine (*Sultr*; Famine, Hunger), Hel's knife: 34
Farbauti (*Fárbauti*; Peril Striker), Loki's father, a giant: 33
Farma-God (*Farmaguð*; God of Cargoes), name of Odin: 20
Farmatyr (*Farmatýr*; God of Cargoes), name of Odin: 20
Father of Armies (*Herjaföðr*; also Father of Men), name of Odin: 38, in a verse
Father of the Slain (*Valföðr*), name of Odin: 15, in a verse; 20
Fenja (*Fenja*), slave woman, probably a giantess: S8
Fenrir or **Fenriswolf** (*Fenrir* [Bog Dweller] or *Fenrisúlfr*), wolf, fathered by Loki: 12, in a verse; 25; 34, his binding by the gods; 38; 51, his getting loose at Ragnarok, called Freki, Hvedrung's son; 53
Fensalir or **Fensal** (plural *Fensalir*, sing. *Fensalr*), Frigg's home: 35; 49
Fili (*Fili*), dwarf: 14
Fimafeng (*Fimafengr*), Ægir's slave: S6, killed by Loki
Fimbulthul (*Fimbulþul*; Steadily Loud), river flowing from Hvergelmir: 4; 39
Fimbulvetr (*Fimbulvetr*; Extreme or Mighty Winter), the beginning of Ragnarok: 51
Finn (*Finn*), dwarf: 14
Finn (*Finn*), son of Gudolf: P3
Finn's Legacy (*Finnsleif*), mail shirt: S9
Fjalar (*Fjalarr*), dwarf: S2, with his brother Galar, kills Kvasir and makes the mead of poetry
Fjolnir (*Fjölnir*; Wise One, Much Knowing): 3, one of the twelve names of Odin; 20
Fjolnir (*Fjölnir*; Wise One, Much Knowing), a Swedish king: S8
Fjolsvid (*Fjölsviðr*; Very Wise One), name of Odin: 20
Fjorgyn (*Fjörgynn*, *Fjörgvinn*), Frigg's father: 9
Fjorm (*Fjörm*; Hurrying), river flowing from Hvergelmir: 4; 39
Folkvang and **Folkvangar** (*Fólkvangr* and plural *Fólkvangar*; Warriors' Field), Freyja's home: 24
Forseti (*Forseti*; He Who Sits Foremost), a god, Baldr's son: 32; S1
Franang's Falls (*Fránangrsfors*), waterfall, Loki's hiding place: 50
France (*Frakkland*; Land of the Franks), ruled by Siggi and Rerir: P4
Freki (*Freki*; Wolf, perhaps Greedy Wolf), Odin's wolf: 38
Freki (*Freki*; Wolf or Greedy Wolf), a name for Fenrir: 51, in a verse
Freovin (*Freovin*), son of Frjodigar: P4
Frey (*Freyr*; Lord), Njord's son: 24, a description of; 34; 37, seeks to marry Gerd, reason he was without weapon when he fought Beli; 43, given Skidbladnir by some dwarves; 49, rides to Baldr's funeral;

51, will fight with Surt at Ragnarok, called Beli's Bright Bane; S1; S5; S6, visits Ægir

Freyja (*Freyja*; Lady, Woman), goddess: 24; 35, a description of; 42, promised as a bride to the builder of Asgard's wall; 49, rides to Baldr's funeral; S1, lends Loki her falcon shape; S3, waits on Hrungnir; S6, visits Ægir

Friallaf (*Friallaf*), Fridleif, son of Finn: P3

Fridleif (*Friðleifr*), son of Skjold: S8, king after Skjold; P5

Frigg (*Frigg*), Odin's wife: 9, daughter of Fjorgyn; 20; 35, is described; 49, exacts an oath from all things that they would not harm Baldr, rides to Baldr's funeral; S1; S4; S6, visits Ægir; P3

Frigida (*Frigida*), a name for Frigg: P3

Frjodigar or **Frodi** (*Frioðigar* or *Fróði*), son of Brand: P4

Frodi (*Fróði*), king in Denmark, grandson of Skjold, son of Fridleif: S8, his mill and peace

Frost Giants (*Hrímþursar*, sing. *Hrímþurs*): 3; 5; 7; 15; 21; 42; 49; 51; S5

Frosti (*Frosti*), dwarf: 14

Fulla (*Fulla*), goddess: 35; 49, a goddess connected with Frigg; S1

Fundin (*Fundinn*), dwarf: 14

Fyri (*Fýri*), a river in Sweden passing through Uppsala: S9

Fyri Plains (*Fýrisvellir*), in Sweden, the plains of the river Fyri: S9

Galar (*Galarr*), dwarf: S2, with his brother Fjalar, kills Kvasir and makes the mead of poetry

Gandalf (*Gandálfr*; Sorcerer Elf, Wand Elf), dwarf: 14

Gang (*Gangr*), giant: S1

Gangleri or **Ganglari** (*Gangleri* or *Ganglari*; Wanderer, Strider, Weary Walker), name of Odin: 20

Gangleri (*Gangleri* or *Ganglari*; Strider, Wanderer, Weary Walker), the assumed name of Gylfi, king of Sweden, journeying to meet the Æsir: 2, Gylfi assumes this name; 3, asks High about All-Father; 4, asks how things began; 5, asks of order of things before man; 6, asks of Ymir; 7, asks of giants; 8, asks about the sons of Bor; 9, asks about the origins of people; 11, asks about the course of the sun and moon; 12, asks who bothers Sun; 13, asks of path from earth to sky; 14, asks of Asgard's completion; 15, asks about the holy place of the gods; 16, asks about Yggdrasil; 17, asks about significant places; 18, asks for the wind's origins; 19, asks of winter and summer; 20, asks which Æsir to believe in; 21, inquires of other Æsir; 22, asks of further Æsir; 25, asks of other Æsir; 26, asks of Idunn's apples; 34, asks for description of fantastic fetter, why Fenriswolf wasn't killed; 35, asks about the goddesses; 37, comments on Frey's gift; 38, asks how Odin's fallen warriors are fed; 39, asks about drink in Valhalla; 40, comments on doors of Valhalla; 41, asks about Einherjar's amusement; 42, asks of Sleipnir's owner; 43, asks of Skidbladnir; 44, asks if Thor was ever bested; 48, asks of vengeance on Utgarda-Loki; 49, asks for more regarding the Æsir; 50, asks if vengeance for Baldr was taken; 51, asks of Ragnarok; 52, asks what comes after Ragnarok; 53, asks where the gods will live after Ragnarok; 54, tells people stories he has heard; 55, Æsir recall stories told to him. *See* ***Gylfi***

Gardrofa (*Garðrofa*), a mare: 35, in a verse

Garm (*Garmr*), Hel's hound that will fight against Tyr at Ragnarok: 41, in a verse; 51

Gates of Hel (*Helgrindr*): 4; 49, Hermod arrives there

Gaut (*Gautr*), name of Odin: 20

Gefjun (*Gefjun*; She Who Gives), goddess: 1, forms Sjaelland; 35; S1; S6, visits Ægir

Gefn (*Gefn*; Giver), one of Freyja's names: 35

Geirahod (*Geirahöð*), valkyrie: 36, in a verse

Geirrod (*Geirrøðr*), giant king: 20, Odin named himself on his visit to King Geirrod; S4, his encounters with Loki and Thor

Geirrod's Courts (*Geirrøðargarðar*): S4, first Loki's then Thor's journey to

Geirvimul (*Geirvimul*; Spear Teeming), river flowing from Hvergelmir: 39

Gelgja (*Gelgja*), attachment on fetter: 34, binds the Fenriswolf and is threaded through Gjoll

Gerd (*Gerðr*), Frey's wife: 37; S1, called a goddess

Geri (*Geri*; Greedy), Odin's wolf: 38

Germany. *See* ***Saxland***

Gevis or **Gavir** (*Gevis* or *Gavir*), son of Wigg: P4

Giant Land or **Jotunheim** (*Jötunheimr* or *Jötunheimar*): 1; 10; 14; 34; 42; 45, Thor's journey to Giant Land with Skrymir; 49; 51; S1; S3

Gilling (*Gillingr*), a giant, father of Suttung: S2

Gils (*Gils*), horse: 15

Gimle (*Gimlé*; Protected from Fire), place where the righteous men will live after death: 3, synonymous with Vingolf; 17, a description of; 52, after Ragnarok

Ginnar (*Ginnarr*), dwarf: 14

Ginnung Sky (*Ginnungahiminn*), the sky or firmament: 8

Ginnungagap (*Ginnungagap*), a void filled with magic power: 5, is described; 8, the world and the stars are put in it; 15, one of the roots of Yggdrasil reaches what used to be Ginnungagap

Gipul (*Gipul*), river flowing from Hvergelmir: 39
Gjallarhorn (*Gjallarhorn*; Resounding Horn, the Horn or Trumpet of Gjoll): 15, Mimir drinks from it; 27, Heimdall's horn; 51, will be blown by Heimdall at Ragnarok
Gjalp (*Gjálp*), one of Geirrod's daughters, straddles the river: S4
Gjoll (*Gjöll*), stone that anchors Fenrir's fetter: 34
Gjoll (*Gjöll*; Noisy), river flowing from Hvergelmir: 4, next to the Gates of Hel; 49, Hermod rides over it
Gjoll Bridge (*Gjallarbrú*): 49, guarded by Modgud
Gjuki (*Gjúki*), king, Sigurd's father-in-law: S7
Gjukungs or **Niflungs** (*Gjukungar* or *Niflungar*), King Gjuki's descendants, chiefly Gudrun's family: S7
Glad (*Glaðr*; Glad or Radiant One), horse: 15
Gladsheim (*Glaðsheimr*; Home of Gladness or Joy, Radiant Home), temple housing Odin's and the Æsir's seats: 14
Glaer or **Glen** (*Glær* or *Glenr*; Shining One?), horse: 15
Glapsvid (*Glapsviðr*; Seducer), name of Odin: 20
Gleipnir (*Gleipnir*), fetter: 25, Tyr loses his hand to bind Fenrir with it; 34, made from six elements, binds Fenrir
Glen (*Glenr*; Shining One), Sun's husband: 11
Glen (*Glenr*). *See* **Glaer**
Glitnir (*Glitnir*; Radiant Place), Forseti's home: 17, description of; 32
Gloin (*Glóinn*), dwarf: 14
Glora. *See* **Lora**
Gna (*Gná*), goddess: 35, associated with Frigg
Gnipahellir (*Gnipahellir*; Jutting or Overhanging Cave), cave leading to Hel's domain, guarded by Garm: 51
Gnita-Heath (*Gnitaheiðr*): S7
God (*Guð*): P1
Goddesses (*Ásynjur* and *Gyðjur*): 14, on Vingolf, their sanctuary; 20; 24, Freyja, the most splendid of the goddesses; 35; 36; S1
Goin (*Góinn*), serpent gnawing at the root of Yggdrasil: 16
Gold Bristle (*Gullinbursti*), Frey's boar: 49. *See* **Sheathed Tooth**
Golden Age (*Gullaldr*): 14, spoiled by women who came from Giant Land
Golden Forelock. *See* **Gulltopp**
Golden Mane (*Gullfaxi*), Hrungnir's horse: S3, given to Magni
Goll (*Göll*), valkyrie: 36, in a verse
Gomul (*Gömul*; Old), river flowing from Hvergelmir: 39
Gondlir (*Göndlir*; Wand Wielder), name of Odin: 20
Gopul (*Göpul*; Gaper, Forward Rushing), river flowing from Hvergelmir: 39

Gothorm (*Gothormr*), Gjuki's stepson: S7, kills Sigurd, and is killed by him
Goti (*Goti*), Gunnar's horse: S7
Gotland (*Gotland*), old name for Denmark, northern Jutland: S8
Grabak (*Grábakr*; Grey Back), serpent gnawing at the roots of Yggdrasil: 16
Grad (*Gráð*; Greedy), a river: 39
Grafvitnir (*Grafvitnir*; Grave Wolf), father of serpents gnawing at the roots of Yggdrasil: 16
Grafvollud (*Grafvölluðr*; Field Burrower), serpent gnawing at the roots of Yggdrasil: 16
Gram (*Gramr*), Sigurd's sword: S7
Grani (*Grani*), Sigurd's horse: S7
Greip (*Greip*), one of Geirrod's daughters: S4
Grid (*Gríðr*), giantess, mother of Vidar the Silent: S4, lends Thor her belt, staff and iron gloves
Grid's Staff (*Gríðarvölr*): S4, Thor uses it on his journey to Geirrod's courts
Grim (*Grímr*; Masked One), name of Odin: 20
Grimhild (*Grímhildr*), Gjuki's wife: S7
Grimnir (*Grímnir*; Masked One), name of Odin: 20
Grimnir, Lay of (*Grímnismál*), Eddic poem: 21; 36; 40
Grjotunagardar (*Grjótúnagarðar*; Courtyards of Rocky Fields), Hrungnir's home: S3
Groa (*Gróa*): S3, pronounces spells to loosen the whetstone stuck in Thor's head, wife of Aurvandil
Grotti (*Grotti*), mill: S8
Grotti's Song (*Grottasöngr*), a poem recited by Fenja and Menja: S8
Gudny (*Guðný*), Gjuki's daughter: S7
Gudolf (*Guðólfr*), son of Jat: P3
Gudrun (*Guðrún Gjúkadóttir*), Gjuki's daughter: S7, marries Sigurd, Atli and Jonak
Gullfaxi. *See* ***Golden Mane***
Gullintanni (*Gullintanni*; Gold Toothed), a name of Heimdall: 27
Gulltopp (*Gulltoppr*; Golden Forelock), horse: 15; 27, Heimdall's horse; 49, Heimdall rides him to Baldr's funeral
Gungnir or **Gugnir** (*Gungnir* or *Gugnir*; Swaying One), Odin's spear: 51; S5, Odin receives it from the dwarves
Gunn (*Guðr* or *Gunnr*; Battle, Conflict), valkyrie: 36, rides with Rota and Skuld to decide battles and choose the slain
Gunnar (*Gunnarr*), Gjuki's son: S7, marries Brynhild

Gunnlod (*Gunnlöð*), giantess, Suttung's daughter: S2, appointed guardian of the mead of poetry, lets Odin drink the mead
Gunnthra and **Gunnthro** (*Gunnþrá* and *Gunnþró*), river flowing from Hvergelmir: 4; 39, Gunnthro, a river from Hvergelmir, perhaps the same
Gunnthrain (*Gunnþráin*), a river: 39
Gylfi (*Gylfi*), Swedish king: 1, the Gefjun episode; 1–54, conversing with the three Æsir; P5, calling himself Gangleri meets the Æsir. *See* ***Gangleri***
Gyllir (*Gyllir*; Golden), horse: 15
Gymir (*Gymir*), Gerd's father: 37
Habrok (*Hábrók*), hawk: 41, in a verse
Hallinskidi (*Hallinskíði*), name of Heimdall: 27
Hamdir (*Hamðir*), son of Gudrun and Jonak, brother of Erp and Sorli: S7
Hamskerpir (*Hamskerpir*), horse: 35, in a verse
Hang Jaw or **Hengikjopt** (*Hengikjöptr*): perhaps Odin: S8
Hanga-God (*Hangaguð*; God of the Hanged), name of Odin: 20
Hapta-God (*Haptaguð*; God of Prisoners, God of Fetters), name of Odin: 20
Har (*Hár/Hárr*), dwarf: 14
Har (*Hár/Hárr*; High One or Hoary One), name of Odin: 20; talks with Gylfi, perhaps Odin. *See* ***High***
Harbard (*Hárbarðr*; Grey Beard), name of Odin: 20
Hati Hrodvitnisson (*Hati Hróðvitnisson*; He Who Hates, Enemy), wolf pursuing Moon: 12
Haur (*Haurr*), dwarf: 14
Haustlong (*Haustlöng*), poem: S3
Hedin Hjarrandason (*Heðinn Hjarrandason*), legendary king: S10
Heidrun (*Heiðrún*), goat: 39, stands on top of Valhalla
Heimdall (*Heimdallr*), god: 27, a description of; 49, rides to Baldr's funeral; 51, will awaken the gods at Ragnarok, fights Loki; S1. *See* ***Gullintanni*** and ***Hallinskidi***
Heimdall's Chant (*Heimdalargaldr*), a verse: 27
Heimir in Hlymdales (*Heimir í Hlymdölum*), Aslaug's foster father: S7
Heingest (*Heingestr*), son of Vitta: P4
Hel (*Hel*; see notes 1 and 2, chapter 3), goddess of the underworld, Loki's daughter: 3, receives wicked men after their death; 34, Odin throws her into Niflheim and gives her authority over nine worlds; 49, tests the Æsir's love of Baldr; 51
Hel (*Hel*; see notes 1 and 2, chapter 3), the underworld: 3, wicked

men go there after death; 50; 53, Baldr and Hod will return from there after Ragnarok. *See* ***Niflhel, Road to Hel*** and ***Gates of Hel***
Helblindi (*Helblindi*; Hel Blind), Loki's brother: 33
Helblindi (*Helblindi*; Hel Blind), name of Odin (perhaps scribal error for Herblindi, Blinder of Armies): 20
Helgeland Genealogies, The (*Háleygjatal*): P5
Heptifili (*Heptifili*), dwarf: 14
Heremod (*Heremóð*), son of Itrmann: P3
Herfjotur (*Herfjötur*; Fetterer of an Army), valkyrie: 36, in a verse
Hermod the Bold (*Hermóðr inn hvati*), Odin's son: 49, travels to Hel to offer her ransom for Baldr
Herran or **Herjan** (*Herran* or *Herjan*; Lord, Lord of Raiders, the First among Warriors): 3, one of the twelve names of Odin; 20
Herteit (*Herteitr*; Glad of War), name of Odin: 20
High (*Hár/Hárr*; High One), one of the Æsir who talks with Gylfi: 2; 3; 4; 5; 6; 7; 8; 9; 11; 12; 13; 14; 15; 16; 17; 18; 19; 20; 21; 22; 25; 34; 35; 37; 38; 39; 40; 41; 42; 43; 44; 48; 49; 50; 51; 53
Hild (*Hildr*; Battle). *See* ***Brynhild***
Hild (*Hildr*; Battle), King Hogni's daughter, abducted by King Hedin: S10
Hild (*Hildr*; Battle), valkyrie: 36, in a verse
Hildigolt. *See* ***Battle Boar***
Himinbjorg (*Himinbjörg*; Heavenly Mountains, Heavenly Cliffs, if singular, Salvation or Protection of Heaven), stands where Bifrost enters heaven: 17; 27, Heimdall's home
Himinhrjot (*Himinhrjótr*), Hymir's ox: 48, Thor makes bait out of its head
Hindafell (*Hindafjall*; Hind Mountain?), a mountain where Brynhild lives: S7
Hjadnings, Battle of the (*Hjaðingavíg*): S10
Hjalmberi (*Hjálmberi*; Helmet Bearer), name of Odin: 20
Hjalprek (*Hjálprekr*), legendary king: S7, Regin becomes his smith
Hjalti the Courageous (*Hjalti hugprúði*), one of Hrolf Kraki's berserkers: S9
Hjordis (*Hjördís*), Eylimi's daughter, mother of Sigurd: S7
Hjuki (*Hjúki*), Moon's follower: 11, taken along with Bil by Mani
Hledjolf (*Hleðjólfr*), dwarf: 14
Hleidra (*Hleiðra*). *See* ***Lejre***
Hler (*Hlér*). *See* ***Ægir***
Hlesey (*Hlésey*; Hler's Island), perhaps Læsø in the Kattegat between modern Denmark and Sweden: S1
Hlidskjalf (*Hliðskjálf*; Doorway, Gatetower or Watchtower): 9, is in

the middle of the Old Asgard; 17; 37, Frey falls in love with Gerd by looking out from it; 50, Odin spots Loki's hiding place from it

Hlin (*Hlín*; Protector): 35, goddess connected with Frigg; 51, name for Frigg

Hlodyn (*Hlöðyn*), name for Earth, Thor's mother: 51

Hlokk (*Hlökk*; Noise, Battle), valkyrie: 36, in a verse

Hlymdales (*Hlymdalir*): S7

Hnikar (*Hnikarr*; [Spear] Thruster, Mover, Inciter), name of Odin: 20. *See* ***Nikar***

Hnikud (*Hnikuðr*; [Spear] Thruster, Mover, Inciter), name of Odin: 20. *See* ***Nikuz***

Hnitbjorg (*Hnitbjörg*), place where Suttung hides the mead of poetry: S2

Hnoss (*Hnoss*; Precious or Costly Thing), Freyja's daughter: 35

Hod (*Höðr*; Warrior), Baldr's slayer: 28, description of; 49, slays Baldr; 53, will return with Baldr from Hel after Ragnarok

Hoddmimir's Wood (*Holt Hoddmímis*), place where two human beings will survive Ragnarok: 53

Hoenir (*Hœnir*), a god: 23, taken as a hostage by the Vanir in exchange for Njord; S1; S7

Hofvarpnir (*Hófvarpnir* or *Hófvarfnir*; Hoof Kicker?), Gna's horse: 35

Hogni (*Högni*), Gunnar's brother: S7

Hogni (*Högni*), legendary king: S10

Horn (*Hörn*), one of Freyja's names: 35

Hoy (*Háey*), island in Orkney: S10

Hraesvelg (*Hræsvelgr*; Corpse Gulper), eagle giant, source of winds: 18

Hreidmar (*Hreiðmarr*), father of Fafnir, Otter and Regin: S7

Hrid (*Hríð*; Snow Storm), river flowing from Hvergelmir: 4

Hrimfaxi (*Hrímfaxi*; Frost Mane), Night's horse: 10, the foam from his bit bedews the earth every morning

Hringhorn. *See* ***Ringhorn***

Hrist (*Hrist*; Shaker), valkyrie: 36, in a verse

Hrolf kraki (*Hrólfr kraki*), legendary king of Denmark: S9

Hronn (*Hrönn*; Wave), a river: 39

Hroptatyr (*Hroptatýr*), name of Odin: 20

Hrotti (*Hrotti*), sword: S7

Hrungnir (*Hrungnir*), giant: S3, his encounter with Odin and his battle with Thor; S4

Hrungnir's Heart (*Hrungnishjarta*): S3

Hrym (*Hrymr*), giant: 51, will steer Naglfar at Ragnarok

Hugi (*Hugi*; Thought, Mind): 46, his running contest with Thjalfi; 47, Utgarda-Loki reveals his identity
Hugin (*Huginn*; Thought, Mind), one of Odin's ravens: 38
Hugstari (*Hugstari*), dwarf: 14
Hunger (*Hungr*), Hel's plate: 34
Hvedrung (*Hveðrungr*), probably a name for Loki: 51
Hvergelmir (*Hvergelmir*; Roaring Kettle), a spring in Niflheim, source of many rivers: 4; 15; 16; 39; 52
Hvitserk the Bold (*Hvítserkr inn hvati*), one of Hrolf Kraki's berserkers: S9
Hymir (*Hymir*), giant: 48, Thor goes fishing with
Hyrrokkin (*Hyrrokkin*; Shrunk in Fire), giantess: 49, launches the ship Ringhorn
Idavoll (*Iðavöllr*; Eternally Renewing Field, Field of Activity): 14, site of Asgard; 53, Vidar and Vali will live there after Ragnarok
Idi (*Iði*), giant: S1
Idunn (*Iðunn*), goddess, wife of Bragi: 26, keeps the apples of youth; S1, is stolen by the giant Thjazi; S6, visits Ægir.
Ingi (*Ingi*), dwarf: 14
Iron Wood or **Jarnvid** (*Járnviðr*): 12
Iron Wood Dwellers or **Jarnvidjur** (*Járnviðjur*), troll women living in Iron Wood: 12
Isarnkol (*Ísarnkol*), bellows that cool Sun's horses: 11
Itrmann (*Ítrmann*), son of Athra, father of Heremod: P3
Ivaldi, Sons of (*Ívaldi*, *synir Ívalda*), dwarves: 43, give Skidbladnir to Frey; S5, make treasures for the gods
Jafnhar (*Jafnhár*; Just-as-High): 20, in a verse. *See* ***Just-as-High***
Jalangr's Heath (*Jalangrsheiðr*), near Jelling in Denmark: S8
Jalg or **Jalk** (*Jálg* or *Jálkr*; Gelding): 3, one of the twelve names of Odin; 20
Jarnsaxa (*Járnsaxa*; Iron Cutlass or Sax), giantess, mother of Magni: S3
Jarnvid and **Jarnvidjur**. *See* ***Iron Wood*** and ***Iron Wood Dwellers***
Jat (*Jat*), son of Biaf: P3
Jonak (*Jónakr*), king: S7, marries Gudrun, father of Erp, Hamdir and Sorli
Jord (*Jörð*). *See* ***Earth***
Jormungand (*Jörmungandr*; Enormous Monster), the Midgard Serpent, fathered by Loki: 34, Odin throws him into the World Ocean; 51, in a verse. *See* ***Midgard Serpent***
Jormunrek (*Jörmunrekr inn ríki*; the Powerful or Great), Ermanaric or Ermenrichus, Gothic king: S7, marries Svanhild

Joruvellir (*Jöruvellir*; Plains of Sand/Pebbles): 14
Jotunheim (*Jötunheimr*, plural *Jötunheimar*). *See* ***Giant Land***
Just-as-High (*Jafnhár*): 2, one of the Æsir who talks with Gylfi; 3, tells how All-Father created the world; 4, describes Niflheim; 5, speaks of Ginnungagap; 8, tells how the oceans are created from Ymir's blood; 15, describes Yggdrasil; 20, tells of the power of the goddesses, Jafnhar, name of Odin in a verse; 44, defers to Third on the matter of Thor's trip to Giant Land
Jutland (*Jótland*), former Reidgotaland: P5
Kerlaugs (*Kerlaugar*, singular *Kerlaug*), two rivers: 15, in a verse
Kili (*Kili*), dwarf: 14
Kjalar (*Kjalarr*), name of Odin: 20
Kor (*Kör*; Sick Bed), Hel's bed: 34
Kormt (*Körmt*), river: 15, in a verse
Kvasir (*Kvasir*): 50, the wisest, recognizes the net in Loki's fire; S2, made by the Æsir and the Vanir, killed by the dwarfs Fjalar and Galar; mead of poetry is made from his blood
Laeding (*Lœðingr* or *Leyðingr*), fetter: 34
Laufey or **Nal** (*Laufey* or *Nál*), Loki's mother: 33; 42, reference to her son; 49, concerning the son of; S5
Lazy (*Ganglati*), Hel's manservant: 34
Leifthrasir (*Leifþrasir*; Life Yearner), one of the two human beings to survive Ragnarok: 53
Leiptr (*Leiptr*; Flashing Bright), river flowing from Hvergelmir: 4
Lejre (*Hleiðra*), place on Sjaelland, seat of ancient Danish kings: S9
Lerad or **Laerad** (*Léraðr or Læraðr*), tree which may be the World Tree, Yggdrasil: 39
Lettfeti (*Léttfeti*; Lightfoot), horse: 15
Lif (*Líf*; Life), one of the two human beings to survive Ragnarok: 53
Light Elves (*Ljósálfar*): 17, description of. *See* ***Elves***
Lit (*Litr*), dwarf: 14; 49, kicked into Baldr's funeral pyre by Thor
Lofar (*Lofarr*), dwarf: 14
Lofn (*Lofn*; Loving), goddess: 35
Logi (*Logi*; Fire): 46, his eating contest with Loki; 47, his identity revealed to Thor
Logrinn (*Lögrinn*; the Water or the Lake), Lake Mälar in Sweden: 1, is formed by Gefjun ploughing land in Sweden
Loki or **Lopt** (*Loki* or *Loptr*): 20, in a verse from *Loki's Flyting*; 33, is described; 34, the fate of Loki's children by the giantess Angrboda; 42, gives birth to Sleipnir; 44, travels to Utgard with Thor; 46, his eating contest with Logi; 47; 49, contrives the killing of Baldr; 50, tries to escape the vengeance of the gods by turning himself into a

salmon, is caught by them and chained to three rocks with a snake fastened above him and dripping poison on to his face; 51, will fight Heimdall at Ragnarok, in a verse from *The Sibyl's Prophecy*; 55, name given to Ulysses by the Turks; S1, the uncooked-meat episode, steals Idunn for the giant Thjazi, makes Thjazi's daughter Skadi laugh; S4, is captured by Geirrod and is forced to bring Thor to him unarmed; S5, cuts off Sif's hair and restores it; S6, visits Ægir, insults gods, kills Fimafeng; S7, kills Otter

Lora or **Glora** (*Lora* or *Glora*), the wife of Loricus: P3, is killed by Tror/Thor

Loricus (*Loricus*), duke, Tror/Thor's foster-father: P3, is killed by Tror/Thor

Loridi (*Loriði*), son of Tror/Thor and Sibyl/Sif: P3

Lyngvi (*Lyngvi*), an island: 34

Magi (*Magi*), descendant of Tror/Thor, son of Moda: P3

Magni (*Magni*; Strong), Thor's son: 53, will survive Ragnarok; S3, lifts Hrungnir's leg off Thor

Malar (*Mälar*). *See* ***Logrinn***

Managarm (*Mánagarmr*; Moon Dog), wolf who fills himself with all who die and will swallow the heavenly bodies: 12

Mani (*Máni*). *See* ***Moon***

Mardoll (*Mardöll*), one of Freyja's names: 35

Mediterranean Sea (*Miðjarðarsjár*): P2

Megingjard (*Megingjarðar*; Belt of Strength). *See* **Belt of Strength**

Menja (*Menja*), slave woman, probably giantess: S8

Mennon (*Mennon*), one of the kings of Troy: P3, marries Troan, the daughter of Priam

Midgard (*Miðgarðr*; the Middle Enclosure [Middle Yard] or Middle Earth), also the wall encircling the world of humans: 8, is formed out of Ymir's eyelashes (or eyebrows); 9, men are given a home there; 12; 42, master builder makes a deal with the Æsir to fortify it; 48; 51, in a verse

Midgard Serpent (*Miðgarðsormr*, also *Jörmungandr*): 34; 47; 48, Thor's encounter with; 51, will blow poison at Ragnarok; 53. *See* ***Jormungand***

Mimir (*Mímir*), owner of Mimir's Well (*Mímis brunnr*), the well of wisdom: 15, on the location of the well; Mimir drinks from the horn Gjall from the famous well and drinks mead in verse; 51, Odin will consult him at Ragnarok. *See* ***Hoddmimir's Wood***

Mist (*Mist*), valkyrie: 36, in a verse

Mistletoe (*Mistilteinn*): 49, found by Loki and used against Baldr

Mjollnir (*Mjöllnir*; probably to do with milling and grinding, hence a hammer that breaks or grinds into tiny fragments), Thor's hammer: 21; 42; 44; 45; 49; 53; S3; S4

Moda (*Móða*), son of Vingenir, descendant of Tror/Thor: P3

Modgud (*Móðguðr*; Furious Battler), maiden guarding the bridge over the river Gjoll: 49

Modi (*Móði*; Angry, Courageous, Eager), son of Thor: 53, will survive Ragnarok

Modsognir (*Moðsognir*), dwarf: 14

Modvitnir (*Möðvitnir*), dwarf: 14

Moin (*Móinn*), serpent gnawing at the roots of Yggdrasil: 16

Mokkurkalfi (*Mökkurkálfi*; Clay Foot), clay giant: S3

Moon (*Máni*): 8, in a verse; 11, description of; 51, caught at Ragnarok

Mountain Giants (*Bergrisar*, sing. *Bergrisi*): 15; 21; 27; 37; 42; 49

Mundilfari (*Mundilfari* or *Mundilfæri*; Mover of the Mill Handle?), father of Sun and Moon: 11, marries Sun to Glen

Munin (*Muninn*; Memory, Thought and Remembrance), one of Odin's ravens: 38

Munon (*Munon*). *See* ***Mennon***

Muspell (*Muspell*, sometimes seems to be the same as *Muspellsheimr*): 4, the first world to exist; 5; 8, stars formed out of its sparks; 11, burning embers from Muspellsheim; 43, owns the ship Naglfar. *See* ***Muspell, Sons of***

Muspell, Sons of (*Muspells synir*): 13, Bifrost will break under them; 37; 51, ride at Ragnarok

Mysing (*Mýsingr*), sea king: S8

Naglfar (*Naglfar*; Nail Ship), Muspell's ship: 43; 51, will be launched at Ragnarok

Naglfari (*Naglfari*), Night's first husband, Aud's father: 10

Nain (*Náinn*), dwarf: 14

Nal (*Nál*). *See* ***Laufey***

Nanna (*Nanna*), Nep's daughter, Baldr's wife, mother of Forseti: 32; 49, dies of grief at Baldr's death; S1

Nar (*Nár*; Corpse), dwarf: 14

Nari or **Narfi** (*Nari* or *Narfi*), son of Loki and Sigyn: 33; 50, gods fashion chains out of his entrails to bind Loki

Nastrandir (*Nástrandir*; as a plural word, Corpse Strands or Beaches, as singular *Náströnd*, Corpse Strand): 52, in prose and in verse, see note 2

Necklace of the Brisings. *See* ***Brisingamen***

Nep (*Nepr*), Nanna's father: 32; 49

Nibelungs. *See* ***Gjukungs***

Nidafjoll (*Niðafjöll*; Dark Mountains, sing. *Niðafjall*): 52

Nidhogg (*Níðhöggr*; Hateful Striker), serpent gnawing at the roots of Yggdrasil: 15; 16; 52, in a verse
Nidi (*Niði*), dwarf: 14
Niflheim (*Niflheimr*; Dark World): 4, made long before the earth; 5, is a source of cold and grim things; 15, is reached by one of the roots of Yggdrasil; 34, Odin gives Hel rule over it
Niflhel (*Niflhel*; Dark Hel), place where some men go after death: 3, note 2; 42
Niflungs (*Niflungar*). *See* ***Gjukungs***
Night (*Nótt*): 10, is married first to Naglfari, then to Annar, finally to Delling. She rides the sky in a chariot drawn by the horse Hrimfaxi
Nikar or **Hnikar** (*Nikarr* or *Hnikarr*; [Spear] Thruster): 3, one of the twelve names of Odin; 20
Nikuz or **Hnikud** (*Nikuz* or *Hnikuðr*; [Spear] Thruster): 3, one of the twelve names of Odin; 20
Niping (*Nipingr*), dwarf: 14
Njord (*Njörðr*): 23, a description of, his marriage arrangement with Skadi; 24, father of Frey and Freyja; 37, sends for Skirnir to find reason for Frey's anger; S1, is chosen by Skadi as her husband; S6, visits Ægir
Noah (*Nói*): P1, the story of the flood
Noatun (*Nóatún*; Enclosure for Ships), Njord's dwelling: 23; 24; S1
Nonn (*Nönn*; Strong), a river: 39
Nordri (*Norðri*). *See* ***North***
Norfi or **Narfi** (*Nörfi* or *Narfi*; Thin or Narrow), Night's father, giant: 10
Nori (*Nori*), dwarf: 14
Norn (*Norn*), female figures who determine people's fate: 15; 16; 36. *See* ***Urd***, ***Verdandi*** and ***Skuld***
North (*Norðri*), dwarf holding up a corner of the sky formed out of Ymir's skull: 8; 14
Norway (*Nóregr*): S9; S10; P5, Odin appoints one of his sons to rule over Norway
Norwegians (*Norðmenn*): S8
Not (*Nöt* or *Naut*), a river: 39
Nyi (*Nýi*), dwarf: 14
Nyr (*Nýr*; New One), dwarf: 14
Nyrad (*Nýráðr*), dwarf: 14
Nyt (*Nyt*), a river: 39
Od (*Óðr*), Freyja's husband: 35; 42, in a verse
Odin (*Óðinn*), the highest and the oldest of all the gods: 2, in a verse; 3, said to have twelve names (but he has many more), creates heaven,

earth, the sky and man with an immortal soul; 6, is son of Bor and Bestla; 9, is father of the family of the gods inhabiting the Old Asgard, begets his first son, Asa-Thor, with Earth, who is both his daughter and wife; 10, gives Night the horse Hrimfaxi and Day the horse Skinfaxi, as well as the chariots on which to ride the sky; 14; 15, gives his eye for a drink out of the Well of Mimir; 17; 20, is described with names; 22; 30; 24, splits half of the slain with Freyja; 34; 35; 36, sends valkyries to battles; 37; 38, description of Odin in Valhalla; 41; 49, drives to Baldr's funeral; 50, finds Loki from Hlidskjalf; 51, talks with Mimir, will fight with Fenrir at Ragnarok; S1, the cooking of an ox, makes stars out of Thjazi's eyes; S2, acquires the mead of poetry; S3, provokes Hrungnir; S5, judges and receives treasures from the dwarves; S6, visits Ægir; S7, the otter's ransom; S8; P3, goes to Reidgotaland, then to Sweden where he establishes twelve rulers and draws up a code of law; P4, his gift of prophecy, sets out on a journey from Turkey, lives in Germany. *See **All-Father***

Odrerir (*Óðrerir* or *Óðrørir*), a kettle holding the mead of poetry: S2

Ofnir (*Ófnir*), serpent gnawing at the root of Yggdrasil: 16

Oin (*Óinn*), dwarf: 14

Okolnir (*Ókolnir*; Never Cold), a place in heaven that never grows cold: 52

Oku-Thor (*Ökuþórr*; Thor the Charioteer or Thor the Driver). *See **Thor***

Old One or **Old Ogress/Giantess** (*In Aldna* or *In Gamla Gýgr*), primeval female, possibly Angrboda: 12. *See **Angrboda***

Olvaldi (*Ölvaldi*), giant, father of Thjazi: S1

Omi (*Ómi*; Resounding or Loud One): 3, one of the twelve names of Odin; 20

Onar (*Ónarr*), dwarf: 14

Ori (*Óri*; Raging or Raving One), dwarf: 14

Orkney Isles (*Orkneyjar*): S10

Ormt (*Örmt*), river: 15, in a verse

Oski (*Óski*; Fulfiller of Desire or Wisher): 3, one of the twelve names of Odin; 20

Otter (*Otr*), Hreidmar's son, brother of Fafnir and Regin: S7, is killed by Loki

Priam (*Priamus*): P3, chief king of Troy

Radgrid (*Ráðgríð*; Counselling Truce), valkyrie: 36, in a verse

Radsvinn (*Ráðsviðr*; Wise in Counsel), dwarf: 14

Ragnarok (*Ragnarøkr*; Darkness or Twilight of the Gods. *Ragnarök*; Doom or End of the Gods): 26, Idunn's apples keep the gods young till Ragnarok; 34, Fenrir awaits it with a sword propped in his mouth; 50, Loki awaits it chained to three rocks; 51, the events of; 52, the world after it; S10

Ran (*Rán*), a goddess, wife of Ægir: S6

Randgrid (*Randgríð*; Shield Truce), valkyrie: 36, in a verse

Randver (*Randvér*), Jormunrek's son: S7

Ratatosk (*Ratatoskr*; Drill Tooth), squirrel carrying messages between the hawk Vedrfolnir and Nidhogg: 16

Rati (*Rati*; Drill or Biter), auger or drill: S2

Raven (*Hrafn*), King Ali's horse: S9

Refil (*Refill*; Serpent?), Regin's sword: S7

Regin the Smith (*Reginn*), Hreidmar's son, Fafnir's brother: S7, is killed by Sigurd

Reginleif (*Reginleif*), valkyrie: 36, in a verse

Reidgotaland (*Reiðgotaland*), a name for Jutland: P5, Odin reaches it and appoints his son Skjold to govern it

Rekk (*Rekkr*), dwarf: 14

Rerir (*Rerir*), son of Siggi ruling over France, Volsungs: P4

Rhine (*Rín*): S7, Gunnar and Hogni hide Fafnir's treasure in it

Rind (*Rindr*), Vali's mother: 30; 36

Ringhorn (*Hringhorni*), Baldr's ship: 49

Road to Hel (*Helvegr*): 4, in a verse; 49; 51, in a verse

Roskva (*Röskva*), daughter of a farmer: 44, becomes Thor's bond-servant; 45

Rota (*Rota*), valkyrie: 36, rides with Gunn and Skuld

Saehrimnir (*Sæhrímnir*), boar used to feed Odin's champions in Valhalla: 38

Saeming (*Sæmingr*), ancestor of the ruling families of Norway: P5

Saga (*Sága*), goddess: 35

Sann (*Saðr*; Truthful), name of Odin: 20

Sanngetal (*Sanngetall*; One Who Guesses Right), name of Odin: 20

Saxland (*Saxaland* or *Saxland*), Saxony, name in old Scandinavia for all northern Germany: P4, Odin reaches it, Veggdegg, a son of Odin, rules over East Saxony; P5, the language of the men of Asia is brought to Saxland

Saxons (*Saxar*): S9

Sekin (*Sekin* or *Sækin*; Advancer), river flowing from Hvergelmir: 39

Seskef (*Seskef*), son of Magi: P3

Sessrumnir (*Sessrúmnir*; With Many Seats), Freyja's hall: 24, is described

Sheathed Tooth (*Slíðrugtanni*), Frey's boar: 49. *See* **Gold Bristle**

Siar (*Síarr*), dwarf: 14

Sibyl or **Sif** (*Sibil* or *Sif*), a prophetess, wife of Tror/Thor: P3. *See Sif*
Sibyl's Prophecy, The (*Völuspá*), eddic poem: 4, on the beginning of things and Surt; 8, on the reckoning of time; 12, on the wolf Managarm; 14, on the creation of dwarves; 15, on Odin's pledging his eye for a drink out of the well of wisdom; 17, on Gimle; 42, on Thor's rage; 51, on Ragnarok
Sibyl's Prophecy, The Shorter (*Völuspá in skamma*), eddic poem: 5
Sid (*Síð*; Slow Moving), river flowing from Hvergelmir: 39
Sidhott (*Síðhöttr*; Drooping Hood), name of Odin: 20
Sidskegg (*Síðskeggr*; Long Beard), name of Odin: 20
Sif (*Sif*; Wife), Thor's wife: 31, Ull's mother; S3, Hrungnir threatens to carry her off; S5, Loki cuts off her hair; S6, visits Ægir; P3
Sigar (*Sigarr*), son of Vitrgils: P4
Sig-Father (*Sigföðr*; Father of Victory or Battle), name of Odin: 20
Siggi (*Siggi* or *Sigi*), son of Odin ruling over France, Volsungs: P4
Sigmund (*Sigmundr*), Sigurd's son: S7, is killed at the age of three
Sigmund (*Sigmundr*), Volsung's son, Sigurd's father: S7
Sigtun (*Sigtúnir* or *Sigtún*), town site in Sweden chosen by Odin for himself: P5
Sigurd (*Sigurðr Sigmundarson Fáfnisbani*), Sigmund's son, the slayer of Fafnir: S7, is adopted by Regin, kills Fafnir and Regin, marries Gudrun, wins Brynhild for Gunnar, is killed by Gothorm
Sigyn (*Sigyn*), Loki's wife: 33; 50, collects the poison dripping on to Loki's face; S1
Silfrtopp or **Silfrintopp** (*Silfrtoppr* or *Silfrintoppr*; Silver Forelock), horse: 15
Simul (*Simul*), pole carried by Bil and Hjuki: 11
Sindri (*Sindri*; Sparkling), hall in heaven: 52
Sinfjotli (*Sinfjötli*), son of Sigmund Volsungsson: S7
Sinir (*Sinir*; Sinewy), horse: 15
Sjaelland (*Selund*), called Zealand in English, the central island in Denmark: 1
Sjofn (*Sjöfn*), goddess: 35
Skadi (*Skaði*), Njord's wife, daughter of Thjazi the giant, ski god or ski lady: 23; 50, fastens a poisonous snake above Loki's face; S1, comes to Asgard to avenge her father; S6, visits Ægir.
Skafinn (*Skafinn* or *Skafiðr*), dwarf: 14
Skeggjold (*Skeggjöld*; Axe Age), valkyrie: 36, in a verse
Skeidbrimir (*Skeiðbrimir*), horse: 15
Skidbladnir (*Skíðblaðnir*), ship: 41, in a verse; 43, description of; 44; S5, is made by the dwarves
Skilfing (*Skilfingr*), name of Odin: 20

Skinfaxi (*Skinfaxi*; Shining Mane), Day's horse: 10, his mane illuminates the earth and the sky

Skirnir (*Skírnir*; Bright One), Frey's servant: 34, sent by the Æsir to the World of the Dark Elves; 37, arranges Frey's marriage with Gerd; 51

Skirpir (*Skirpir*), dwarf: 14

Skjaldun or **Skjold** (*Skjaldun* or *Skjöldr*), son of Heremod: P3

Skjold (*Skjöldr*; Shield), son of Odin, king of Denmark: S8; P5, rules over Reidgotaland. *See* **Skjaldun**

Skjoldungs (*Skjöldungar*), kings of Denmark descended from Skjold: S8; P5

Skogul (*Skögul*; Shaker?), valkyrie: 36, in a verse

Skoll (*Sköll*), wolf pursuing the Sun: 12

Skrymir (*Skrýmir*; Braggart?), Utgarda-Loki: 45, travels to Utgard with Thor

Skuld (*Skuld*; Obligation, Necessity or Future), norn: 15; 36, rides with the valkyries Gunn and Rota to choose the slain

Sleipnir (*Sleipnir*; Fast Traveller), Odin's horse: 15; 41, in a verse; 42, his birth; 49, Hermod rides him during his trip to Hel; S3

Slid (*Slíðr*; Dangerous, Fearsome), river flowing from Hvergelmir: 4

Slothful (*Ganglöt*), Hel's maidservant: 34

Slungnir (*Slungnir*), King Adils' horse: S9

Snotra (*Snotra*; Wise or Courtly [*Snotr*]), goddess: 35

Soeg (*Sœgr* or *Sægr*), pail carried by Bil and Hjuki: 11

Sokkvabekk (*Søkkvabekkr*; Sunken Bank or Bench), Saga's home: 35

Sol (*Sól*). *See* **Sun**

Son (*Són*), one of the vats holding the mead of poetry: S2

Sorli (*Sörli*), son of Gudrun and Jonak, brother of Hamdir and Erp: S7

South (*Suðri*), dwarf holding up a corner of the sky: 8; 14

Summer (*Sumarr*): 19

Sun (*Sól*), daughter of Mundilfari: 8, in a verse; 11, the gods make her drive the chariot of the sun; 12, is pursued by the wolf Skoll; 35

Surt (*Surtr*; Black One), Muspell's guardian, possibly a fire giant or demon: 4; 17; 51, will lead the sons of Muspell at Ragnarok; 53

Suttung (*Suttungr*), giant: S2, obtains the mead of poetry as compensation for the death of his parents and hides it

Svadilfari (*Svaðilfari* or *Svaðilfœri*), master builder's horse and father of Sleipnir: 42

Svafnir (*Sváfnir*; Put to Sleep/Kill), name of Odin: 2

Svafnir (*Sváfnir*), serpent gnawing at the roots of Yggdrasil: 16

Svanhild (*Svanhildr*), Sigurd's daughter: S7, is killed by Jormunrek

Svarin's Burial Mound (*Svarinshaugr*): 14
Svartalfaheim (*Svartálfaheimr*). *See* ***World of the Dark Elves***
Svarthofdi (*Svarthöfði*; Dark Head), ancestor of sorcerers: 5, in a verse
Svasud (*Svásuðr*; Delightful), Summer's father: 19
Svebdegg or **Svipdag** (*Svebdegg* or *Svipdagr*), son of Sigar: P4
Sviagris. *See* ***Swedes' Pig***
Svidar (*Sviðarr* or *Sviðurr*; Spear God?): 3, one of the twelve names of Odin; 20, Svidur
Svidrir (*Sviðrir*; Spear God?): 3, one of the twelve names of Odin; 20
Svipal (*Svipall*; Changing or Shifting One), name of Odin: 20
Svipdag (*Svipdagr*), one of Hrolf Kraki's berserkers: S9; P4. *See* ***Svebdegg***
Svol (*Svöl*; Cool), river flowing from Hvergelmir: 4; 39
Sweden (*Svíþjóð*): 1; S8; P5, Odin reaches it, the language of the men of Asia is brought to Sweden
Swedes' Pig or **Sviagris** (*Svíagríss*): S9
Sylg (*Sylgr*; Swallower), river flowing from Hvergelmir: 4
Syn (*Syn*; Refusal), goddess: 35
Syr (*Sýr*; Sow), one of Freyja's names: 35
Tanngniost (*Tanngnióstr*; Tooth Gnasher), one of the goats that pulls Thor's chariot: 21
Tanngrisnir (*Tanngrisnir*; Snarl Tooth), one of the goats that pulls Thor's chariot: 21
Thekk (*Þekkr*; Clever? Pleasant?), name of Odin: 20
Thekk (*Þekkr*), dwarf: 14
Third (*Þriði*), one of the Æsir who speaks with Gylfi: 2; 3, talks of man's creation and good and evil men; 4, describes Muspell; 5, tells of Ymir's origins; 8, describes the creation of the sky; 20, gives the names of Odin; 44, is said to give the true account of Thor's journey to Giant Land; 52, describes the world after Ragnarok
Thjalfi (*Þjálfi*), son of a farmer: 44, becomes Thor's bondservant; 45, carries Thor's knapsack; 46, his running contest with Hugi; 47; S3
Thjazi (*Þjazi*), giant, Skadi's father: 23, in a verse; S1, forces Loki to abduct Idunn and is killed by the Æsir, his daughter seeks vengeance
Thjod (*Þjóð*), name perhaps corresponding to the Danish province of Thy in northern Jutland: S7
Thjodnuma (*Þjóðnuma*; People Grabber), a river: 39
Thjodolf of Hvin (*Þjóðólfr inn hvinverski*), skald: 2, a verse from him regarding Valhalla; S3
Thokk (*Þökk*; Thanks or Gratitude), giantess, Loki: 49, refuses to weep for Baldr
Tholl (*Þöll*), a river: 39

Thor (*Þórr* also *Ásaþórr* [Thor of the Æsir] and *Ökuþórr* [Oku-Thor, Thor the Charioteer or Thor the Driver]): 9, is born from Odin and Earth; 15, his journey to the gods' court of justice; 21, is described; 29, strength compared to Vidar; 31; 42, slays the master builder; 44, acquires his bondservants Roskva and Thjalfi; 45, encounters Skrymir; 46, goes through the tests put to him by Utgarda-Loki; 47, hears the truth of Utgarda-Loki's deceptions; 48, goes fishing for the Midgard Serpent with the giant Hymir; 49, threatens the giantess Hyrrokkin, blesses Baldr's funeral pyre, kicks dwarf in; 50, catches Loki, who has turned himself into a salmon; 51, will fight with the Midgard Serpent at Ragnarok; in verse, the son of Earth or Hlodyn; 53; 55, called Ector; S1; S3, battles with Hrungnir; S4, his encounter with Geirrod and his family; S5, receives Mjollnir from the dwarves; P3, son of Munon or Mennon and Troan, kills Loricus and his wife

Thorin (*Þorinn*; Daring or Bold One), dwarf: 14

Thracia (*Thracia*; Thrace): P3, Tror/Thor is brought up there. *See* ***Thrudheim***

Thrid (*Þriði*), one of the names of Odin: 20. *See* ***Third***

Throin (*Þróinn*), dwarf: 14

Thror (*Þrór*), dwarf: 14

Thror (*Þrór*), name of Odin: 20

Thrud (*Þrúðr*; Powerful), valkyrie: 36, in a verse

Thrudheim (*Þrúðheimr*), a name for Thracia: P3

Thrudvangar (*Þrúðvangar*; Plains or Place of Strength), Thor's domain: 21; 47; S3

Thrymheim (*Þrymheimr*; Thunder or Noisy Home), Thjazi's dwelling: 23; S1, Thjazi takes Idunn there

Thund (*Þundr*; Roaring One or Rumbler), name of Odin: 20

Thunn (*Þunðr*), name of Odin: 20

Thviti (*Þviti*), rock anchoring the fetter that holds Fenrir: 34

Thyn (*Þyn*; Frothing), a river: 39

Troan (*Troan*), daughter of Priam, married to king Mennon: P3

Tror (*Tror*), a name for Thor, son of Mennon and Troan: P3. *See* ***Thor***

Troy (*Troja*): 9, a name for Asgard; 55; P3, is built in what is now known as Turkey; P5, Sweden is governed after the manner of Troy

Turkey (*Tyrkland*): P3, a region near the world's centre; P4, Odin sets out on his journey from Turkey

Turks (*Tyrkir*): P5; 55

Tyr (*Týr*), a god: 25, a description of; 34, loses his hand chaining Fenrir; 51, fights Garm at Ragnarok; S1; S6, visits Ægir

Ulixes (*Ulixes*), Ulysses, a name for Loki by Turks: 55

Ull (*Ullr*), Sif's son: 31; S1

Unn (*Uðr*), name of Odin: 20
Uppsala (*Uppsalir*), the seat of the ancient Swedish kings: S9
Urd (*Urðr*; Fate or Destiny), a norn: 15
Urd, Well of (*Urðarbrunnr*; Well of Destiny or Fate): 15; 16, in verse and prose; 17
Utgard (*Útgarðr*; Outer Enclosure): 45, Thor travels there
Utgarda-Loki (*Útgarðaloki*; Loki of the Outlying Regions), a giant king: 45, concerning his retainers; 46, puts Thor and his companions to tests; 47, reveals deceptions to Thor; 48. *See* ***Skrymir***
Vaeni (*Væni*), a lake, probably Vänern in Sweden: S9
Vafthrudnir (*Vafþrúðnir*; Mighty Weaver, possibly Strong in Difficult Riddles), giant: 5
Vafud (*Váfuðr*; Dangling One?), name of Odin: 20
Vak (*Vakr*; Alert or Vigilant One), name of Odin: 20
Valaskjalf (*Valaskjálf*), Odin's hall: 17
Val-Father (*Valföðr*; Father of the Slain), name of Odin: 15, in a verse; 20
Valhalla (*Valhöll*; Hall of the Slain), Odin's hall: 2, with reference to its being roofed with shields; 20, Odin mans it with the Einherjar; 36, the valkyries serve mead in it; 38, with reference to the feeding of the host of Odin's champions; 39, description of creatures of; 40, the doors of; 41, the daily battles of; 42; 49; S3
Vali (*Váli*), dwarf: 14
Vali (*Váli*), son of Loki: 50, kills his brother when the Æsir turn him into a wolf
Vali or Ali (*Váli* or *Áli*), son of Odin and Rind: 30; 53, will survive Ragnarok; S1
Valkyrie (*Valkyrja Valkyrjur* plural; Chooser of the Slain): 36, sent by Odin to battle where they choose the slain for Valhalla; 49, with Odin at Baldr's funeral; S7, Brynhild was a valkyrie; S10
Van (*Ván* or *Vón*; Hope or Expectation), river from the Fenriswolf's saliva: 34
Vanaheim (*Vanaheimar*; Home of the Vanir), place where Njord was brought up: 23
Vanir, the (*Vanir*), a race of gods: 23, give Njord to the Æsir as a hostage; 35, Freyja the goddess of; S2, make a truce with the Æsir
Var (*Vár*; Beloved), goddess: 35
Vartari (*Vartari*), thong used to sew Loki's lips: S5
Vasad (*Vásað* or *Vásuðr*; Damp Cold, Sleety), father of Vindloni, the father of Winter: 19
Ve (*Vé*), son of Bor and Bestla, brother of Odin: 6

Vedrfolnir (*Veðrfölnir*; Wind Bleached), hawk sitting between the eyes of the eagle in the branches of Yggdrasil: 16
Veggdegg (*Veggdegg*), son of Odin ruling over East Saxland: P4
Vegsvinn (*Vegsvinn*; Way Swift), in some manuscripts, river flowing from Hvergelmir: 39
Veratyr (*Veratýr*; God of Men), name of Odin: 20
Verdandi (*Verðandi*; Becoming or Being), norn: 15
Veseti (*Véseti*), one of Hrolf Kraki's berserkers: S9
Vestri (*Vestri*). *See* ***West***
Vid (*Víð*; Broad), river flowing from Hvergelmir: 4; 39
Vidar (*Víðarr*; Wide Reigner, called the Silent, *Inn Þögli*), a god, Odin's son: 29; 51, his shoe kills Fenrir at Ragnarok; 53, survives Ragnarok; S1; S4, his mother; S6, visits Ægir
Vidblain (*Víðbláinn*; Wide Blue), third heaven: 17
Vidfinn (*Viðfinnr*; Finn of the Woods), father of Bil and Hjuki: 11
Vidolf (*Viðólfr*; Forest Wolf), ancestor of seeresses: 5, in a verse
Vidrir (*Viðrir*; Ruler of Weather): 3, one of the twelve names of Odin
Vidur (*Viðurr*), name of Odin: 20
Vig (*Vigr*), dwarf: 14
Vigrid (*Vígríðr*; Battle Plain), plain: 51, site of Ragnarok
Vili (*Vili*), son of Bor and Bestla, brother of Odin: 6
Vilmeid (*Vilmeiðr*), ancestor of wizards: 5, in a verse
Vimur (*Vimur*), river: S4, Thor crosses it
Vin (*Vin*), a river: 39
Vina (*Vína*), a river: 39
Vindalf (*Vindálfr*; Wind Elf), dwarf: 14
Vindloni or **Vindsval** (*Vindlóni* or *Vindsvalr*; Wind Chill), father of Winter: 19
Vingenir (*Vingenir*), son of Vingethor: P3
Vingethor (*Vingeþórr*), son of Einridi: P3
Vingnir (*Vingnir*), a name for Thor: 53, in a verse
Vingolf (*Vingólf*; Friendly Quarters): 3, connected with Gimle; 14, is the sanctuary of the goddesses; 20, Odin mans it with the Einherjar
Virpir (*Virpir*), dwarf: 14
Vitr (*Vitr*; Wise), dwarf: 14
Vitrgils (*Vitrgils*), son of Veggdegg: P4
Vitta (*Vitta*), son of Vitrgils: P4
Voden (*Voden*), son of Friallaf, Odin: P3
Vogg (*Vöggr*), a small boy: S9, gives King Hrolf Kraki his name
Volsung (*Völsungr*), a legendary hero: S7, father of Sigmund. *See* ***Volsungs***

Volsungs (*Völsungar*), descendants of Volsung: S7; P4, family originating in France. *See* ***Sigurd*** and ***Volsung***

Voluspa (*Völuspá*). See ***Sibyl's Prophecy*** and ***Sibyl's Prophecy, The Shorter***

Vor (*Vör*; Careful), goddess: 35

Vott (*Vöttr*), one of Hrolf Kraki's berserkers: S9

West (*Vestri*), dwarf holding up a corner of the sky formed out of Ymir's skull: 8; 14

Westphalia (*Vestfal*): P4, is ruled over by Beldegg, son of Odin

Wigg (*Wigg*), son of Freovin: P4

Winter (*Vetr*): 19

World of the Dark Elves (*Svartálfaheimr*): 34, Skirnir is sent there; S7, Loki travels there. *See* ***Elves***

World Tree. *See* ***Yggdrasil***

Ygg (*Yggr*; Terrible One), Odin: 20

Yggdrasil (*Yggdrasill*; Ygg's Horse), the Ash Tree or the World Tree: 15, a description of; 16, the creatures of; 41, in a verse; 51, will tremble at Ragnarok. *See* ***Lerad***

Ylg (*Ylgr*; Swelling), river flowing from Hvergelmir: 4

Ymir (*Ymir*), primeval giant: 5, is formed in Ginnungagap, a male and female form under his left arm and one of his legs begets a son with the other, the frost giants coming into being; 6, lives off Audhumla's milk; 7, killed by the sons of Bor; 8, the world is created from his body, the wall of Midgard is formed from his eyebrows (or eyelashes); 14, dwarves find life in his flesh

Ynglings (*Ynglingar*), descendants of Yngvi: P5

Yngvi (*Yngvi*), son of Odin, rules over Sweden after Odin; is progenitor of the Ynglings: P5

Yrsa (*Yrsa*, the name Yrsa, unusual in medieval Norse narrative, may be related to Latin *ursa* (she bear)), Hrolf Kraki's mother and his sister: S9

Zealand (*Selund*). *See* ***Sjaelland***

read more 

PENGUIN CLASSICS

THE SAGA OF GRETTIR THE STRONG

'The most valiant man who has ever lived in Iceland'

Composed at the end of the fourteenth century by an unknown author, *The Saga of Grettir the Strong* is one of the last great Icelandic sagas. It relates the tale of Grettir, an eleventh-century warrior struggling to hold on to the values of a heroic age as they are eclipsed by Christianity and a more pastoral lifestyle. Unable to settle into a community of farmers, Grettir becomes the aggressive scourge of both honest men and evil monsters – until, following a battle with the sinister ghost Glam, he is cursed to endure a life of tortured loneliness away from civilization, fighting giants, trolls and berserks. A mesmerizing combination of pagan ideals and Christian faith, this is a profoundly moving conclusion to the Golden Age of saga writing.

This is an updated edition of Bernard Scudder's acclaimed translation. The new introduction by Örnólfur Thorsson considers the influence of Christianity on Icelandic saga writing, and this edition also includes genealogical tables and a note on the translation.

Translated by Bernard Scudder

Edited with an introduction by Örnólfur Thorsson

read more 

PENGUIN CLASSICS

EGIL'S SAGA

'The sea-goddess has ruffled me,
stripped me bare of my loved ones'

Egil's Saga tells the story of the long and brutal life of the tenth-century warrior-poet and farmer Egil Skallagrimsson: a psychologically ambiguous character who was at once the composer of intricately beautiful poetry and a physical grotesque capable of staggering brutality. This Icelandic saga recounts Egil's progression from youthful savagery to mature wisdom as he struggles to defend his honour in a running feud against the Norwegian King Erik Blood-axe, fights for the English King Athelstan in his battles against Scotland and embarks on colourful Viking raids across Europe. Exploring issues as diverse as the question of loyalty, the power of poetry and the relationship between two brothers who love the same woman, *Egil's Saga* is a fascinating depiction of a deeply human character, and one of the true masterpieces of medieval literature.

This new translation by Bernard Scudder fully conveys the poetic style of the original. It also contains a new introduction by Svanhildur Óskarsdóttir, placing the saga in historical context, a detailed chronology, a chart of Egil's ancestors and family, maps and notes.

Translated by Bernard Scudder

Edited by Ornulfur Thorsson

THE STORY OF PENGUIN CLASSICS

Before 1946 …'Classics' are mainly the domain of academics and students, without readable editions for everyone else. This all changes when a little-known classicist, E. V. Rieu, presents Penguin founder Allen Lane with the translation of Homer's *Odyssey* that he has been working on and reading to his wife Nelly in his spare time.

1946 *The Odyssey* becomes the first Penguin Classic published, and promptly sells three million copies. Suddenly, classic books are no longer for the privileged few.

1950s Rieu, now series editor, turns to professional writers for the best modern, readable translations, including Dorothy L. Sayers's *Inferno* and Robert Graves's *The Twelve Caesars*, which revives the salacious original.

1960s The Classics are given the distinctive black jackets that have remained a constant throughout the series's various looks. Rieu retires in 1964, hailing the Penguin Classics list as 'the greatest educative force of the 20th century'.

1970s A new generation of translators arrives to swell the Penguin Classics ranks, and the list grows to encompass more philosophy, religion, science, history and politics.

1980s The Penguin American Library joins the Classics stable, with titles such as *The Last of the Mohicans* safeguarded. Penguin Classics now offers the most comprehensive library of world literature available.

1990s The launch of Penguin Audiobooks brings the classics to a listening audience for the first time, and in 1999 the launch of the Penguin Classics website takes them online to a larger global readership than ever before.

The 21st Century Penguin Classics are rejacketed for the first time in nearly twenty years. This world famous series now consists of more than 1300 titles, making the widest range of the best books ever written available to millions – and constantly redefining the meaning of what makes a 'classic'.

The Odyssey continues …